CHANEY LAW

Chaney Brothers 4

ROBERT VAUGHAN

Paperback Edition

Published in the United States by Wolfpack Publishing, Las Vegas

Wolfpack Publishing
6032 Wheat Penny Avenue
Las Vegas, NV 89122

wolfpackpublishing.com

Paperback ISBN 978-1-64734-503-7
eBook ISBN 978-1-64734-502-0

CHANEY LAW

CHAPTER 1

Blanco County, Texas

Had Colin MacDonald any inkling or suspicion that he would not live to see another sunrise he probably still would have done the same thing he did every day since arriving in Blanco County with six thousand head of sheep he'd brought up from Mexico.

Even before reaching the decision to make the move, he knew that when he did it, trouble would ensue, with Texas cattlemen hating woollies with a passion. After getting over the initial shock of learning that he was staying, the county cattleman's association called a meeting to discuss their course of action for eradicating the Scotsman and his damned stinking sheep.

A message was promptly dispatched by telegraph and made its way across the wires to a town called Perdition in South Texas where it was received and taken down by the telegrapher there. He hurried along to the Longhorn Saloon and handed it to a well-dressed man known as Jim Coleman.

When Coleman took the piece of paper, he unfolded it and perused its contents coolly, then got to his feet instantly, excusing himself from the company seated around the poker table. "I'm sorry, my friends, but duty calls."

After packing provisions in his saddlebags and saddling his horse, the hired killer spent the next six days traveling from Perdition to the township of Bell, where he came to stand before the Cattleman's association to hear what they wanted to be done.

On completion of their instructions, Coleman nodded to the gathered men and said, "I can take care of the problem for you, but it is going to cost you two thousand dollars for my services."

At the mention of such an astronomical figure, the chairman of the association, an older, bullish man named Hank Conker appeared to be on the verge of apoplexy. "Damn it, sir," he growled. "If I had known you were going to charge so much for a simple job, I'd have had one of my hands take care of it."

Coleman's cool reply came as he turned to leave, "You are quite welcome to do so."

The owner of the Broken C ranch stared daggers at Coleman's receding back, seething briefly before he capitulated and blustered, "All right. But you better be good at what you do."

Turning back to run his eyes over the gathered men, stopping when he landed on the face of the chairman once more, his face showed no emotion as he spoke. "I am. You'll not see me again. However, you will wire the money to this bank," he handed over a piece of paper with the details written on it, "once the job is done."

Then Coleman left them and set about accomplishing what he had been engaged to do.

Macdonald sat slumped in the saddle on his horse, watching listlessly as his sheep grazed peacefully. To the east of the flock stood a Mexican hand named Manuel Ortega. He'd brought his wife Carmella north with MacDonald when the sheep had been purchased. Carmella had been hired by the

Scotsman to cook and clean. Their daughter, Louisa, and two shepherds, Antonio, and Eduardo had also made the trek and were now forging a new life for themselves in Texas.

The sound of a dog's deep-throated bark drew MacDonald's attention and he saw the large Maremma Sheepdog racing across to the east where Manuel knelt to pat it, roughing its thick white coat. The Scotsman smiled.

MacDonald felt the skin at the back of his neck prickle. A sensation was a curious one that caused him to turn his head and focus on a low rise dotted with trees and large granite boulders. He frowned for a moment, unable to specify exactly what had drawn his attention, then shrugged the feeling off and was about to turn back to his flock when a heavy caliber bullet ripped through the air from a good distance away, and punched the sheep man from the saddle.

Toppling sideways, he hit the ground hard, stunned and unable to draw breath since the impact of the bullet. MacDonald's eyes stared up at the cloudless sky as he tried to comprehend what had happened. The thought remained as darkness enveloped him.

Texas

Buck Chaney fumbled with blood-slick fingers trying to reload the Winchester. He was pretty sure that he'd slipped in another six cartridges and that the three Carter brothers were closing in on him. Their number had decreased from four, the blond-headed deputy marshal from Barlow Texas having already sent the oldest brother Hank to meet his maker. More than likely Hell, but one could never be sure.

"We're coming for you, Marshal. You hear me?"

Buck was reasonably certain that the voice

belonged to Jack Carter, the second oldest of the siblings, but now the eldest living. Chaney edged around the corner of the boulder and peered through the brush, his steel-gray eyes searching, trying to ascertain the direction they were coming from.

"Looks like you done got yourself in a right fix this time, Buck," the younger Chaney brother murmured to himself, wishing that his older Brother Lance was with him instead of off doing a job for County Sheriff Deke White. Working the lever of the Winchester to rack a round into the chamber, he winced with the movement, a searing pain tearing through his side where a bullet remained buried beneath the flesh.

A flurry of gunshots hammered splinters from the rock that Buck had taken refuge behind. With stiff movements and grimacing with pain and the effort, he leaned out and fired the carbine before retreating to the safety of cover. He was rewarded with a yelp of pain and hoped that one more of the Carter brothers was out of the fight.

A seriously bad bunch, the Carters had come out of Kansas, hit a stage running south through Indian Territory, then moved on into Texas where they'd proceeded to rob two more stages, leaving behind three dead in their wake.

A telegram for Buck had arrived from Chief Marshal Mike Dodge up in Van Buren, Arkansas, advising that the Carter brothers were on their way south. Unfortunately, Buck missed them by a whole day, and when they became alerted to the fact that someone was on their back trail, they vanished suddenly over rocky ground.

The deputy had spent the better part of another day searching before he managed to pick it up again. From that point, he'd been playing catchup while the Carters went about their business.

After the second of the stage robberies, Buck's

luck changed. The brothers had escaped with two thousand dollars from the strongbox and killed the guard. However, one of their horses picked up a stone bruise not long after and went lame, giving the deputy time to catch up and run them to ground.

But proximity also brought with it a need for heightened need for awareness of the killers, and Buck hadn't suspected that he was so close until the bullet from Hank's Winchester had slammed into his side.

Now though, Hank was dead and at least one other brother was wounded. It wasn't Jack because he was still shouting at Buck. Which left Joe or Sam.

Buck winced at a stabbing pain and shouted. "Which one was that, Jack? Joe or Sam?"

"Shut your mouth, Chaney. It weren't neither of them."

So they knew who he was.

"It was me, Jack," a pained voice called out. "He shot me. I need doctoring."

"Didn't sound like nothing to me! I'll take a guess and say it was Sam."

"Damn it, Sam, shut up!"

Easing out cautiously from behind the rock, Buck moved just far enough to get a look at the terrain before him. The whiplash of a rifle coupled with the ricochet of a bullet was enough to force him to withdraw to cover once more. Sharp splinters from the boulder peppered his exposed flesh, adding to the pain the deputy was already feeling.

"Did I get you, Chaney?" Jack Carter called out.

"Not even close, Jack!"

"Jack, Sam needs a doctor or he ain't going to make it."

"Christ, Joe, we got him pinned down. We ain't about to put our tails between our legs and run out now."

An uneasy silence settled over the vicinity. While Buck waited to see what would happen next, the pain from his wound radiated outward through his body. After ten minutes with no further gunfire or movement, the deputy began to get suspicious. He eased around the rough surface of the boulder he was hiding behind and moved cautiously out into the open. The distant drumming of retreating hoof-beats reached his ears. After all of the bluster about not going to run with his tail between his legs, it looked as though the remaining Carter brothers had done just that.

A wave of relief washed over Buck as he slumped against the boulder's hard surface. Leaning the Winchester on the rock beside him, he began to look down at the wound in his side. His shirt was slick with fresh blood and he tore at the hole in it so he could see more of the wound.

Buck winced with the effort but eventually accomplished what he set out to do. The rent in his shirt was now large enough to examine the dark hole which continued to leak what seemed to be a whole lot of blood.

The deputy poked around it gingerly before reaching around behind himself. He felt the lump of the bullet beneath the skin. He guessed it would be fine until he could make it to see a doctor, however, what concerned him the most was the amount of blood he was still losing.

Wiping his bloody hands on his shirt—it was ruined anyway—Buck retrieved the Winchester and began making his way back to his horse. When he reached into his saddlebags, his horse swung its head back to smell the blood, its withers giving a violent shiver. Buck patted his mount to reassure him that he was going to be OK, then withdrew a clean shirt from the worn and battered leather. Bundling it up into a tight ball, he tucked it inside his torn shirt and pressed it firmly against the wound, the pressure taking his breath away.

After taking several minutes to regain his senses,

he struggled to mount the bay. The action sent a searing pain ripping through his body, and for a moment Buck thought he might pass out. He grabbed the saddle horn to steady himself, breathing deeply as darkness began descending. After several deep, calming breaths, his vision started to clear.

"I hope you know your way, horse, because things ain't too good at the moment," Buck muttered shakily to the animal.

He then urged it forward into a walk, closing his eyes for a little rest, and before they had traveled a hundred yards, the deputy's chin was slumped to his chest and he was sleeping seated in the saddle.

Southwest of Barlow, Texas

Lance Chaney drew his buckskin horse to a halt and hipped in the saddle. The faint wisp of dust rising into the clear blue Texas sky told him that they were still there. A high-pitched cackle was followed by, "They's going to get you, Marshal. Cut you open and eat your liver while it's still warm. Old Iron Guts don't like it when white men upset him."

The Barlow marshal ignored the man on the bay horse he was leading. He tied the rope around his saddle horn and drew the Winchester from his saddle scabbard, ensuring that there was a round under the hammer.

"Old Iron Guts" the man was referring to was a renegade Comanche warrior who rode with five or six warriors throughout West Texas, raising all kinds of hell. His name was actually Iron Shirt derived from the old Spanish Conquistador armor that he wore.

The rider on the bay hawked loudly and spit a gob of phlegm on the ground beside the horse. His cold blue eyes sparkled as he chuckled. "Make peace with your maker, Chaney. You'll be shaking his hand before sundown."

"Shut up, Shad," Lance snapped. "Or I'll shoot you here and leave your stinking corpse for the buzzards."

Shad Croft laughed even louder this time at the threat. The outlaw was crazy, Lance was certain of that, and he shook his head that it was just his luck to get stuck bringing him in. The man was wanted for running guns and alcohol to the Comanches. Deke White had received word that Croft was running a new batch of weapons to the Indians somewhere southwest of Barlow and asked Lance to check it out for him. Even though the older Chaney's powers stopped at the Barlow town limits, occasionally he was deputized by the county sheriff to perform extra jobs. This being one of them.

Croft looked more like a Comanche than a white man, his hair worn long with a buzzard feather tied into it. There was a scar on his cheek, and when he laughed he revealed a gap-toothed smile, a space where one of his incisors had broken off.

Lance removed his low-crowned hat and sleeved the sweat from his forehead before plopping it back atop his blond haired head, similar to that of his brother's.

"What you going to do, Chaney? Old Iron Guts has got you outnumbered."

"Wouldn't be the first time," Lance shot back at him referring to numerous different instances during the Civil War when he was a major in the Union Cavalry. Unlike Buck who had been a captain in the Confederate Cavalry. Brother against brother never rang truer for the Chaney boys. But their homecoming had been bittersweet, and the siblings united in a common cause, gradually rebuilding a relationship that had been torn apart by the war.

"Maybe if you let me go, he might stop, let you live."

"Not going to happen, Shad."

"Well, I guess you're going to die then."

Ignoring the older man's taunts, Lance turned his horse, back along the trail, and the pair had ridden no more than a hundred yards further when Lance stopped again. This time, however, he dismounted and replaced the Winchester in its scabbard.

Croft was confused and it showed on his face as he gave the marshal a quizzical look, asking, "What are you doing?"

Lance ignored the man's question, instead, he walked over to the outlaw and yanked him roughly from the saddle. "Hey...what the–"

Starting to struggle against the abrupt and forceful treatment, Croft became still only after a slap, up the back of his head as Lance snapped, "Settle down or I'll bend a gun barrel over your head."

The outlaw's look challenged the marshal as he spat, "You wouldn't dare –"

The retort was cut short as Lance's Navy Colt swept upward from its holster and cracked audibly against the side of Croft's head. The man staggered momentarily, but Lance held him upright in his strong grip. "You were saying?"

"Son of a bitch, you hit me." Trying to retain a defiant tone, but unable to keep an uncertain edge from his voice.

"And I'll do it again too if you don't shut your yap. Get over there behind those rocks."

With a solid shove, Croft was propelled forward, lurched a few steps, and then gathered himself. When he reached the large gray slabs of granite the marshal ordered him to sit down with his back against one.

"Now what?" Croft spat.

"You sit there and be quiet or you'll not see the sun go down. You give me any trouble I'll place a bullet between those beady eyes of yours. Understood?"

The outlaw's growing uncertainty crept into his

eyes. The marshal had made good his claim that he would hit him, so maybe, just maybe, he would follow through with this threat too. Croft nodded and slid down the rock face to sit on the ground. "Alright."

Lance put the horses out of sight, returning with his saddlebags and bedroll, fumbling with the ties on the latter. He placed it on the dry ground before unfurling it to reveal an 1863 Sharps .54 caliber carbine.

"What are you going to do with that?" Croft asked as he watched Lance open the breech and feed a cartridge into it.

"Kill a renegade."

From his saddlebags, the marshal removed a spyglass and extended it to full length. After studying the vicinity of the raised dust cloud for several moments, he noted the riders that began to appear at its base. First one, then another, until they were all visible. There were six in total.

Lance put the spyglass back into his saddlebags and picked up the Sharps. He stared at the outlaw and suddenly asked, "Why?"

"Why what?"

"Why sell guns to the Comanche so they can kill whites?"

Croft's top lip curled. "Money, why else?"

"Well, you're about to lose a customer."

The outlaw smiled and said, "Maybe."

"What are you smiling at?"

"Just wondering."

"Wondering what? Stop talking in riddles and keep it plain."

"Fine," Croft said with a nod. "I was wondering what you were going to do about them."

Lance followed the outlaw's gaze to a low ridge to the south. A chill ran through his veins when he saw perhaps ten more mounted warriors.

"Who are they?"

Croft shrugged. "No idea. But I'm sure happy to see them."

The Comanches started forward allowing their horses to pick the way down the slope. Lance turned to look at the other Comanches under Iron Shirt. They were getting nearer but still remained out of range. The marshal hurried across and took the Henry from the saddle scabbard and leaned it against the boulder he'd been using for cover.

"You're looking mighty nervous, Marshal," Croft taunted with more than a subtle hint of glee. "I guess I would too if I was about to lose my hair."

"Shut up, Croft."

"Yep, getting mighty tetchy too. I hope they kill you slow, Marshal; it'll be nice to hear you scream."

After a glance in either direction, Lance gave an abrupt nod then moved swiftly across to Croft's position beside the rock. At the marshal's sudden movement, the outlaw's eyes widened with fear and his jaw dropped open to cry out. Before the escape of any noise from his throat, the stock of the Sharps swept in a powerful arc, striking the outlaw a brutal blow under his chin.

Croft's teeth clicked together, narrowly avoiding the tip of his tongue, and his eyes rolled back in his head before he slumped sideways, unconscious. "I warned you," Lance muttered. And turned away to await what was coming in relative peace.

A bead of sweat ran down Lance's nose and dripped into the dirt at his feet. The sound of hoofbeats grew steadily louder as both groups of riders drew closer. Lance gripped the Henry tighter. He'd swapped it with the Sharps because of the weapon's superior firing capacity.

It wouldn't be long before they found him and he knew that when it happened, the best he could hope for was a quick death.

Lance watched on as the two groups almost converged. They stopped within a few yards of each other and the older Chaney could hear their voices from his position; calm at first then growing steadily louder. "Obviously a mutual dislike there," Lance muttered to himself.

For a minute or so longer the voices continued at a raised level before Iron Shirt turned his band and rode away. The Indian's actions brought a frown to the marshal's face as he wondered what had happened to make the renegade Comanche ride off.

That was about the time that something strange happened. The leader of the new arrivals turned his pony and headed straight toward Lance's refuge.

Lance tightened his grasp on the Henry and brought it up ready to use, when the rider stopped and called out, "He is gone, white man. You can come out now."

A surge of adrenaline coursed through Lance as he considered his limited options. Try to run? Fight? "Maybe just see what he wants."

He stepped out of cover and held the Henry across his chest in a non-threatening gesture. The Comanche urged his horse further forward until there was less than twenty feet between them.

The Indian carried a feathered lance and was bare-chested. His high cheekbones sat either side of a large hawkish nose. "You are lucky we came along when we did," the Comanche said. "Iron Shirt would have killed you."

"He would have tried," Lance rebuked him.

The Indian just shrugged broad shoulders. "How are you called?"

Lance hesitated.

"Do not worry, if I wanted you dead it would be so."

"I am Lance Chaney, marshal from over Barlow way."

"I have heard of you," he grunted and left it at that. "I am called Little Wolf."

"I have heard of you also."

"Iron Shirt said you have the one called Croft. Is that true?"

Lance nodded. "That is true. I'm taking him in. Most likely he will hang."

Little Wolf nodded. "Good. He has only brought trouble to my people. Maybe you could give him to me, and I will take care of him for you."

"I can't do that."

"Too bad."

"So, what now?"

"You go, do not come back."

Lance nodded but said, "Can't promise you that."

"This is Comanche land. You do not belong here," said Little Wolf with a stern voice.

"We should be able to live together."

The Comanche snorted in disgust and wheeled his pony around, giving it a savage kick in the flanks. It lunged forward into a canter. Lance watched the other Comanches join him and as they disappeared in a cloud of dust, he said, "Nice meeting you."

CHAPTER 2

Barlow, Texas

It took Lance the better part of two days to reach Barlow, thankfully avoiding further trouble—notwithstanding Croft's constant yammer, which brought Lance's temper to the brink of boiling over and wanting to put a bullet in the man's head just to shut him up.

As he rode into town, he heard the lonesome whistle of the train about to depart Barlow's station. Oddly enough, the tracks had been laid through the main street, and above the buildings he could see the black smoke roiling in a plume as it pulled away from the station on its journey to the Comanche County seat of Brenham.

The country beyond where the train terminated was serviced by a regular stage run between the smaller towns.

Once Lance had Croft locked away, he would wire Deke to organize himself to come down and collect his prisoner.

Drawing up in front of the jail, he dragged Croft from the saddle. The outlaw once more protested his rough treatment, but the marshal was beyond listening. Instead, he manhandled him up the steps onto the boardwalk, pushing him sufficiently hard through the jail doorway to cause him to stagger.

"You here, Pete?" Lance called out as he placed his Henry on the battered desk strewn with papers.

When there was no answer, Lance crossed the room to the hook where the cell keys were normally kept. With a muttered curse at finding them missing, he started back across to the desk to check the drawers but turned abruptly to face the opening door that led to the cages out back. A sheepish looking deputy with red hair emerged.

"There you—"

Lance got no further before the face of a young lady appeared behind the deputy, her long blonde hair a little mussed. She appeared to be in her late teens and was wearing a pale blue dress. Her cheeks were flushed, and she seemed to be short of breath.

The marshal frowned before saying, "I don't want to know. But you, young lady, need to get out of here before your father comes looking for you."

"Marshal Chaney, I—"

Shaking his head, Lance cut her off by saying, "I don't want to know, I already said, Millie."

Millie Cravens nodded.

"Tell me, sweetness, I'll listen."

Lance turned a withering gaze on the outlaw wearing a leering grin. "Shut up, Croft! Pete, put him out back. If he gives you any trouble, shoot him."

"Yes, sir."

Pete disappeared into the back room with his prisoner, while Millie made her way hurriedly towards the office door, patting her hair into place. As she reached for the door handle, the wooden door swung inward, almost collecting her with its arc. As she recoiled, she looked up to see the figure of her father blocking the opening.

"I knew it! Where else would you be except down here mooning over that Pete Brown?"

Cravens was a portly man who favored black suits and a ridiculous top hat. His hot gaze burned holes through his startled daughter who stood there opening and closing her mouth, failing to conjure the words that might help her cause.

"She's only just walked in the door, Mayor," Lance lied. "Nothing has been going on."

Millie glanced at Lance, her eyes wide with surprise, but thankful for his intercession.

"Really?" the mayor blurted out. "Really? Millie, go home."

"Pa—"

"Now!"

Millie ran out the door, tears rolling down her cheeks. Lance said, "Bit hard on her, Mayor, weren't you?"

"You leave the raising of my daughter to me," he snapped at Lance, somehow doubting the veracity of the marshal's words.

Lance nodded with casual indifference, sat in his chair, and began looking through some wanted fliers. He looked up again as Pete came through the rear door and saw the Cravens standing there. As Pete turned back to retreat down the passage, the mayor barked, "Hold it right there, you little weasel!"

With that, Pete stopped and turned to stare at the irate man. "What do you want?"

"A little respect, for starters," Cravens fumed. "And you can stay the hell away from my daughter."

The marshal watched on waiting to see what the young deputy's response would be.

"She's old enough to make her own decisions," Pete said insolently.

With an imperceptible nod of agreeance, Lance remained where he was, watching on with interest, knowing what would happen next. The mayor's face turned purple. "Why, you blamed insubordinate young pup!" He took a step forward, his arms outstretched. "I'll break your damned neck. Just see if I won't."

Lance moved swiftly to insert himself between the pair before things became too heated. "All right, that'll do. Go home, Mayor."

"Get out of the way, Chaney."

"Nope. Go home or I'll lock you up until you cool down."

"You wouldn't dare."

"Try me."

Cravens was getting nowhere, and he not only knew it but rankled at the fact. After several heartbeats of grinding his teeth together, he snarled, "Keep him away from my daughter or I'll break his neck."

"Goodbye, Mayor."

With that, Cravens whirled about and stalked from the jail, slamming the wooden door behind him hard enough that it rattled the pane of glass in the window.

"Thanks, Lance," Pete said with a grin, thinking that it had gone better than he'd expected. When the marshal's withering gaze settled upon him, the grin faded from his face and he knew it wasn't over.

"What were you thinking?" Lance growled. "What if it had been Cravens who walked in here instead of me? What do you think would have happened then?"

"Nothing did."

"He sure as shooting wouldn't have thought that," Lance snapped. He pointed at the gun rack on the plank wall. "There's no lock on that. He could have just picked up one of the rifles and shot you dead right here."

"But—"

"I don't want to hear your excuses, Pete. If you want to keep working for me, you don't let Millie back in this office. Now, get the lock back on them guns and then go along to the telegraph office and

send word to Deke that we have Croft."
"Yes, sir."

Blanco County, Texas

Manuel Ortega saw the horse before he made out the body lying in the grass beside it. A cold shiver ran down the Mexican's spine as he edged closer, memories of the recent death of his friend, Colin MacDonald, spinning through his mind. The shock of it remained with him, along with the shock of learning that the man had bequeathed the land and all of the sheep to him in his will.

His wife Carmella had pleaded with him not to stay, but for them to return to Mexico. But there was nothing in Mexico to go back to. Here he was now a rich man. Rich in land and stock, which was what he told his beautiful Carmella, yet all she wanted was for them to leave, for him to take them far away. It was no good to them if he was dead too.

Now there was this.

Manuel dismounted and walked cautiously forward. He gripped the old Spencer carbine in his hands, prepared to use it if required. Upon reaching the body, he peered down into the face of a man. He lay on his back and the lower part of his shirt and pants was black with dried blood.

The face was pallid but something about the way it looked urged Manuel to check him. He leaned down and touched the man's cheek. It was cool to touch, but not cold. The man was still alive.

Manuel crossed himself. "Jesucristo."

An hour later, after struggling to get the man over his horse's saddle, Manuel finally walked it back to the ranch house. Carmella met him in the yard, her flawless face etched with concern as she saw the man on the horse.

"Manuel! What has happened?"

He took her hand in his and said reassuringly, "I do not know what has happened. This man needs our help. He has been shot. I will send one of the others for the doctor. Maybe Eduardo. Look at this."

Manuel held out his hand and opened it showing his wife the marshal's badge he had. She gasped. "He is a lawman?"

"So it would seem."

"Who would shoot this man?" Carmella asked her husband. "Do you think it was Senor Conker?"

Manuel reached up and tucked a long strand of his wife's lustrous black hair behind her ear. "I don't know. Maybe if he lives then we will know the truth. Hurry, tell Eduardo what he must do."

"Si."

Carmella hurried away to find the shepherd. Behind Manuel came a low moan and he turned to look at the man on the horse. He needed to get him inside, now.

Barlow, Texas

"You're back," a soft voice said with the hint of a southern drawl. Lance felt a hand on his arm, and he turned to see Lily Montgomery standing there. He leaned down and she kissed him on the cheek. "Are you having a drink?" she asked.

"Maybe a couple," he told her.

"When you get it come over to my table."

"Sure."

"Bert, give the marshal my bottle."

"Yes, ma'am," the slender barkeep said.

Lance watched her walk over to her table, her long copper-colored hair hanging down her narrow back. He wondered whether the emerald green dress she wore was new as he didn't think he'd seen it before.

Bert placed the bottle on the polished bar top and said, "Helps if you know the boss."

"It sure does," Lance said with a grin before turning to head for Lily's table.

He sat down with Lily and let out a long sigh. She studied him closely before saying, "You look tired. Are you OK?"

"I'll be fine. I just had a slight disagreement with Cravens about Pete and Millie. Damned young fool thought it would be OK to do his sparking in the jail."

Lily smirked.

"It ain't funny. He threatened to take my job."

"He wouldn't do that. He's all bluster."

"I don't know if I would care if he did. There's plenty of other towns."

Lance noticed the alarm in her eyes. And he hurriedly added, "But none like this one."

He drank his whiskey and then poured another. Outside, the sun was all but gone and there was now a steady flow of customers coming in. The kerosene lamps on the wall shone a dull orange and the cigar smoke was starting to build along with the noise.

"You heard from Buck at all?" Lily asked.

The marshal shook his head. "Not as yet."

"He's been gone a while."

"I expect he'll be gone a while longer."

Lily could see that Lance was troubled by it. It wasn't unusual for Buck to be gone for long periods but there was usually some word. "Do you want another drink?"

"Not yet. I wouldn't say no to a meal though."

Lily nodded. "Are you staying here tonight?"

"No."

She looked disappointed.

"I've got a prisoner to look after. Pete did the last one so I should take my turn."

"OK. I'll come visit you."

He raised his eyebrows. "In the jail."

"Yes, in the jail. You've been away for almost a week."

He chuckled. "I'll anticipate your presence with the eagerness that it deserves."

"You be careful, Lance Chaney," Lily scolded. "I'll bring a horse pistol with me."

He held his hands up to shoulder level. "No. Please, no. Not that."

She burst out laughing. "You are awful."

Lily was about to say more when she noticed that Lance's expression had changed. He was frowning and his eyes were directed towards the entrance. She looked that way and saw Pete walking towards their table, a concerned look on his young face.

"What is it?" Lance asked him.

"Judge Dyson wants you to go to Brenham," he said. "Deke White is dead."

Once Lance had finished pulling his black boots on, he stood up and stomped his feet to make sure they were on properly. He reached out and took the gun belt from the back of the chair and started to buckle it on.

"What do you think Judge Dyson wants?" Lily asked from where she sat in the bed, back against the wood bedhead.

"I guess I'll find out when I get to Brenham," he answered.

"How long do you figure to be gone?"

"I don't know."

"Damn it, you only just got back."

"It's the job."

"No, it isn't," she snapped. "Your job is here in Barlow, not riding all across Texas."

He turned and stared at her. He loved the way her hair framed her face when it was down. "I have to go."

"I know, damn it."

He thought for a moment then said, "Why don't you come with me?"

Lily chuckled. "I can't do that. I have a place to run."

"So. Let Bert run the place. I'm sure he's quite capable."

Lily remained silent and he could tell she was giving the idea serious consideration. "Come on, I'll buy you dinner at one of their fancy cafés."

A smile split Lily's face. "OK, I'll do it."

"You'll have to ride a buggy because there's no train again until tomorrow. And you'll have to put up with Croft and his moaning."

"I can do that."

"Then it's settled. We'll go together."

Ortega Homestead, Texas

The doctor closed the door of the room and walked down the wide stairs to the living area. Manuel and Carmella waited for the gray-headed man to speak.

"I don't know. The infection is going but he doesn't seem to want to wake up. I guess it is something that only time will tell."

Manuel nodded. "What should we do for him, Senor Walker?"

"Just keep an eye on him. If his temperature goes up again, let me know and I'll come and check on him. I'm afraid there isn't much more I can do."

"Thank you, Doctor," Carmella said with a warm smile.

"How is everything else?" Walker asked.

Manuel and Carmella glanced at each other before the Mexican said, "It is OK."

"No trouble with the association?"

"No."

"There is a whisper around town that they are going to try something. I think that they thought that once MacDonald was gone, that would be the end of it all and you would be gone too. Not hang around like you've done."

"I have tried to convince him to go," Carmella said. "But he is too stubborn."

"Listen to your wife, she shows sense."

Manuel shook his head. "This is our land now. I will fight to keep it."

Walker nodded. "Yes, but tell me this, are you willing to die for it?"

"If I have to."

There was a gasp from Carmella and the doctor said, "You just may well at that."

An uncomfortable silence descended upon the room and with a sigh, Walker said, "I'll head back to town now. I'll be back in a few days to check on him again."

"Thank you, Doctor," Carmella said.

"In the meantime," he said to Manuel. "Think seriously about leaving. These men have already proven their willingness to kill to achieve their outcomes. Like as not, they will not think twice about doing it again."

They walked the doctor out and watched him climb into his buggy. He turned the horse and flicked the reins across its back, causing it to walk on. Once he was gone, a timid voice spoke from behind them, "Has he gone?"

Manuel and Carmella turned to see their eight-year-old daughter Louisa standing there holding a book. Like her mother, she had long black hair and gentle eyes. Also, like her mother, she had flawless features.

Carmella nodded. "Yes, he's gone."

Louisa's face fell. "I was hoping to read to him before he left."

Her mother walked across the porch and took her daughter by the hand. "Come, read to me."

"Really?"

"Yes. I would rather do nothing else than listen

to you read to me."

Manuel watched them walk back inside and for the first time questioned his wisdom in choosing to stay.

Brenham, Texas

The platform was busy, many of those waiting to catch the train to travel further along the line. Lance helped Lily disembark and then said to her, "Wait here while I go and get Croft."

Lance returned to the carriage and unshackled the outlaw from the hard seat, escorting him outside and onto the platform. The marshal stopped Croft next to their carpetbags and said, "Pick them up."

"What?"

"The bags. Pick them up."

"Do it yourself."

Using his right hand, Lance gave the outlaw a hefty clip which brought forth a howl of protest, and the outlaw turned to lunge at the marshal. He was brought up short, however, when Lance drove the hard barrel of his Colt into the man's middle. "Pick them up."

Croft muttered something under his breath and leaned down to pick up the carpetbags. Lance nodded. "Now, start walking."

From the platform, they made their way along Rail Street, across Third, until they reached Main. Once there they turned left and began walking along the busy boardwalk, past the Cactus Flower Saloon.

They kept on until they reached the Brenham Cattleman's Trust and Loan where they were forced to cross over Yard Street which ran perpendicular to Main.

After they were across and returned to the boardwalk once more, they stopped outside the main doors of the Brenham Hotel. Lance looked at Lily and asked, "You want to get us a room while I take care of this one?"

Lily nodded. "I can do that."

"Give her the bags."

Croft dropped them onto the rough boards and Lance whacked him again. "No manners."

"I'll be waiting for you," Lily said.

"I won't be long. I hope. Come on, Croft, let's get you locked away."

The marshal and the outlaw continued along Main past the double-story boarding house and then across the street to the sheriff's office where they found Deputy Hardy Walsh sitting at what was once Deke White's desk. He climbed to his feet and shook hands with Lance. "Good to see you, Lance. I wish it was under better circumstances, though."

Walsh was a solid man in his mid-twenties with dark hair. Lance nodded. "Me too, Hardy. You got a place for Croft here and we can have a talk?"

"Sure," Walsh said, opening the top drawer of the cluttered desk and took out the cell keys. Lance followed him out the back and they locked the outlaw in a nine-by-nine cell. Once back in the main office area Lance asked Walsh, "What happened to Deke?"

"Horse throwed him. Busted his damned neck," Walsh replied.

"Just like that?"

"Uh-huh."

Lance found it hard to believe that Deke White's life could be over just like that. All due to a horse and not an outlaw bullet. But things like that happened. "Hard luck."

"Yeah," Walsh allowed. "Hard luck."

"You know what the judge wants to see me about?"

"I've an idea."

"What?"

"I'll let him tell you."

Lance was puzzled but shrugged his shoulders and then started towards the door. "Catch up later for a drink?"

"Sure, you buy."

The marshal left the jail and went next door to the brick-built courthouse. He walked up the steps and through twin wood doors. The interior of the courtroom was lit by six lamps placed around the wood-paneled walls. A large bench presided over by Judge Granville Dyson was made from the same wood. In the center of the room hung a large chandelier, operated by a rope pulley system that lowered and raised it when the lamps needed to be lit.

The judge was seated at his bench, seemingly elbow deep in papers, which in itself was unusual because he had his own chambers to work in. Sensing that he wasn't alone, he looked up to see Lance standing back watching him. "Come closer, Chaney so I don't have to shout at you."

Lance nodded and made his way along the walkway between the pews. "Working out here now, Judge?"

"Better light out here. I swear my eyes are getting worse by the day."

Judge Granville Dyson was somewhere in his sixties and his hunched shoulders attested to his advancing age, along with his gray hair and lined face. Not to mention his grumpy demeanor. Lance stopped in front of the bench. "What can I do for you, Judge?"

"You know about Deke White," it was a rhetorical question, but Lance acknowledged it anyway.

"Yes, sir, I know."

"Bad stuff. Terrible for the county. And a pain in the ass for me," Dyson growled. "I have to find a replacement for him."

"Hardy Walsh should be a good fit," Lance pointed out.

"One would have thought so, but no, he doesn't

want to do it. Instead, he gave me another name. Yours."

Lance was taken by surprise. This was the last thing he expected. "I have a job, Judge. In Barlow, remember?"

"I know that, damn it. But I want you here, for the county. If you're worried about that lousy town of yours, take satisfaction in the knowledge that as county sheriff you'll still be able to keep an eye on it."

"I thought county sheriffs were elected."

"They are," Dyson allowed. "But I can choose whoever I want to fill in until then. I choose you."

"Whoa now, Judge. What if I decide to take the work and get voted out next election?"

"You won't. You're a good man, Chaney. Good record too. On top of what you'll earn from the county, I'll throw in ten percent of all fines, as well as the bounty money on any outlaw you bring in."

Lance let out a long breath. "That's a mighty handsome offer –"

Dyson's eyes narrowed. "Damn right it is."

"Can I think about it?"

"All right. I'll give you until the end of the day."

"That's not very long."

"It's all you're going to get. And just to help you with your decision, you brought in that varmint Croft on the train today, didn't you?"

"I did."

"How much bounty did he have on him?"

"I don't know."

"Well I do," Dyson growled. "Five-hundred. It's yours. Whether you take the badge or not."

"I don't know what to say, Judge."

"Say yes, damn your eyes."

"I'll think about it."

"Then get out of my courthouse. I've got work to do."

The room was small but tidy. Deep in thought about the judge's proposition, Lance sat on the iron-framed bed atop the lumpy mattress. Pouring water from the jug into the dish on top of the polished wood sideboard, Lily turned her head to look at him. "What is it?" she asked as she washed then dried her hands, the tension finally getting the better of her. "You've looked that way for the past hour."

"Hmm?"

"Lance Chaney, did you hear anything I just said?"

"Yes."

"If that's true, what did I say then?"

"That – ah...I don't know."

She walked across the floor, her steps light and almost silent, and took his hand. "Tell me what's wrong."

"Judge Dyson wants me to take over as county sheriff."

"And?" Lily asked noncommittally.

"And I told him I would think about it."

"What does that mean?"

Lance shook his head. "I don't know."

"Would it mean that you have to leave Barlow?"

"Yes."

"Oh."

He stared at her, the uncertainty on her face evident. "I've sat here and thought about it long and hard and there is only one way that I would accept his offer."

"And that is?"

"If you would come to Brenham with me."

Lily opened her mouth to speak but Lance cut her off. "I know it's a lot to ask, which is why I'm going to tell him no."

"Don't you dare."

The older Chaney frowned.

"Do you want to do the job?"

"I guess it would be good, and the extra money would come in handy."

"Then tell him yes."

"What about you, us?" Lance asked.

"I'll come with you."

He was taken by surprise. "You'll what?"

"If you don't realize what I feel for you by now, Lance Chaney, then you never will and I may as well stay in Barlow," she scolded him.

"What about your saloon."

"I'll sell it and buy or build something else here."

"You're sure?"

"I said as much didn't I?"

He came off the bed and scooped her up in his arms. Lifted her clear of the floor and twirled her about before kissing her on the lips. "You've just made me the happiest man in Texas."

Lily gave him a broad smile. "Put me down and go tell the judge you'll do it. Then come back and take me out for supper. If you can afford it."

He remembered the reward he had coming. "I'll afford it."

"I'll wear the star," Lance told Dyson, a grinning splitting his face.

The judge smiled too. "Good. How long will it take before you can be back here?"

"Two, three days. I need to settle a few things in Barlow."

"Fine, fine. What about that woman of yours?"

"What woman?"

Dyson chuckled. "You know who I'm talking about. The saloon owner. Lily isn't it?"

"It is."

"What's she going to say when she finds out?"

It was Lance's turn to give a laugh. "She's here in Brenham. In fact, she was the one who convinced me to take the badge on."

"And she's willing to let you go?"

"Nope. She's coming too. Going to set up a business here in town."

"Good Lord, just what we need. Another saloon."

CHAPTER 3

Blanco County, Texas

"Sam needs a doctor, Jack," Joe Carter pointed out to his brother. "I've done all I can, but the infection is getting worse. It's been a good few days since the marshal shot him, and he ain't getting no better."

"Give it a few more days," Jack said.

"He ain't got a few more days. There is a town west of here which will have a doctor. How about I ride into town and bring him out here?"

With no sign of pursuit, the brothers had relaxed a little and taken the opportunity to rest up so they could tend their brother in the stand of cottonwoods next to the slow-moving creek. But now things were worse.

"What if you get recognized?" Jack asked. "It's too risky."

"I'll go in after dark. Ask around for a doctor and then bring him here."

"What's the name of the town?"

"Bell."

"Bell you say?"

"Yeah."

"We'll all go."

"What?" Joe asked incredulously.

"I know the sheriff there. We rode some together a while back. Before he decided to pin on a badge."

"You mean he's like us?"

"Used to be."

"What if he ain't anymore."

"He will be. Get Sam on his horse. We'll leave now."

"You'll need to give me a hand; he passed out a while ago."

Jack Carter gave a sigh, indicating his annoyance at the inconvenience. "Fine."

After five minutes of pushing and shoving, they finally managed to secure their brother to his horse.

Bell, Texas

Sheriff Ben Kennedy saw the three riders coming along the dusty street from a way back. He frowned because it looked like the two outside riders were supporting the one in the middle. Out of habit he reached down and placed his right hand reassuringly on the butt of his Navy Colt.

Bell was a cattle town, always had been. Hell, it was said that when Hank Conker first came to the range years before with his herd, the town sprouted from the shit they left behind. But now the scent of bovines had been overpowered; contaminated by the rancher's worst nightmare. The stench of sheep. And he was almost certain that war would break out soon if the damned Mexicans didn't pull up stakes and get gone.

The damned woolies had already been the cause of one death, and if Manuel Ortega refused to leave, the cattlemen would more than likely have him killed. Shame though, his wife sure was pretty. Then again...

Kennedy's gaze wandered back to the riders. He squinted his eyes and raised his left arm to shade them from the glare of the sun. Then opening them wide with surprise, he muttered, "Surely not."

But the closer the riders got the more it became obvious. Jack Carter had hit town.

The horses stopped and Jack stared at Kennedy. "It's me all right, just in case you're still wondering."

"What the hell are you doing in my town?" Kennedy asked, a hard edge to his voice.

"Nice to see you too, Ben," Jack Carter quipped.

"You ain't answered my question yet."

"My brother Sam needs a doctor."

Kennedy glanced around and noticed some of the townsfolk were beginning to stop and stare. "Get him off the horse and inside. There's an empty cell out the back. Put him in there."

Easing the wounded outlaw down from his horse, they moved him inside and placed him on the cot in the cell out back and turned to Kennedy. "Where's the doc?" Jack asked.

"I'll get him in a moment, but first you need to get out of town, Jack, before someone realizes who you are and puts me in an awkward position."

"Ain't going nowhere without our brother," Joe growled.

Kennedy's eyes narrowed. "I want your opinion I'll give it to you."

The outlaw's hand dropped to his six-gun and Jack said, "Ease up there, brother, think before you go off halfcocked."

"I'll have your brother took care of Jack, but like I said, you need to leave. I've an idea where you can go if you're not afraid of a little work."

"If it can keep that marshal off our trail then I'm willing to look at it," Jack told him.

"What marshal?"

"Buck Chaney. He was the one who shot Sam. Killed Hank, too."

Kennedy let out a low whistle. "Hank's dead? Can't say I'm surprised."

"Whatever. Where do we find this place you're

thinking of?"

"It's west of town," Kennedy said. "Ranch called the Broken C. The owner is a man named Hank Conker. Tell him I sent you."

"All right then. I'll be back in a few days to check on Sam."

The sheriff shook his head. "I'll send word on how he's doing. If he dies, I'll have him buried."

"If he dies, I'll have you buried," Joe hissed.

Kennedy stared hard at the unshaven outlaw whose black hair hung down to his collar. "Don't push me, boy, I've ate worse than you for breakfast."

"Take it easy, Ben," Jack soothed.

"Get gone, Jack. Having you here is bringing out something in me that's been buried for a while now, and I don't like it."

"All right, we're going. But I'll be expecting word."

"You'll get it when I send it."

Kennedy watched them leave and then turned to look at the wounded man lying on the straw mattress of the cot. He walked across the cell and studied him for a few moments then made his decision. He reached down and picked up the stained pillow before placing it over the now unconscious Sam Carter's face.

Broken C, Ranch

"Who did you say you were?" Broken C foreman, Max Gilbert asked.

"Nobody in particular," Jack Carter replied. "Ben Kennedy said we should be able to find some work here for a while."

"He did, did he?" Gilbert asked as he eyed them with caution.

"Sure, he did. Now, was he right or are we wasting our time? If we are, then we'll just ride on out again."

"That won't be necessary," a new voice joined the conversation and Conker stepped outside on the large wooden porch. "What do you men do?"

"Pretty much anything?" Jack told the Broken C owner.

Conker studied them for a moment before he nodded and said, "All right, stow your stuff in the bunkhouse. Max will be over there shortly to give you jobs to do."

After they rode over to the bunkhouse, Conker asked Gilbert, "What do you think?"

"They've got killer written all over them," Gilbert told his boss.

"Then we may have a use for them."

Gilbert nodded. "It's possible."

The Broken C owner shifted his gaze and letting it drift out across the rolling hills to the east. Somewhere out there, nestled Bell. To the ranch house's west, the terrain changed, flattening out a little. This had been Conker's home for the past ten years, and his plans were to be there at least another twenty or until he died, whichever came first.

Maybe these men would serve a purpose, especially if that Mex son of a bitch insisted on staying put with his sheep on the range to the north of his. At least that way he wouldn't have to use Coleman again. He'd discuss it with the association members. It was about time that Ortega learned in no uncertain terms that he needed to go.

"See how they turn out, Max. There's going to be a meeting of the association members in a couple of days. They might just come in handy."

"You know who that older one was, right?"

"Not a clue," Conker said.

"He's Jack Carter. I knew his name, but I wanted to hear him say it."

"Do you figure that our friend Sheriff Kennedy knows who he is?"

"A man with his past, yeah, I'd say so."

"Go into town tomorrow and have a chat with him, find out if he does."

"OK."

Ortega Homestead

Buck wasn't aware of much when he first woke up. It was dark, his head swam, and he could smell food. Not freshly cooked food, but the leftover scent of food that had been cooked earlier in the day. He tried to move, and pain shot through his side. A low groan escaped his lips and he lay there, barely breathing, with his eyes squeezed shut until the pain subsided.

"Hello?"

Buck's voice wasn't much more than a harsh whisper. His throat was dry, and his mouth tasted like a horse had taken a dump in it. Searching his fuzzy brain, he tried to remember what had happened to him. Where he was, but everything was blank. At least he still knew who he was, so that was a good starting point.

"Carters," he muttered softly. He'd been hunting the Carters when he'd been wounded. But everything after that was gone.

Closing his eyes, Buck's breathing became shallower and overwhelming fatigue swamped him and he drifted back to sleep.

Carmella Ortega gasped, startled to find Buck staring back at her through the open curtains when she turned around.

"Sorry, ma'am, didn't mean to startle you."

"Madre de Dios, you are awake."

"Yes – yes, ma'am," he nodded and cleared his throat. "I wouldn't mind a little water if you have some."

"Of course, I'll get you some from the kitchen."

He watched Carmella cross the room to the door and disappear. A mighty fine-looking woman, that's for sure. He was enough in control of his senses to notice that. A few minutes later she returned with a jug of water and a glass, and a man. Husband, Buck guessed.

"My Carmella said you were awake, Marshal. It is good to see. We did not think that it would happen. The doctor was even doubtful for a time."

Carmella poured the water and assisted Buck so he could drink. He could smell the sweet scent of freshly bathed skin as she wrapped an arm around him in support. Once he was finished, she eased him back down.

"Where am I?" Buck asked.

The marshal noticed the Mexican's chest puff out a little with pride as he said, "You are in the home of Manuel and Carmella Ortega, Señor."

Buck frowned, his mind working but coming up empty. "Am I in Mexico?"

Ortega chuckled. "No, no. You are in Blanco County, Texas."

"That's something, I guess. How long have I been here?"

"Enough of the questions," Carmella said to Buck. "Get some rest."

"What is your name, Marshal?" Ortega asked glancing at his wife.

"Chaney. Buck Chaney."

"Are you hungry? Perhaps my wife could get you something to eat?"

Buck thought about it for a moment, assessing the growling of his stomach against the pressing urge to sleep, deciding that at this moment he was too tired to eat. "Maybe later. Thank you."

Carmella said, "I'll be back to check on you after, Marshal Chaney."

"It's actually Deputy Marshal, ma'am."

She smiled. "Deputy Marshal."

Buck watched them leave and then closed his eyes, giving in to the blackness and blessed relief of sleep.

Brenham, Texas

John Ferguson tossed back his last drink and put the glass back on the scarred tabletop with perhaps a little more force than was necessary. The blonde whore sitting expectantly across from him jumped a little then noticed he was climbing to his feet. "Where you going, Johnny?"

"Back to the Circle D," Ferguson informed her eliciting an annoyed frown.

"But why? The sun has only just gone down."

The cowhand straightened up before picking his stained and dusty Stetson from the table then turned to her to say, "It is for that very fact, Daisy my dear, that I should be getting back. Mister Denham ain't going to like it if I'm late up in the morning."

Daisy smiled. "You could stay up late with me."

Ferguson returned her smile and looked around the dimly lit Railway Saloon. He shook his head. "As inviting as that sounds, and a poke with you does sound mighty good, I need my job more."

She pouted at him and then said, "Are you coming to town on Saturday?"

"Uh-huh."

"Will I see you then?"

"Sure. I'll come and have that poke then."

"I'll hold you to that, Johnny Ferguson."

"I wouldn't expect anything else."

Ferguson made his way between tables and across the sawdust-covered floor towards the door. He pushed out through it, placing his hat on his head, and straight away felt the slight chill in the air. It brought back memories of the cold nights he'd spent under the stars during the war. He shivered and pulled his coat collar up.

The cowhand walked along South Street, kicking up dust with each step, then crossed Third, continuing until he reached Main. He stopped at the intersection, looked right, and then turned right. Halfway along the last block, he crossed over the street, avoiding several wagons drawn by teams of bullocks. On the far side was a laundry run by a Chinese man named Lim. The livery was next to the laundry and the hand needed to get his horse before he went anywhere.

Outside the large double-doors, a lit lantern hung from a wooden corbel, lighting the way for travelers who may arrive late at night. Ferguson opened the door, the unoiled hinges screeching their protest. There were two more coal oil lanterns hanging from the stable's uprights, casting eerie shadows throughout the gloomy interior. "Franklin, you here?"

The snort of an animal greeted him. The hand stepped inside. "I've come to collect my horse!"

In the dusty stillness, Ferguson shrugged and muttered, "Guess I can fix it next time I come to town."

He wandered down the line of stalls on his right until he came to his horse. "Hey, boy. Time to go home."

Although most men left their mounts tethered to hitch racks outside the saloons while in town, Ferguson wasn't one of them. He believed that he and his horse were partners, reliant on the beast at all times, and that earned him a modicum of respect. He, therefore, thought that no matter his business, the animal should be well cared for. So, on every visit to town, he always put him up at the livery to be fed, watered, and rubbed down by Franklin, the hostler.

Ferguson's hand had just touched the top of the stall gate when his horse let out a warning nicker. The man whirled about, his hand dropping to his six-gun. In the shadows, he could make out nothing unusual, but saw only horses on the other side staring back at him.

He turned back. "Damn it, horse –"

The last thing Ferguson ever felt was the bite of the knife across his throat.

Hardy Walsh was waiting for Lance when he stepped down from the train just after noon the following day. "Are you on your own?" he asked the new county sheriff.

"Yeah. I've got my horse in the stock car and some things in baggage –"

"I'll have someone take care of it."

"What's up?"

They started dodging between milling passengers, as they walked along the platform, waiting until they were alone before Walsh went on. "A cowhand from the Circle D, John Ferguson, was found a short time ago with his throat cut."

"Where?" Lance asked.

"Under some hay in the livery."

"Welcome to Brenham."

"Yeah, something like that."

Walsh stopped and spoke to one of the local bums that haunted the rail station around train time looking for a little work for pocket change. He explained what needed to be done for the new lawman and then the two of them kept going.

They walked along Rail street and then down Third to South before turning that way and onto Main. A small crowd had gathered outside the livery, and the two men had to force their way through. "Move aside," Walsh growled as he pushed one of the onlookers aside.

"Hey!" the man grunted. "What are you doing?"

He turned to glare at the deputy but instead locked gazes with Lance. The older Chaney brother said, "You have a problem, friend?"

His mouth opened, but the words that were forming in his brain were suddenly caught in his throat, and with a shake of his head the man said, "No, sir."

Entering the livery, they found two men waiting there. One was unmistakably the Brenham doctor, the other was dressed in wool pants and a gray shirt. At their feet was the body of a man, his shirt stained black with dried blood from the gaping wound in his throat.

Walsh said, "This is Doc Harding and livery owner Buster Franklin. This is the new county sheriff, gents. Lance Chaney."

"Not the best thing to greet you upon your arrival, Sheriff," Harding said pointing at the corpse.

"What can you tell me, Doc?"

"Not much I'm afraid. He was killed last evening and hidden under the hay in there." He pointed towards the vacant stall. "Throat has been cut clean which tells me that the knife was very sharp."

"Who found the body?"

Franklin cleared his throat. "I did. The horses were kicking up a fuss all morning. I never really thought much of it until I caught sight of the blood spray on one of the stall gates."

"Where?"

Franklin took him along the stalls to where the bloodstained gate stood closed. "I don't know how many times I walked past it this morning without seeing it. When I finally did, I got to thinking and looking around. That was when I found Ferguson."

"Where's he from?"

"Out at the Circle D. He left his horse here yesterday when he hit town. Hell, he always leaves it here. Thinks more of the animal than he does of people, I swear."

"You know of anyone who would want to kill him?"

"Nope."

Lance nodded and stared at the spray pattern on the gate. He guessed in the dim-lit light of the livery's interior it would be easy to miss. He walked back over to where the corpse lay. "Have you checked his pockets, Hardy?"

"No."

Lance leaned down and went through Ferguson's pockets. He came up with some loose change, two dollars, tobacco, and not much else. "It doesn't look like he was robbed. His gun is still in its holster."

"So why would someone kill him?" Walsh asked.

"That's something we'll have to figure out," Lance answered. "Hardy, see if you can find out what he did while he was in town yesterday."

"Yes, sir."

"Have you finished with the body, Doc?"

Harding nodded. "Not much else I can do."

"All right. Franklin, get the undertaker and have him take care of the body."

"Sure, Sheriff."

Lance walked back outside to where the crowd waited. They jostled to see what was happening. "Everybody go about your business."

There were a few grumbles of dissent, but recognizing the authority of their new lawman, did as instructed and dissipated quickly. Lance glanced to his left and saw the Chinaman standing outside of what looked to be a false-front store with a large canvas-covered main building area. The sheriff walked over to him, touched his hat brim. "Howdy. Name's Chaney. I'm the new county sheriff."

The man eyed him warily and said, "I am Lim. This is my laundry."

Lance looked up at the sign which told him just as much. Lim's hair was fastened in a long queue down his back, and he was dressed in what Lance thought were gray nightclothes. "Did you hear anything last night, Lim?"

The Chinese man shook his head. "No. Hear nothing."

"You sure?"

He nodded. "Hear nothing."

"All right. Thanks."

"Welcome."

Two hours after leaving the livery, Hardy Walsh walked into the jail and reported to Lance what he'd found out.

"It ain't much, Lance," he started. "Ferguson came into town yesterday and did a couple of jobs for Clive Denham and then went to the Railway Saloon where he spent the rest of the afternoon. I asked around everywhere in town but that was all I could come up with."

"What jobs did he have to do for Denham?"

"He placed an order at the dry-goods store and then stopped at the freight and stage outfit to check on some things that Denham was waiting on. After that he went to the saloon."

Lance thought for a moment and then said, "You want to ride out to the Circle D and talk to Denham?"

"I can do that."

"Just the usual questions. Maybe check with some of those he worked with to see if they know anything."

"I'll saddle up and ride now."

"Thanks, Hardy."

"Before you go, do you know anything about his past?"

Walsh shook his head. "Other than he fought in the war, no. But that covers every second man in town."

"All right. I'll see you when you get back."

Once Walsh left the office, Lance did too. He wanted to ask some follow-up questions at the saloon. If there was one place where everyone's business was known, the saloon was it.

The Railway was quiet when he entered. The barroom smelled of stale beer and tobacco smoke. The patrons were outnumbered by soiled doves, and while the only two customers were being entertained, the remaining three ladies looking bored, lounged at a corner table.

Lance crossed to the bar, his bootheels clunking on the wooden floorboards. The barkeep looked up from his work disinterestedly polishing glasses, grateful to see a prospective customer, and asked, "What can I get you?"

"Answers would be good," Lance replied.

The dark-headed man shook his head, his bushy mustache hiding the downturn of his mouth. "You want answers, go find them somewhere else. A drink? That's what I can give you."

Lance pulled his coat lapel back to show the barkeep the badge. "Try again. The name is Chaney."

"Damn it. Twice in one day. I told the deputy I don't know nothing, OK? Now leave me be."

"When I'm done. Now, what was Ferguson doing here last evening? Was he on his own?"

"Yes."

Lance looked around the room. Without looking at the barkeep he said, "Which girl was he with?"

"What?"

"He was here on his own. Your girls wouldn't be doing their jobs if they left him sitting there all on his own. Which one?"

"Daisy."

"Where is she?"

"At the table over there with Monk," the barkeep said, pointing.

"Thanks. What's your name?"

"Posey."

"Someone sure hated you, didn't they?"

"Tell me about it."

Lance walked across to the table where Daisy was using her feminine wiles on a big bear of a man Posey had identified as Monk. The man looked up and glared at Lance. "Go away."

"I need to speak to the lady," Lance told him.

"Go away, she's with me," Monk grunted.

"And I told you I need to talk to her."

Monk came erect and unfurled to his full height somewhere above six and a half feet. "You might want to reconsider that."

Lance showed him his badge. "So might you. I promise I won't keep her long."

"I guess I ain't got no choice then."

"Not really."

The big man shuffled off and Lance sat down. "Just want to ask a few questions is all and I'll let you get back to work."

"Is this about Johnny?"

"Yes. He was with you here last evening?"

"Uh-huh. I tried to get him to stay for a poke, but he wanted to get back to the Circle D. If he had he'd still be alive."

"You don't know that," Lance said. "Do you know of anyone who would want to hurt him?"

"No."

"He didn't mention anything?"

"No. Sometimes he had nightmares about the war, but that was it."

"How do you know that?"

"He stayed the night with me every now and then."

"How could he afford that?"

"For free."

"So he said nothing."

"No, sir."

"OK. But if you think of something, let me know."

She nodded. "I will."

Lance climbed from the chair and walked towards the door.

Circle D

"Well, I'll be a son of a bitch," Clive Denham growled. "That damn Ferguson was always a good worker. Who am I going to get to replace him?"

"Clive," Martha Denham scolded her 62-year-old gray-haired husband. "I'll not have that kind of cussing in this house."

"Well, he was," Denham reiterated.

"The young man isn't even in the ground yet and you're already giving his job away."

"A ranch won't run itself, Martha," Denham growled. "I lose a hand and I lose money."

"I don't believe you, Clive, I really don't," his wife scolded him. She turned her gaze on Walsh. "You will tell the undertaker, Mister Hathaway, that we will pay for the young man's burial."

Clive Denham almost choked on his wife's words. His eyes bulged and he blurted out, "Just hold on a dang minute, woman. Who said I was going to pay—"

"Oh, shush up," his wife growled. "A young man who worked for you is dead. The least you can do is pay to see he's buried right."

The rancher glared at his wife but then nodded. "I guess so."

Walsh asked, "Is there any reason that you can think of why someone would want to kill him?"

They both shook their heads. Denham said, "No. He seemed to get on with everyone. Even that saloon girl. He seemed to be moon-eyed over her. Never affected his effort none though. Did his work, was out of bed early and always one of the first out of the yard. Couple more years and he would have made foreman."

"So you can't think of anything?"

"Like I said, he was all good. If he had enemies, then we never knew about them."

"He had nightmares every now and then," one of the hands spoke up.

Walsh turned to him. "What about?"

The blond-headed cowboy shrugged. "Not sure. War stuff mostly, I think. Like most of us who fought."

Walsh nodded. "If you can think of anything you consider we should know, can you let the sheriff know?"

Denham frowned. "Sheriff? I thought Deke got hisself killed?"

"New county sheriff now. Lance Chaney."

"I've heard of him," Denham acknowledged. "Good man they say. Heard Deke speak of him."

Walsh nodded. "He's a good man all right. I'm sure he'll do a good job."

"What about you, Hardy?" Martha asked the deputy. "Why not you?"

Walsh smiled. "The judge asked me, Martha. I told him I was happy just the way things were. In fact, I told him to ask Lance."

"You're a good man, Hardy Walsh," the woman said reaching out and taking his hand. "You'd make a nice husband for our Mary."

"Damn it, woman," Denham growled. "The man is out here on law business."

Walsh smiled. "Is she here, Martha?"

"She's in the kitchen."

"Maybe I can talk to some of the other hands and then call upon her?"

"I'd be right cross if you didn't, Hardy," Martha scolded.

Walsh talked to some of the other hands and came up with no more than what he already knew. When he returned to the ranch house, he found Mary and her mother in the large kitchen. He took his hat off and placed it on the table.

"Good, you're here," Martha greeted. "Did you find out anything more?"

"No, ma'am." He looked at Mary who was also looking at him. She was in her mid-twenties, a few years younger than Walsh, had long black hair, and a slim figure. "Hello, Mary."

"Hello, Hardy."

A drawn-out silence was broken by Martha Denham. "Shall I leave the room so you two can talk more freely?"

Mary blushed a shade of deep red, embarrassed by her mother's forthrightness. "Ma!"

"Oh, hush child. Any fool can see that I'm in the way. I might as well go and collect the eggs before the chickens hatch them."

After she'd left Mary said, "I'm sorry about that."

"Don't be. I'm kind of glad she's gone."

"I saw you talking to Pa before. Did he mention that he's going to run for governor next year?"

"No," said Walsh, a little surprised. "I'd have thought he'd be too busy here to run for office."

"This ranch virtually runs itself. He says he can make a difference, so Ma said she was happy enough for him to do it."

"I'll remember to wish him luck."

Another silence was followed by Mary asking if he was going to the church dance the day after next. Walsh said, "I will if you'd go with me?"

"We were going anyway. Pa figured it would be a good time to tell everyone that he was running for governor. But I'd be happy to be going with you. Maybe we could meet there?"

"I'd like that."

"Then I'll see you there."

He picked his hat up off the table. "You will."

He turned to leave when Mary clearing her throat stopped him. He turned back. "Is there something you've forgot, Hardy?"

He gave her a confused look. "I don't think so, ma'am."

"Oh, damn it," Mary huffed and strode forward,

her grey dress swirling. When she reached the deputy, she grabbed his shoulders and kissed him on the lips, standing on tiptoe to do it. When she pulled back, she said, "There, now you can go."

He nodded, taken by surprise. "Yes, ma'am," he gasped.

"And don't you be late, Hardy Walsh," she warned him. "I expect the first dance and every one after that."

"Yes, ma'am," he said again and stumbled from the kitchen.

Bell, Texas

Max Gilbert rode into town, crossing the wooden bridge over Wash Creek and along Main Street. His journey took him past Settlement and Yard streets, across Holt and eventually to the T-intersection at the far end of town where Law Street was. Aptly named because it held the jail and courthouse on it, situated side-by-side.

The Broken C foreman rode up to the hitch rail and climbed down. He looped the reins of his bay around the crossbar and climbed the steps onto the uneven boardwalk. The day was hot, and the sun was at the right angle for the gray boards to kick heat back up into his face. Sweat began forming on his cheeks and he took his hat from his head, revealing black hair with a smattering of silver flecks through it.

Inside the office he found Kennedy seated at his desk, constructed of dark wood, with more scratches than a flea-infested coon dog. The sheriff sat up taller when he saw Gilbert, giving him an unwelcoming glare. "What can I do for you?" he asked abruptly.

"The boss sent me into town to ask about the new men you sent out to the ranch."

"Uh-huh. What does he want to know?"

"You seem to know them. You tell me."

Kennedy nodded. "All right. Jack Carter and his brother Joe. Mean sons of bitches who need killing. But they will take orders as long as there's a dollar in it for them. They arrived in town with another brother, Sam. He was wounded. They left him here so the doc could take a look at him."

"And?"

"He died," Kennedy said without going into any details. "You might want to tell his brothers when you head back to the Broken C."

"Anything else. Like how you know them?"

"Jack and I rode some together back in the day. Had to part ways with him. Crazy mean at times. Didn't want to wake up one night with a knife in my chest. You want my advice, shoot them and bury them deep. Just to make sure they can't climb out."

Gilbert walked over to a potbellied stove in the corner where a coffee jug sat on the hot plate. He touched it and found it cold. He turned back to the sheriff and asked, "Then why would you send them out to the ranch if they're as crazy mean as you say?"

"Conker is looking for help. Like I said, they'll follow orders it there's a dollar in it for them. Plus, they wanted a place to lay low. Seems they had a marshal named Chaney on their trail."

The foreman shook his head. "And you sent them out to the ranch? What the hell were you thinking?"

"You don't talk to me like that, Gilbert. Conker wanted men. I sent them. End of story. You want to get rid of the sheep, use them. They'll do it cheap."

"The boss ain't going to like this, Kennedy."

"He likes anything that gets him results."

Broken C, Ranch

"What do you mean he's dead?" Jack Carter growled.

"Just what I said," Gilbert replied. "Your brother died."

"Damn it," Joe snarled. "I bet that son of a bitch let him die instead of getting a doctor for him like he said he would."

"I wouldn't know anything about that," Gilbert said. "All I know is that he died and was buried in the cemetery."

"I guess there ain't much point to us hanging around then," Jack surmised.

"We can still go into town and shoot the damned sheriff for letting Sam die."

"Just rein your horses in a moment," Gilbert said. "You both could stay around and earn some money, if you want?"

Jack guffawed. "Nursing cows ain't something I'm apt to do, Gilbert. No offense. I'm better at stealing them."

"I didn't say it would be legitimate wages. Might be a mess of shooting involved."

Jack looked at his brother. "Might be easier than robbing banks."

"Maybe."

"All right, Gilbert. We'll put down roots for a while. But we ain't nursing cows, like I said. You need to understand that right from the get-go."

"Then you're staying?"

"I guess we are."

CHAPTER 4

Ortega Homestead, Texas

Buck spent the whole of the day in bed resting and eating, his strength returning in waves. That evening he summoned the strength to rise and sit at the table for dinner, joining Manuel, Carmella, and their daughter Louisa. The fare was simple, a lamb stew with potatoes and vegetables. It was followed by blueberry pie baked fresh that afternoon and washed down with rich black coffee. When he was finished Buck said, "That was mighty fine cooking, ma'am. I reckon I could almost eat another three courses."

Carmella smiled. "I'm glad you enjoyed it, Deputy Marshal."

"If I'm going to be resting up here for a couple of days until I can ride, you might as well get my name right. It's Buck. Buck Chaney."

Ortega nodded. "Buck it is. And you will call us Manuel and Carmella."

"What about this little princess?"

Louisa beamed. "My name is Louisa."

"Pleased to meet you, Louisa."

Carmella got up from the table. "Louisa, come with me. We will do the dishes while the men talk."

"Yes, Mama."

Once they were gone Buck said, "You have a nice family, Manuel."

"Thank you, Buck. Although I wish they were not here at such a time."

"Trouble?"

"More than I think I can handle on my own," Ortega said. "But what about you, Marshal? Why are you here?"

"I was trailing some men. Killers. I caught up to them and I was wounded in a gunfight. Once I'm well enough I'll go after them again. But what about your troubles? Is there anything I can do to help out?"

"We are sheep farmers."

Buck nodded. He knew what that meant. Sheep farmers in cattle country were almost as bad as having a herd with Spanish Fever. It was a good bet to get yourself hung just thinking about bringing sheep into cow country.

"It wasn't us who brought them here," Manuel said. "It was but we didn't own them. A Scottish man named Colin MacDonald brought them up from Mexico. He hired us to work for him. A short time ago he was murdered. Shot from ambush no more than a mile from where we sit."

"Did the law get who done it?" Buck asked.

"We are sheep people in cattleman's country," Manuel said bitterly. "The sheriff is in the pocket of the cattlemen, and I have heard some say he was once an outlaw himself. What do you think happened?"

Buck understood. "Nothing at all."

"Now the cattlemen are threatening us."

"Why don't you leave?"

"We have nowhere to go. We gave up everything to come here with MacDonald."

"So, you're going to see it through to the end?" Buck asked.

"Yes," Manuel said.

"Be careful your pride don't get you killed, Manuel. Remember your family."

"It is for them that I do this."

"Who is the he bull of the woods?" Buck asked.

The Mexican looked at him confused.

"The boss? The biggest rancher? The man who's causing all your problems?"

"A rancher called Hank Conker. He is also the head of the Cattleman's Association."

"Fine. Once I'm back on my feet I'll have a word to him and see if I can't sort something out."

Manuel shook his head. "You would be wasting your time, Buck. That man is not an understanding one. I'm afraid the only thing he deals in is lead."

"You figure he was behind this MacDonald feller getting killed?"

"Yes. Of that I am certain. And if you interfere, he will almost certainly try to kill you too."

Buck chuckled as he remembered all that he'd been through in recent years. "I'm a mighty hard man to kill, Manuel."

"Let us hope so."

Brenham, Texas

The Cactus Flower saloon became busier as the sun went down. Now, a couple of hours later, it was more than half full. Lance sat at a scarred-top table with Hardy Walsh, a partial bottle sitting between them.

The piano player sitting at an out of tune upright, seemed determined to get right a new tune from back east much to the chagrin of those within the confines of the saloon's walls, as well as those outside in the immediate vicinity of the saloon.

Brass lamps on the walls cast their dim light, and the chandelier hanging above the main bar had the same effect, creating a cozy ambiance of flickering shadows in the recesses. The bar was a polished hardwood slab, and a brass footrail ran the length of its base. Typical of many bars of the time, a large wall mirror hung on the back wall, a diagonal crack ran left to right across it. Rows of bottles and glasses were stacked on several wood shelves of the same dark timber that comprised the railings on the staircase running up to the second floor.

Two four-seater card tables were sited against the far wall with no vacant chairs around either, the men there engrossed in a game of Five Card Stud. A heavily-painted whore had draped herself across one of the players at the second table, and he was rubbing his free hand along her rump, causing her to giggle. Lance frowned.

"Did you have any luck with Daisy?" Walsh asked.

"Nope. All she could give me was nightmares."

The deputy nodded. "That's about all the Denham's gave me, too. That and the news Clive is running for governor. Making the announcement tomorrow night at the church dance."

"Church dance?"

"That's right, you going?"

"Can't say that I am."

"You mind if I do?"

Lance studied him for a moment and then said, "You stepping out with someone?"

"Mary Denham."

"Good luck to you."

"You mind if I join you for a moment?"

Both lawmen looked up at Judge Dyson and nodded. Lance pointed at the spare chair. "Be our guest."

The judge sat down and asked, "You have anything about the murder yet?"

"Not a thing."

"Blast it. There are already rumors getting around town about a killer in our midst. Making everyone nervous."

"Sorry Judge," Lance apologized. "But after asking around town and even the ranch, we've come up with an empty bucket."

Lance looked back over at the card table and saw the gambler rub the butt of the whore once more.

"What are you going to do now?" Dyson asked.

Lance flicked his gaze back to him. "Keep asking around. Someone must have seen something."

"I pray you find that someone Lance. I really do."

The judge got up from his seat. "I'll bid you good evening, gentlemen."

"Evening, Judge."

Dyson was halfway to the door when a thin man wearing a white shirt and a green vest, sidled through the gathering crowd, making a beeline for the table where the two lawmen were sitting. He had a piece of paper in his hand.

Stopping in front of them he looked at Lance. "Sheriff, I have a telegram for you."

"Who are you?"

"Burns, Western Union," the man supplied.

Lance held out his hand and took the piece of paper. He reached into his pocket, took out a quarter, and flipped it to the telegrapher who turned and left. Lance unfolded the paper and read the message. He smiled.

"Good news I take it," Walsh guessed.

"The best. Lily is coming tomorrow. She's sold her saloon in Barlow and is going to buy one of the ones here."

"Which one?"

"I don't know, she didn't say. But whichever one it is, I know she'll make a go of it."

"Some of the owners around here ain't going to like a woman moving in on their territory."

"Too bad," Lance said. Then added, "Wait here."

Walsh watched him get up from the chair he sat in and make his way over to the table where the whore was still draped across the gambler. Three of the gamblers looked up at him as he stopped behind the woman and her player. He asked, "Having a good evening, gents?"

"Sure Sheriff," a red-headed gambler said. "The company is good, but the cards aren't so hot. Not to worry. You win some, you lose some."

"What about you, Mister?" Lance said. "Your friend bringing you any luck?"

The woman unwrapped herself from the gambler so he could turn to face Lance. She had strikingly blue eyes accentuated by her blonde hair. The low-cut green dress she wore which drew focus to her voluminous breasts which threatened to spill out over the top. Lance studied her for a moment and a hint of uncertainty flickered across her face when she saw the badge pinned to his chest.

The man looked up at the sheriff. His face was clean-shaven except for a pencil-thin mustache. His face was pale, almost sickly looking. He was about to speak when the redhead said, "He's about the only one having any luck tonight."

"Is that so. What's your name, Mister?"

"Chet Miller."

"Uh-huh. So, how much you won tonight, Miller?"

"Couple of dollars."

"Couple?" one of the other gamblers said. "More like twenty."

Lance nodded. "What's your name, Miss?" he asked the whore.

"Sylvie."

"You mind if I touch you for luck, Sylvie?"

Now her alarm grew. "Why?"

"Just want to see how lucky you are."

Lance reached out and she took a step back. Before she was out of reach, he grasped her arm with his left hand and then dragged her close. "Where you going?"

"Let me go."

Miller came out of his seat, but the sheriff was expecting the move. His right hand filled with his Navy Colt and his thumb eared the trigger back. "You try for that hideout gun you have and I'll gut-shoot you."

Miller froze.

From where he sat, Walsh witnessed the start of the trouble and came to his feet. He drew his six-gun and walked across to the table. "Having some trouble, Lance?"

"Think our friend here was cheating at cards. I was just about to prove it. Check him for a hideout gun, Hardy."

The deputy stepped forward and checked Miller for weapons. He found a small Derringer and an Arkansas Toothpick tucked in the man's boot. Walsh held it up. "Interesting."

Lance nodded. "We'll get to that." He then held Sylvie firmly while he felt around her rump. He found the split in her dress and reached inside. A moment later his hand emerged with four cards.

"Well I'll be a son of a bitch," the red-headed gambler said in wonderment. "They were cheating us."

"Empty your pockets, Miller."

The gambler emptied them out onto the table. A small pile of money sat in the center next to the pot. Lance reached forward and took a ten-dollar note. He tucked it in the gambler's hand and said, "The rest of you split what's left."

"You can't do that," Miller blurted out as the others started to divide up the money. "There's more money there than what I won."

"I guess you'll learn not to cheat, won't you? I mean I can let them have you. See how they deal with you."

Miller went silent.

"No? You can spend the night in jail anyhow.

Then you'll be put on tomorrow's westbound stage."

"I have a horse."

"Not anymore you don't. Hardy, take him to jail. I'll be there directly."

"Sure, Lance. Come on, you," he said giving Miller a shove.

Lance turned to Sylvie who looked suddenly scared. Before he could speak, the saloon owner arrived. "What is going on?" he demanded.

"Who are you?"

"Jacobs. I own this place," the portly man said.

"Seems your girl here was working with a card cheat," Lance informed him.

The owner turned a hot glare on the whore. "You damned bitch. Get upstairs and wait for me there. I'll give you what for when I get there."

"Just hold on there, Jacobs," Lance said. "While I don't cotton to cheats, I like women beaters even less. I'm going to check back on Sylvie over the coming days and if there's so much as a hair out of place I'm going to come down on you like an avalanche of rocks. Understand?"

The saloon owner nodded. "Fine."

"How much did he give you to help out?" Lance asked her.

"Ten dollars."

"Give it here," Jacobs demanded.

Sylvie started to reach into her corset top when Lance stopped her. He knew that ten dollars was a lot of money to her and more than tempting. "Keep it. I have a feeling business will be slow for a while until people start to forget."

He heard Jacobs mutter something under his breath and turned to face him. "Remember what I said, Mister Jacobs. Not a hair out of place."

Lance left the saloon then, but not before taking his bottle from the table. Outside, the air was cool and crisp. A buggy rattled along the street, a young couple sitting in it. No doubt courting. Then he thought of Lily. It would be good to have her here. He let out a sigh and closed his eyes for a moment taking in the sounds of nighttime Brenham. Then he stepped down onto the street and headed for the jail.

He found Walsh waiting for him inside. The deputy had himself a hot cup of coffee. Lance placed the bottle on the scratched and marked desktop and said, "You got a spare cup?"

Walsh nodded. "Sure. Give me a minute."

He found the tin mug and filled it from the pot on the potbellied stove. He gave it to Lance who thanked him and asked, "Where's that toothpick?"

Walsh opened the top drawer of the desk and reached inside. He took the wicked-looking weapon out and passed it over to the sheriff. Lance looked it over and said, "Sharp enough to do the job."

"That it is."

"Let's go and have a talk to our friend."

They went out to the cells where Miller sat on a bunk. The cell next to his was empty, Croft having been transferred the day before Lance arrived. Studying the man for a moment in silence, the sheriff then asked, "How long you been in Brenham, Miller?"

"Why?"

"Just answer the question," Walsh snapped.

"Got in two days ago."

"Where were you last night?" Lance asked.

"Railway Saloon playing cards."

"Did you go anywhere near the livery last night?"

"No, why?"

"Just want to know is all," Lance said.

Miller's expression changed as he realized what the sheriff was getting around to. His eyes widened and he blurted out, "Is this about that feller getting killed?"

"What if it is?"

"I never killed no one. Sure, I might play a little loose with the cards but I'm no killer."

"Give us some names so we can check your story," Walsh said.

"I can only remember one. Man named Betts. Never really caught his first name."

Lance looked at his deputy. "You know him."

Walsh nodded. "Porter Betts. Local. I'll rustle him up in the morning and ask him some questions."

"Fine."

"What about me?" Miller asked.

"You're here until the stage leaves, remember?" Lance told him. "But if your story doesn't check out, then me and you are going to have another talk."

The two men left the cells and walked back through to the main office. "What do you think?" Walsh asked Lance.

"I think he's telling the truth. Like he says, he's a cheater, not a killer."

"Which means our killer is still out there somewhere."

"Or is long gone."

Lily Montgomery stepped down off the train and threw herself into Lance's arms, planting a kiss on his lips. "Easy woman," he said to her. "It's only been a couple of days."

"Couple of days be damned," she shot back at him. "It's been too long."

He was about to say something else to her when movement caught his eye and Maggie Pine stepped down from the carriage. "Well, I'll be," he muttered.

Lily turned her head and glanced at Maggie. "Oh, I forgot to tell you, Maggie is going to live here too. I hope you're OK with that?"

"I've no problem with it. What about Buck?"

"We've not heard from him. I was hoping you

might have."

Lance shook his head. "No, not a word."

The sheriff released Lily and stepped towards Maggie. He wrapped his arms around her slim frame and pulled her close. "Good to see you, Maggie."

She stepped back and looked up at his face, her brown eyes sparkling. "You too, Lance. I'm so excited about this. A bigger town, more opportunity."

"It sure is that."

Maggie fingered a strand of her long black hair. "Lance—"

"I've had no word from Buck, Maggie."

Her face fell. "Oh."

"I'm sure he's fine."

Lily slipped in beside her and put an arm around her waist. "You know Buck. He always comes back."

Lance chuckled. "He's like a bad smell that way. Come on, I'll have someone take care of your bags and we'll head into town."

Lily caught him looking around the platform. "Are you expecting someone else?"

"Kinda thought you might have brought your harem with you."

She smiled at him. "New town, new start."

"Who bought the saloon?"

Lily's eyes opened wide. "Bert, can you believe it?"

Lance was as surprised as she had been when the barkeep had made the offer. "Really? Where did he get the money?"

"I don't know but obviously I was paying him too much. No, I'm glad it was him. At least he will look after the saloon."

Lance started along the platform, a woman on each arm. "Oh, I forgot to tell you, there's a dance tonight."

"Tonight?" Lily gasped.

"Yes, and I guess I'm going to have my dance

card filled with two lovely ladies to keep occupied."

"Oh, no," Maggie exclaimed. "I couldn't intrude on you both like that."

"Nonsense," said Lily. "It's a good way to meet new people. It'll be fun."

"That's settled then," Lance said. "We're going. I might even have to have a bath."

"If you don't, Lance Chaney, I'll not come within ten feet of you."

"Are you saying I smell, my dear?" he inquired, feigning indignance.

"Oh no, heaven forbid. I like horse smell on a man."

All three broke out into laughter as they walked along together.

"Why didn't our friend in there leave on the stage, Hardy?"

"Stage ain't leaving until tomorrow, Lance," Walsh explained. "It has a busted axle."

"The driver say how?"

"Now that's just the strangest thing," Walsh replied. "He's saying that someone sabotaged it."

"Why would they do that?"

"Hell, I don't know. I think he's been drinking again. He's been known to overdo it the night before a run."

"Did you have a look at it?"

Walsh shook his head. "Didn't see the point. I just thought he was – do you want me to head down to the stage depot and have a look?"

Lance shook his head. "No, it's fine. I'll do it myself. Like you said it could be nothing. If you want, you could clean up around here. Go over all the weapons and give them a clean."

"Sure."

"That way you won't be too tired to go courting tonight."

Walsh shook his head. "Son of a—"

"Be nice, or I'll have you walking patrol tonight."

"There's something you might want to consider, Lance?"

"What's that?"

"Hiring a second deputy," Walsh suggested. "We've been working one short ever since Nils Bennett was killed down in Barlow."

Lance nodded. He couldn't count on Buck because he'd be away more times than not working for Mike Dodge. "You got someone in mind, Hardy?"

"Feller called Holt Carmody. Served with the Texas Cavalry in the war. Good man. Works on one of the ranches. But he'd be better suited to doing what we do."

"Why didn't Deke hire him?"

"Deke tried but he wouldn't do it."

"What makes you think he will this time?"

"Maybe if you ask him, he might change his mind."

"I can try. Where'll I find him?"

Walsh smiled. "I saw him ride into town a while ago. He's probably at the Railway Saloon."

"Uh-huh, why do I feel like that was a setup?"

"I've no idea what you mean, Sheriff."

"Go find yourself a mop."

The railway saloon was quiet, only a few patrons were within the walls and only one barkeep behind the bar. Lance had only just walked through the door when the door to the back room opened and two people appeared. One he'd never seen before. The other he knew well. "You don't take long getting down to business, do you?"

Lily looked over at Lance and gave him a smile. "Girl's got to make a living."

"Uh-huh. Can I assume you've made an offer on this place?"

"Let's just say that Mister Cleve and I are in the early stages of negotiations."

The man beside her smiled a greeting. He wore a suit and a bowler hat. He held out his hand. "Ray Cleve, pleased to meet you, Sheriff. I heard you were in here yesterday. On business."

Lance gripped his hand and the two shook. "Likewise, Cleve. I hope you're making her earn it?"

"She's a tough negotiator, Sheriff. Very tough indeed. But I think we might be able to come to some kind of arrangement."

"Glad to hear," Lance said looking around. The place had possibilities. Two-story, twisting staircase, a long hardwood bar with brass footrail. Solid walls and a reasonable area for customers.

"Were you looking for me, Lance?" Lily asked.

"Nope. I was looking for a man named Holt Carmody. He here, Cleve?"

The saloon owner cast his gaze around the room and nodded in the direction of a table closest to a large mullioned window at the front of the barroom. "Over there drinking water."

"Water?"

Cleve nodded. "Yep, no matter how much I try, there's no liquor passes that man's lips."

"Is there a reason for that?" Lance asked warily thinking the man may have a drinking problem.

"No. I guess he's not a drinking man."

"Thanks. Lily, I'll see you after?"

"I'll call by the jail."

"I'll be there. I've got one more call to make after here and then I'll head back."

Lily stepped forward and kissed his cheek. "Bye."

Lance walked over to the table where Carmody sat. The man looked up at his visitor and saw the badge pinned to his shirt. "Something I can do for you, Sheriff?" he asked in a Texas drawl.

The sheriff figured him to be in his late twenties. He had a square jaw with dark stubble and brown eyes. The stubble matched his hair and Lance was sure that once the man stood erect, he'd be as broad across the shoulders as himself and probably just as tall. "Hardy Walsh suggested I come see you. I'm Lance Chaney."

Carmody said, "I heard of you. But if it's the deputy job you're looking to fill I ain't interested."

"Mind if I sit?" Lance asked.

"I ain't got no objection."

"But you have to pinning on a badge?" Lance asked as he sat down.

"I been shot at enough for one lifetime," Carmody replied.

"Heard you served with the Texas Cavalry? Which lot?"

"The eighth Texas," Carmody said.

"Terry's Texas Rangers. Run across them more than once. Tough as they come, back then."

Carmody nodded. "We were that."

"Officer?"

"Captain. You Cavalry too?"

"Yes. Major. Fourth Missouri."

"Uh-huh."

Lance sighed. "I can use you, Carmody. At least think about it? You'll earn more than you get as a cowhand and have a share in any bounties that are on any outlaws we arrest."

"All right, I'll think about it, but no promises."

Lance climbed to his feet. "If you want the job you can start tomorrow. Thanks for hearing me out."

"Any time, Sheriff."

Lance left the Railway and called at the stage and freight company. The wood-framed building looked like it could use stand some regular maintenance but overall it wasn't too bad. Beside it stood a pair of large gates that opened into a doorless barn which enabled the stages to drive straight through and out to the large corral at the rear. The barn also doubled as storage for feed, and a repair shop. It was here that Lance found the driver working on the busted axle with a second man.

"You have a minute?" Lance asked the driver. "I'm Lance Chaney, the new county sheriff."

"Lane Trevor," the driver, a short man with a large mustache, in his late twenties said. He indicated the second man. A rail-thin hombre with a graying beard. "This here is Milt Reynolds. He looks after the horses and does repairs."

"Pleased to meet you, gents," Lance said.

"What can we do for you, Sheriff?" Trevor asked.

"Hardy was telling me you think the axle was sabotaged," Lance said.

"It was," Reynolds replied.

"Can you show me why you think that?"

"Come over here," Trevor told him. He picked up the busted axle and showed Lance. "See that? When an axle snaps it splinters. However, even though this one has some splinters you can also see where it hasn't."

Nodding, Lance said, "It looks like it was cut some of the way to weaken it."

"Damned right it has."

"Why would anyone do that?" the sheriff asked.

"The only reason I can think of is to stop the stage from leaving," Reynolds replied.

"But why? We're you meant to be carrying a shipment of money? A payroll that's in the Cattleman's Trust and Loan?"

Trevor shook his head. "We were just to carry passengers."

"I'll ask around and see if anyone saw anything," Lance told them. "It happen last night?"

"Not sure. It could have happened anytime up until mid-morning."

"OK. I'll see what I can come up with. Before you leave in the morning."

CHAPTER 5

Bell, Texas

Four men sat around the table in the backroom of the Stockman's Saloon which sat conveniently across the street from the Cattleman's Association offices. Cigars were jammed in their fists, and whiskey—the good stuff—was poured in four glasses in front of them. Hank Conker took a pull of his and placed it heavily onto the polished tabletop. "We need to act, gentlemen. We'll need the grass before winter and I'm not willing to let those damned sheep have any more of it."

"What do you propose we do, Hank?" Red Samson from the Slash S asked. "Even after having the Scotsman killed, they still stayed put."

Samson was named after his shock of red hair atop his head. Conker nodded. "Yes, I was surprised by that. I figured that once MacDonald was gone they would take the sheep and leave. It seems I underestimated the Mexican's resolve."

"You still haven't said what you want to do, Hank." This time it was John Peters who spoke. Peters' JP Connected was the closest to Conker's Broken C.

"We're going to send some of our riders over there tonight and burn the homestead down around their ears. I'll have Max lead them."

Harv Wilson was the fourth rancher on the Cattleman's Association committee. The four of them were the biggest ranchers in the county. Wilson's Rocking W bordered the county line to the east. He was a sad-looking man with a droopy mustache. His wife had up and died on him ten years before, leaving him to struggle with raising a young son on his own. Once the boy had hit ten, he'd sent him east for better schooling. And that's where the boy had stayed.

"I'll send four of my men over. It's all I can spare," Wilson said.

Samson blew a cloud of cigar smoke at the coal oil lamp on the table. "I'll do the same."

Conker looked at Peters a questioning look on his face. "What about you, John?"

Peters hesitated. He'd already gone along with one killing. But this was a family. "We don't have to kill them, Hank. There's a woman and child in the mix."

"Who said anything about killing?" Conker asked. "We're just going to burn them out. If the Mex starts shooting, then..."

"No killing the woman and child."

Conker stared at the JP Connected owner for a moment before he nodded and said, "No killing the woman and child."

"Fine, I'll send four men too."

"Good. Have them at my ranch come early evening."

"Hank what are we going to do with all them sheep if the Mexicans do run off?" Samson asked.

"With a little luck, maybe they'll take them along," Conker replied.

"And what if they don't?"

"We turn them into fertilizer."

Broken C Ranch

Conker looked at the two men who sat on the long sofa before him drinking his best whiskey. Jack Carter and Max Gilbert waited for the rancher to tell them why they had been called before him. On the large wood mantle, a small clock chimed two, a sound that echoed through the living room. Behind the clock was a large stone chimney, below the mantle, a wide-open fireplace, black from years of use.

Finally, Conker spoke. "There was a meeting of the Cattleman's Association earlier today and we voted unanimously to give the Ortegas some encouragement to remove themselves and their sheep off the range. Therefore, you both will ride tonight, along with some men from the other ranches. They should be here soon. Max, you'll be in charge."

Gilbert nodded. "Fine. What if Ortega fights back?"

"Then you kill him. Same with those other Mexicans."

"And the woman and kid?"

"I can't help it if they get in the way. The association needs that grass. If those sheep stay there, they'll disease it for cows."

Jack Carter snorted derisively drawing Conker's attention. "You have something to say?" he growled.

"Sheep don't disease the land," he stated. "What fool told you that?"

The rancher's stare grew hard, cold. "Listen good, Carter. As long as you work for me, you do as I say. And if I say they will disease the land, they will. Do you understand?"

The outlaw set his jaw firm, his lips thinned as he considered just killing the man before him and walking from the room. Then he thought of the money and the sanctuary the ranch was providing for him and his brother. "Yeah, I understand."

"Good. Remember your place or you'll find yourself out the gate," Conker growled. He turned back to Gilbert. "Get it done, Max."

"Yes, sir, Mister Conker."

The pair left the house and walked outside before Gilbert stopped halfway across the yard. Jack stopped too and turned to face him. "Your brother stays here tonight."

Anger simmering just below the surface flared in the outlaw's eyes. "Why?"

"Because I said. I want men who are going to take orders, and from what I've seen, he's not one of them."

"He'll be fine. I'll keep him on a short rein."

"He's trouble."

"I said, I'll keep an eye on him," Jack's voice was full of menace as he took a step forward, his hand on his Colt Army.

Gilbert cast a glance over the outlaw's right shoulder and shook his head. Jack noticed the movement and whipped his head around, years of being on the run not helping his reaction. He felt the cold barrel of a six-gun pressed up underneath his jaw. The ruse had worked, and Gilbert leaned in close and said in a low voice, "You ever try to threaten me like that again and I'll put a bullet in your brain. You do not scare me, Carter, no matter how big and bad you are. I've met a dozen men like you and I'm still here."

"All right, all right. Just take it easy. My brother stays here."

"No, bring him along. Maybe he'll catch a stray bullet. Hell, maybe you both will."

Gilbert let the hammer down on the gun and slid it back into his holster. "Go tell your brother to get ready. Tell Ingram and Wicklow too. They'll come with us."

The foreman watched Jack walk away and knew that he might have just painted a large target on his back.

Brenham, Texas

The evening was cool, the moon big and round in the night sky surrounded by thousands of stars already. Footsteps clunked on the boardwalk as Lance escorted his "two lovely ladies" as he called them, Lily wearing a red dress and Maggie a blue one, to the church dance. The church itself was on the northeast edge of town, built next to a stand of large cottonwoods. The cemetery, full of headstones and wooden crosses, lay adjacent to it.

"It's a lovely evening, Lance," Lily said as she squeezed his left arm tightly.

"It is that. And what better way to spend it than in the company of two wonderful ladies."

"Flattery, sir, will get you everywhere," Maggie told him.

"If Lily thinks like that then it just might," he replied.

Lily elbowed him in the ribs. Lance grunted and she said to him, "Behave yourself."

"Speaking of behaving, I've hardly set eyes on you all day. What have you been up to?"

Lily looked across at Maggie. "Should I tell him?"

"I guess he'll find out sooner or later. I'm not sure that he'll like the fact you bought a ranch though."

Lance's head whipped around. "You what?"

Lily chuckled. "Hold on, darling, before you burst. I bought the Railway Saloon today. It's mine and I take over tomorrow."

On the other side of him, Maggie burst out laughing. He looked at her and said, "That was a good way to give a man heart failure."

"Why is that?" Lily asked. "Don't you think I could own a ranch?"

"No – I mean yes – I mean – oh hell."

Now they both burst out laughing. "Would you still love me if I did buy a ranch?" Lily asked.

"I'd love you if you bought nothing."

"Good answer."

The trio continued their leisurely stroll along Main Street then turned left onto Rail Street. From there they went past Brenham's second hotel, the Rest A Spell then down past a number of well-kept houses, and across Second Street, along the next block to First. The church stood on the opposite corner, diagonally across the intersection.

Gathered outside was a milling group of townsfolk, as well as buggies, horses and other carriages of varying sizes. Lance escorted the two ladies across the street and walked towards the church steps.

"There you are. About time you got here, the music is about to start." Hardy Walsh stepped forward with a young lady on his arm. Lance nodded. "I've been waiting on two women; double the trouble, double the time."

Walsh chuckled, especially when Lily elbowed him once more. "We weren't the ones who had to go by the jail to check on a prisoner."

The deputy introduced Mary Denham to each of them. "Pleasure, Miss Denham," Lance said.

"Do call me Mary," she begged.

"OK, then. Mary, it is."

Lily stepped forward and took Mary by the hand. "My name is Lily Montgomery; this is Maggie Pine. I'm Lance's—" she paused and stared at the sheriff. "His fiancée I guess you could say."

"You could say that," Lance agreed.

"Pleased to meet you both," Mary said. She frowned and turned her gaze to the sheriff. "Don't you have a brother, Sheriff?"

"That's right, Buck."

"And where is he this night?"

"That is a good question. He's off somewhere doing deputy marshal duties."

"Oh."

"Shall we go inside?" Lily asked.

"Yes, lets," Mary replied. "Hardy has promised to dance with me all evening."

"Well good for him," Lance laughed. "Just what he needs for tomorrow, sore feet."

Walsh grinned. "Very funny,"

"They began making their way inside the entryway when a man dressed in a suit approached from behind them. "Could I have a word, please, Sheriff?"

Lily glanced at Lance, her face a mask of concern that her night was about to evaporate. He nodded at her and she followed the others inside. "What can I do for you, Mister—"

"Fellows," the rotund man replied. "It's actually Mayor Fellows."

"Mayor? I thought I would have had a visit from you before now."

"Yes, well, I've been busy," Fellows grunted. "Town council business."

"What can I do for you, Mayor?" Lance asked.

"I want to know what progress you've made in finding the murderer of young Ferguson." It was more of a demand than an inquiry.

"Not much I'm afraid. No one has seen or heard anything and if they have, they're not being very forthcoming."

"Then find something. I have women coming up to me in the street, telling me how scared they are to even venture outside."

"I can't see what's not there, Mayor."

"Maybe you're not cut out for this job, Sheriff Chaney."

The hidden meaning was there and although he tried to hide his emotions, Lance knew he was a good lawman and the words burned. "If you think you can do a better job, Mayor, then go right ahead. If you have any more complaints, I'll be in my office tomorrow."

With that, Lance left the open-mouthed Fellows standing there.

Inside the church, all the pews had been moved aside to form one large dancefloor which was more than ample for the number of people who were there. At the front, the band was in full swing, set up on the raised altar where they could be seen over the heads of those on the dancefloor.

Lance found Lily and Maggie still talking to Mary Denham. Walsh stood to one side looking like he'd been rejected. "Get used to it, Hardy. Women are a breed who seem to be able to talk all day and night about nothing and make sense of it."

"I'm beginning to see what you mean," Walsh replied.

"I see you made it," Judge Dyson said as he approached them, a lady around his age and stature on his arm.

"I don't think I had much choice in the matter, Judge."

"Mmm, yes," he said by way of agreement giving the woman beside him a sidelong glance. "This is my wife, Maybelle."

"You never told me you had a lovely wife, Judge," Lance said making the woman blush.

"You keep talking like that, Chaney and I'm not likely to have one much longer."

"Hush, Granville, let the man speak."

"See what I mean? Now, introduce these lovely ladies to me."

With the introductions out of the way, Dyson turned his focus and attention on Lily. "A little bird told me that you made yourself an investment today."

"Just a little one, Judge," Lily replied.

"I hope you can keep a better lid on it than the last proprietor."

"You'll find I can keep my establishments on a tight rein," Lily said.

The judge nodded stiffly. "Good. You do that and you're apt to see more of me."

"Ahem?"

Dyson looked at his wife. "What? A man deserves to have a little alone time every-now-and-then, Maybelle."

"I know your alone time, Granville. It costs us money every time you have it," she scowled.

"Yes, well..."

Suddenly the band started up and Lily grasped Lance by the hand. "If you'll excuse us, Judge."

"Why yes, by all means."

Once out on the floor, Lily said, "He seems like a nice man."

"Under that exterior lies a tough man, my dear. Straight, fair, but tough."

She smiled wickedly. "We'll see how tough."

The evening went by quickly and it was drawing towards a close when the Mayor drew near to where Lance and the others were all standing having a breather from the dancing, looking for Mary Denham. "Where's your father," he asked rudely interrupting their conversation.

"I–I'm not sure," she replied taken aback.

"What seems to be the problem, Craig?" Walsh asked.

"It's Mayor to you, Deputy," Fellows shot back.

"What's the problem, Craig?" the deputy asked again.

Fellows glared at Walsh but then said, "He's meant to be making his announcement and I can't find him."

"I saw him outside talking to Elroy Ansel, the barber a while ago. Maybe they're swapping war stories."

The mayor grumbled and said, "I'll go and look, shall I?"

As he left, Lance said, "I can see he's going to be an absolute joy to know."

"His bark is much worse than his bite," Mary told them. They all laughed.

There was some commotion at the door and Mary Denham's father appeared, making his way through the crowd. "There he is," she said.

As Denham passed townsfolk, he began shaking hands and greeting them on his way to the front. When he reached the altar, he stepped up onto it, acknowledging the band with a smile, then turned to face the crowd, looking about for his wife and daughter. He signaled them both to join him on the stage.

"I'll be right back," Mary said to Walsh.

Mother and daughter, similar in looks and bearing, made their way up to the raised dais amidst a cheer from those around it. After several moments of tentative applause from the rest of the room, most unsure what was happening, the noise finally abated, and Denham began to speak.

"Friends, neighbors, most of you know me. I've lived around here since Brenham became Brenham. I started a family here, watched and guided my children as they grew into adults here, even lost one trying to keep it safe from the Yankees."

This brought a cheer from the Texas crowd. Lance looked at Walsh. "He lost his son in the war. Mary's older brother, Denham was a colonel. Commanded his own regiment."

"This town has given me so much over the years, and I believe that the time has now come to give something back to it; to Texas. So tonight, I am here to announce that I shall be running for the office of governor of the great state of Texas!"

This announcement brought forth another roar of approval.

"I pledge to you, every last one of you, that I shall work for you and your families to make our state a better and safer place for us all to live. And to not let the Yankees up north—"

"Sheriff."

Lance turned at the voice at his shoulder and

found Reynolds from the stage and freight standing there, a pained expression on his face. "What is it, Milt?"

"You have to come. Right now. It's bad. Real bad."

The sheriff nodded. "All right, lead the way." He turned to Lily. "I have to go."

"Yes, go. Be careful."

"Hardy, you'd best come too."

The deputy looked torn for a moment before Lily said to him, "I'll tell Mary where you've gone. I'm sure she'll be fine."

"Thanks, Miss Montgomery."

"You call me that once more and she'll never see you again. Now go."

They followed Reynolds outside and onto Rail Street. He was hurrying away from them at a good clip when Lance called after him. "Milt, slow down. Tell us what's happened."

The man from the stage and freight stopped in the middle of the street and turned towards them. "It's bad, sheriff. Real bad."

"You have already told me that. Now tell me what is bad?" Lance pressed again.

"He's just hanging there. Dead. He—"

"Who is?" Lance asked.

"It's Lane. He's dead."

CHAPTER 6

Brenham, Texas

Lance looked up at the body of Lane Trevor as it hung from the cross beam of the barn, the dim lantern light making his corpse throw an eerie shadow against the wood wall. His head was lolled to one side and his eyes were closed. Beneath the dead man's boots was an old stool tipped onto its side. Everything pointed towards Trevor having done this to himself.

"What do you think, Doc?" Lance asked Clifford Harding.

"Get him down so I can take a better look."

Lance nodded grimly. "Hardy, get him down."

Walsh walked over to where the rope was tied off to a wall post, and began to untie the knot. As he did so, Lance frowned. Something wasn't right. "Wait, Hardy."

The deputy stopped. "What is it?"

The sheriff walked over to the stool and put it upright. He then slid it under where the body hung. Trevor's boots hung three inches clear of it. "You see that?" Lance asked.

"The boots do not touch," the doctor said.

"He couldn't have done this to himself," Walsh

pointed out.

"We'll see, but it certainly seems that way," the sheriff agreed. "Get him down."

Walsh laid Trevor on the straw-covered floor and stepped back as the doctor stepped forward, waving his hand for more light as he said, "Would one of you hold the lantern for me please while I have a closer look?"

Lance grabbed it and held it over the body while Doc Harding examined the corpse more closely. "The neck isn't broken but you'd expect that being the way it was done. There're marks on his skin from the rope, but there is also additional bruising as well."

Next, he looked at the man's wrists by pulling his sleeves up. "There's nothing remarkable there to indicate that his hands were tied. Help me roll him over."

Lance helped the medico flip the corpse then stepped away, looking at the back of the body, awaiting the doctor to continue his examination. After a quick probe with his fingers, Doc Harding said, "He has been hit from behind. I would say that he was unconscious when he was strung up."

"So, he was definitely killed by someone else, Doc?" Lance asked.

"Yes. I can confirm that he was murdered."

"I'll go and get Wilf Hathaway," Walsh said to the sheriff. "I think he was at the dance."

Lance nodded. "Fine. But do it quietly. I don't want this all over town just yet."

"Sure thing."

"What are you going to do now, Sheriff?" the doctor asked. "Two murders in our normally quiet town within the space of a few days isn't good."

Agreeing with the doctor's statement of the obvious, Lance got down to business. "What can you tell me about him, Doc? Did you know him?"

"Sure. His job has been a stage driver since returning from the war."

Lance thought for a moment. "Did Ferguson and Lane serve together?"

The doctor frowned, giving the question some consideration. "I don't know. Why?"

"I'm trying to figure out whether there is a connection between the two deaths."

"You think they were killed by the same person?"

"It's possible, and right at this point I've got very little to go on. What I need to do is find someone who saw something."

"The Lone Star Saloon is across the way; maybe someone there saw something."

"Maybe. Do you mind waiting here for the undertaker?"

The doctor shook his head. "Not at all."

Lance left the stage and freight and walked across Third Street to the Lone Star. Pushing in through the double doors, he stopped just inside and looked around the main bar area which was only half full of customers. Three soiled doves were working different sectors of room, plying drunks to part them from their money. Lance guessed there would be a couple more upstairs with clients.

The walls were constructed of paper-thin wood planks, numerous coal oil lamps hanging from brackets providing dim light and giving off an oily smoke that added to the room's smoky atmosphere. The large window at the front was smudged, and the stairs leading up to the second floor were against the far wall.

Heads turned to check out the new arrival, staring at him through the tobacco smoke that hung gray-blue beneath the ceiling. Many eyes fixed on the badge that he wore, some dropping quickly to their drinks or cards to avoid direct contact with the law who made his way towards the battered bar. Two men moved their drinks to the right, making room for the sheriff. Behind the bar stood a tall, dark-haired man with a mustache to match.

"What can I do for you, Sheriff?" he asked.

"What's your name?" Lance asked.

"Pete Mellow. This my place."

Lance waved him along the bar to a quieter place. "Have you heard or seen anything unusual tonight?"

"Nothing more than usual," Mellow replied. He frowned. "Why?"

"Lane Trevor was found dead tonight, and—"

"Really!" the saloon owner exclaimed.

"Easy," Lance whispered harshly. "I don't want everyone to know just yet. I want you to keep an ear out if anyone says anything."

"Sure, I can do that. But damn, I can't believe Lane's gone. He used to drink here all the time."

"He did?"

"Sure."

"What did you know about him?"

"Some. He worked odd jobs around the town before the war and when he came back, he went to work for Joe Wyatt."

"Joe Wyatt?" Lance asked.

"The owner of the stage and freight company. Does he know?"

The sheriff said, "Not that I'm aware of."

"Damn."

"Did Lane know John Ferguson?"

Mellow nodded. "Yeah. Before the war they used to drink together all the time. They even joined up together. Funny thing as, when they come home, never really saw them together, like they never mixed. Like something happened."

"They'd changed?" Lance asked.

The saloon owner nodded. "Yeah. But hell, who didn't change that went off to fight?"

"True," Lance agreed.

"Anything else you can think of?"

"Nope. If I do, I'll come see you."

"Do that. Thanks."

"Anytime, Sheriff."

"Where you going, Sheriff?" a voice called out.

Lance turned around and saw a man standing near the bar, facing him. "Do I know you, friend?"

"You don't remember me? I sure as hell remember you, Major Lance Chaney."

"You seem to have the advantage of me," Lance said, his mind whirling as he tried to put a name to the face. Ratty thin lips, pointed nose, deep-set eyes.

"My name is Titus Emery," the man whined. "That ring a damned bell?"

The sheriff noted the way Emery's hand dangled close to his six-gun and was all too aware that he didn't have his on. He'd taken it off for the dance. Lance nodded slowly. "I seem to vaguely remember the last name."

"You ought to. It was the same name my brother Cletus had in sixty-four when you had him hanged," Emery snarled.

Now he remembered. Lance was leading a patrol through the Shenandoah Valley when they had come across a small farm. The Emery brothers had killed the owner and were about to have some fun with his young wife when the patrol found them. The second brother had escaped. Run like a scared rabbit, but they'd managed to capture the first. Lance made the decision to hang him.

"You're the brother who ran," the sheriff said.

"I didn't run so far that I didn't see you murder my brother."

"You and your brother were horse thieves and murderers. You'd have raped that man's wife if my patrol hadn't happened along."

"I've been waiting for the day we'd meet up. Now it's come and I aim to kill you, you son of a bitch."

The patrons in the bar parted like the Red Sea as everyone moved aside to give them room and move out of the firing line. Someone was about to die, and the citizens of Brenham were going to see whether their new sheriff was as tough as they'd heard.

"I don't have a gun, Emery," Lance pointed out.

"Well, you better get one 'cause I aim to shoot you whether you're armed or not."

"Here, Sheriff," a cowboy said and stepped forward offering Lance a six-gun.

He reached out to take it, but Emery snapped, "Wait. Tuck it into his belt. Keep your hands away from your body, Chaney."

Lance did as he was ordered, allowing the cowboy to tuck the six-gun into his pants before looking him in the eye and saying in a low voice, "It pulls to the left a touch, but she's reliable."

"Thanks."

"Alright, get away from him and stop talking," Emery ordered, licking his lips as the anticipation of squaring things with his brother's killer began rising within him.

The cowboy backed off and left Lance standing there alongside the bar. "You can still stop this right now, Emery," the sheriff told him, knowing that he was wasting his breath, but that he had to try. "Just walk away. I'll give you until morning before I come after you. No need for you to die tonight on a sawdust-covered floor."

"I ain't the one who's dying, Chaney," Emery hissed and went for his gun.

Lance's shoulder dipped as his hand streaked towards the six-gun in his waistband. His hand wrapped around it his finger settled on the trigger. As the weapon came up, he cocked the hammer which was all the way back when the gun leveled.

The saloon filled with the roar of a single shot and Emery staggered, his own six-gun nowhere near level. The slug punched into his chest forcing the rat-faced man up onto his toes. His six-gun discharged into the floor at his feet before clattering to the wooden boards, following by his body as it slumped on top of the weapon.

Lance walked over to the killer and stared down at him, making sure he was dead. When he was satisfied, he said, "Someone tell the undertaker that he's wanted. You'll find him across the street."

A man disappeared and a loud buzz of voices began an excited hum. Lance looked for the cowboy who'd loaned him the gun. Holding it out, he said, "Thanks."

"Couldn't let him shoot you down for no reason."

"Thanks anyway."

Ten minutes later, once the undertaker had arrived, Lance left the saloon and stepped out onto the street. He stood there in the half-light of lanterns that spilled from doorways and windows, mulling over what he knew so far as he looked across at the stage and freight. Two men, both murdered, they knew each other, were friends but had changed upon their return from the way. And both had been killed within days of each other. There was some connection and Lance meant to find out what it was.

Later that evening, a little before midnight, both Lance and Hardy Walsh were in the jail having a mug of steaming hot coffee. They'd returned to the dance to escort the ladies home only to find that the dance was over and that Lily and Maggie had found their own way back to the hotel.

"You knew that feller who tried to kill you tonight, huh?"

The sheriff nodded. "Him and his brother. Well, his brother mostly considering he was the one I had hung."

"Everyone has someone on their backtrail," Walsh theorized.

"You, Hardy?"

"Yes."

"Hardy, did you know that Ferguson and Lane

Trevor knew each other before the war?"

Walsh frowned thoughtfully. He scratched at his jaw and said, "No, can't recall as I do."

"According to Mellow at the Lone Star they used to be friends. Left to fight together but when they came back things weren't the same."

"OK. That's nothing strange though."

Lance sipped his coffee. "No, no it's not. What is strange is that two men who are connected to each other are now dead. Murdered within a couple of days of each other."

"So, you think that somehow—"

Walsh's words were cut off by a commotion outside the jail on the street. The two men gave each other confused looks. "Get us a couple of rifles, Hardy," Lance suggested as they placed their mugs on the desk.

Walsh took two Henrys down from the rack on the wall and passed one to the sheriff. They stepped out onto the boardwalk to see a small crowd gathered before them on the street. At the forefront stood Fellows, the mayor. "Good, you are here. Saved me the air from calling you out."

"What do you all want?" Lance asked cradling the Henry in front.

"We want to know what you're doing about the two murders which have our fine town on edge?" the mayor demanded.

Lance scanned the crowd before him and saw the proprietor of the Lone Star standing amongst them. He now knew that the man had a big mouth, and would remember that for future reference. "We're working on it."

"What about my girls?" the only woman in the crowd called out. "How am I supposed to keep them safe?"

"Who are you?"

The woman stepped forward. She had a hawkish face and was clothed in a red dress, cut low to accentuate her ample cleavage. "Celestine Sparks."

"What do you do?"

"I have the joy house on the corner of First and South."

Lance nodded. "Maybe you could tell your girls to bathe their customers before they have a roll with them."

"Do you think this is funny?" Fellows blustered.

"Not in the least, Mayor. Neither is this mob gathering. All I can suggest for the time being is that if you have to go out of a night, take someone with you. As for the ladies of this town, be accompanied or don't go out after dark."

"You mean we are to be hostages in our own town?" the mayor demanded.

"If that's the way you want to interpret it."

"Then what good are you?"

"Rest assured, Fellows, I'll find your killer. Now go home."

"That's Mayor Fellows."

"Go home before I lock you all up for disturbing the peace."

The crowd started to disperse slowly, and it wasn't long before the street was empty once more and the lawmen looked around one last time before turning to go back inside. Footsteps approaching along the boardwalk made them turn to see the judge coming towards them.

"Why didn't you just shoot him?" Dyson asked.

"He's scared like the others," Lance surmised.

"He's an ass."

"Maybe," Lance replied with a smile.

"What happened?" the judge inquired.

"Come inside and I'll explain."

Walsh said, "I might take a turn around the town, Lance. Make sure things are quiet."

"Fine. Be careful, Hardy."

"Always am."

Once inside the jail the judge asked, "What is it I

hear about a second murder?"

Lance cursed under his breath. "It's all over town already?"

"Don't feel bad about it. Word around this place spreads like a stiff breeze on the plains."

The sheriff explained the events of the evening.

"And you think they're connected somehow?"

"Yes."

The judge looked grim. "And I heard you had some trouble in the Lone Star."

"Nothing I couldn't handle."

"The man have paper on him?"

"I don't know."

"Find out and if he has, collect the reward. It's yours."

"I'll see what happens."

"Well, I'm going home. Come see me tomorrow and let me know how you're getting on."

"I'm hoping I'll have a new deputy tomorrow," Lance told him.

"Oh? Who?"

"Holt Carmody."

"Good man," the judge said approvingly. "Good night."

"Good night, Judge."

"You look tired," Lilly greeted him as he entered their hotel room.

"You waited up," he said.

"Of course," she replied and walked forward, wrapping her arms around him and placing her head upon his muscular chest.

"It's not been the best of starts, that's for sure."

"I heard there was another murder."

Lance released her and walked across the room to look out the window and down onto the street. "Yes. A man from the stage and freight business."

"How terrible. Have you any idea who did it?"

He turned and looked at her. Shaking his head, he replied, "No idea. Now I have the mayor jumping all over me wanting answers that I don't have."

"I'm sure you'll find something."

"I hope so," he said with a sigh suddenly feeling weary beyond his years. "And I hope it's soon."

Ortega Homestead, Texas

Buck came awake.

The deputy marshal lay there on the bunkhouse bed, listening intently to work out what it was that had brought him alert so suddenly. The last time he'd experienced a feeling like that he'd been a Johnny Reb. Maybe it was his new surroundings. With his strength growing, he'd offered to move out into the bunkhouse with the two shepherds, Antonio, and Eduardo.

Buck lay there concentrating his hearing on the sounds outside. Then ever so faintly he heard it. It began as a tremor in the bunkhouse floor, growing steadily more audible. The first thing that came to mind was cavalry. The thought was quickly dismissed at the knowledge that no cavalry would come thundering up to the homestead in the middle of the night. But that left another possibility and he was immediately filled with alarm by that. Nightriders!

The deputy swung his legs over the side of the bunk and hurriedly pulled his boots on. He moved over to the bunks where the two Mexicans slept and shook them awake. "Get up, we've got company."

"Qué?"

"I said get up, damn it, there's riders coming in."

Buck found his Colt and strapped it on. Next came the Winchester. He made sure there was a round under the hammer and walked over to the window. Looking out through the glass, he could make out faint pinpricks of light in the distance.

Torches. The bastards were going to burn them out.

He turned around to see the two shepherds standing in the middle of the room. "Do you men have weapons?"

"No," replied Eduardo shaking his head to emphasize his answer.

"Damn it," the deputy cursed as he reached for his Colt and unbuckled the belt. He tossed it to the Mexican. "Can you use that?"

"Si."

"At least that's something. Antonio, I don't have a weapon for you. Keep your head down. Eduardo, stay here at the window. If shooting starts, you shoot back. Understood?"

"Si." Both men nodded their assent.

There were fifteen rounds in the Winchester which Buck hoped would be sufficient. If not, then he was in trouble; they all were. He levered one of the .44 Henry rounds in ready to fire and lowered the hammer. Without time to raise the alarm to the ranch house, he slipped out through the door and hurried toward the barn, taking refuge in the shadows to its right. The last thing he wanted to do was get caught in a burning barn.

As he waited, the drumming of the hoofbeats grew louder like the rumble of a distant storm rolling over the range. Within seconds, galloping mounts thundered into the yard. Men bearing firebrands, hauled back on reins bringing their horses to a stop. Some pranced around eager to keep running.

Two men rode forward, stopping a horse length ahead of the others who sat brandishing their torches.

"Ortega!" one of the riders called out. "Get your Mex ass out here before we burn the house down around your ears."

Buck adjusted his grip on the Winchester.

"Ortega! Now, damn it. I don't care if you have a

woman and kid in there. I'll blasted well burn you out anyway."

Still nothing happened. The lead rider looked around impatiently before muttering something to his men, motioning one of the torch bearers forward. Buck raised his Winchester and centered it on the black shape before him.

"Wait!" The voice was Ortega's. The door of the ranch house opened, and he stepped out, a rifle in his hands. "What do you want, Gilbert?"

Gilbert? He'd remember that name.

"You've got the time it takes for my men to set fire to your house to get your family out," Gilbert barked. He motioned to two of his riders and they headed toward the bunkhouse. "The same goes for the bunkhouse and your other Mex friends."

"Why are you doing this?" Ortega asked.

"You've had enough warnings. Just like MacDonald had. Mister Conker and the others in the Cattleman's Association have been right patient with you. It's time for you and those stinking sheep to go. It'll take a month for the stink to be gone from the range and the disease as well. It'll be no use to cows until it is."

"Sheep are not diseased. Who told you this?" Ortega asked dumbfounded.

"Shut up and do as you're told," Gilbert snarled.

"But—"

"Burn the barn," the foreman snapped. "Show him we are serious."

A rider turned his horse and rode towards the barn. He shaped to throw the torch up into the loft but froze when a low voice said from the shadows, "You throw that, and it'll be the last thing you ever do."

The man stopped, astounded by the words he'd heard. "Wh—what?"

"You heard me, hombre. Throw the torch and I'll kill you."

"Who are you?"

"I'm the night wrangler."

"What's the holdup?" Gilbert called out.

"Ah—"

"Damn it, Burt, is there a problem? Set the barn alight."

"He's got a slight problem," Buck called out. "You see, if he tries it, I'll kill him and then I'm going to start shooting until I empty this Winchester I'm holding."

Gilbert was stunned. "Who are you, Mister?"

"I'm the feller who will kill your men if you don't turn around and get gone."

"Step out into the light where I can see you," Gilbert demanded.

"Nope, I'm right just where I am."

"I don't believe you, stranger. You ain't even armed."

It was an open invitation and the deputy marshal took him up on it. The Winchester roared and one of the riders with a torch let out a yelp of pain, the firestick dropping to the ground. While the rolling echo of the shot disappeared into the night, Buck had already worked the lever of the rifle and was ready to fire again. "You believe me now?"

"I believe you," the foreman snarled.

Beside him, Jack Carter said in a low voice, "Some of the men could circle around him and get behind the barn."

"No, stay where you are," Gilbert whispered harshly before calling across the yard. "You can't get us all, stranger."

"Maybe not, but you make a mighty fine target. So does that feller next to you. What do you think will happen if I cut the head off the snake?"

"It'll just grow another, meaner one," the foreman replied. "Might as well leave now, save a whole world of hurt later on. Might even save the lives of the woman and the kid."

Buck knew he was right about one thing. He couldn't kill them all but thought that he might buffalo his way out of it. "Your call," Buck called out. "You can leave now or die in the dirt beside your horse. Make your choice and hope that it's the right one."

The foreman thought about the ultimatum in silence before saying, "All right, I thought about it. We're going."

"What the hell are you doing?" Jack whispered.

"What I said."

"We can take him."

"You heard the man, Carter; he's got the drop on us. You want to die tonight? I sure don't. This ain't over, now turn your horse around and start riding."

Buck heard the name and froze. The Carters were here. He thought he knew the voice.

"The hell with this," one of the other riders snarled and went for his gun.

"Joe, no!" Jack cried out but it was too late. The hot-headed Joe Carter was already pulling iron.

The rifle whiplashed and the muzzle flash lit the dark shadows once more. Joe Carter grunted as the .44 Henry slug burned deep into his chest from the side. He dropped his six-gun and hunched over with a groan. Then he slid sideways and fell to the hardpacked earth of the yard with an audible thud.

"Joe!" Jack cried out and started to dismount.

"Stay where you are," Buck shouted. "No one moves."

The outlaw stopped. "You're dead, you son of a bitch. I'll kill you."

"People have tried, I'm still here, Carter."

"Do I know you?"

"Maybe. I know you."

"Get out here and face me like a man so I can kill you."

"Be thankful I'm letting you ride out of here."

"The hell I am. I'm not going anywhere until I get

a chance to put a bullet in your stinking hide."

"Suit yourself," Buck said resignedly and stepped out into the dim moonlight. It wasn't much but enough to elicit a reaction from the killer outlaw.

"Son of a bitch! You!"

Jack Carter clawed at his six-gun but had not cleared leather before the Winchester whiplashed again and the slug punched him from the saddle. By the time he hit the ground he'd already joined his brothers in hell.

The deputy worked the lever on the rifle and rammed a new round into the chamber. "Any more of you mule-heads want to get dying over and done with while we're at it?"

"Hold it!" Gilbert snapped before any of his riders did something stupid. "We're leaving, whoever you are. But this ain't over. We'll be back."

"We'll be ready."

"Get the bodies on their horses."

"No," Buck growled. "Leave them be."

"Suit yourself. Come on."

The Broken C foreman wheeled his horse around and rode out of the yard, the rest of the nightriders following him.

Buck walked out into the middle of the yard. Manuel Ortega did the same, his steps heavy, leaden, jerky. "Thank you, Marshal," he managed to get out.

"Don't thank me yet. Like he said, they'll be back. This has just turned into a shooting war and we don't have that many guns. Who was he?"

"Max Gilbert," Ortega replied. "He is Hank Conker's foreman."

There was movement near the bunkhouse as Eduardo and Antonio stepped out into the yard. Buck said, "You need weapons for your shepherds. Take the ones off those dead men. Take their horses and saddles too."

"My men are not fighters," Ortega protested.

"They are now," Buck affirmed. "If you want to hold onto this place, then you'll need every able-bodied person in the fight."

"Cannot the law help. Once they know you are a marshal will they not stop?"

Buck shook his head. "They've already killed to get what they want. Me wearing a badge won't deter them. But you're right, we're going to need more help. I'll wire for some tomorrow."

"Thank you."

"Go see to your family, Manuel. I'll get rid of these bodies and see to the rest of it."

Once Ortega had gone inside, Buck turned to the two shepherds. "Eduardo, give me a hand. Antonio take the saddle gun from that horse over there and get out and watch over the sheep. If something happens, come and get me, understand?"

"Si."

"Good, get going."

Buck sighed. Three Carters were dead but that still left one more out there to find. And he couldn't go home until he found him. Now he was mixed up in a sheep war. But these people had saved his life. He owed them a great debt; one that he meant to repay.

CHAPTER 7

Bell, Texas

The horses' hooves clattered across the boards of the bridge. Beneath it a lazy, almost still creek was in need of rain to flush it out. Bell's main street began at the end of the bridge, and was flanked by the livery on the left and the cathouse on the right.

It was early in the morning and the Texas sun had already poked its head above the horizon in the east. On the second-floor balcony of the cathouse, a redhead, dressed in no more than pantaloons and a loose-fitting chemise, watched the stranger ride past, the pair of horses carrying the Carters draped over their backs trailing behind.

The undertaker was the next building on his right, and he could have stopped there to offload the bodies. But wanting to make a point to the sheriff, Buck kept riding, across Settlement street, past a café, saddler, and various other stores. The next cross street was Holt and it was flanked by the Stockman's Saloon on one corner and the Cattleman's Association opposite. On the far side of Holt was a brick-built bank, and a pool hall.

At the end of the main street was a T intersection to which Law Street ran perpendicular. It was here that the jail and the court were located. The courthouse was also constructed of brick-like the bank; the jail, a framed wood one.

As he'd ridden along the street with the corpses of the outlaws, the macabre procession had picked up numerous followers who traipsed along the boardwalks.

Stepping down from the saddle, Buck tied his horse to the hitch rail then led the other two horses around to it, tying them off before starting to untie the bodies.

"What the hell do you think you're doing? Get them out of here."

The deputy stared up at the solid man with narrowed eyes and a badge, standing on the boardwalk, demanding answers. "I've brought in a couple of outlaws."

"Who are you?"

"You'll find paper on them."

"I asked you a question, Mister."

"Their name is Carter. Jack and Joe," Buck continued still ignoring the question. A body hit the ground.

"Damn it!" Kennedy exploded.

"They were part of a bunch of nightriders who attacked the homestead of Manuel Ortega last night with the intent of burning it to the ground and running them off their land."

"Sheep don't belong here. This is cattle country," Kennedy growled.

"Spoken like a true cattleman."

"Who the hell are you?"

"Who are you?" Buck asked.

"Ben Kennedy. I'm the county sheriff."

"Any deputies?"

"No. Small county."

The second body hit the ground.

"You better damned well tell me who you are, stranger, or I'm going to lock you up for murder."

Buck was about to answer when the sound of horses echoed out from along the main street. The deputy looked down the way Buck had just come, and saw the tight bunch of riders headed toward where the two men were. He walked over to his horse and placed a hand on the Winchester in the saddle boot. He thumbed back the hammer so he wouldn't have to do it later should he require it in a hurry. Sure, he had his Colt in his gun belt, but there was something about staring down the barrel of a rifle which had more effect than that of a six-gun.

There were six riders led by an older man with almost gray hair. On a horse beside him was another man. Solid built, straight-backed. When the riders halted, he was the one who spoke first. "It has to be him, Mister Conker."

"Are you arresting this man for murder, Ben?" Conker growled.

"Not yet, Mister Conker. Is there a reason I should?"

"Yes, damn it. He killed two of my men"

"He claims that they were trying to burn the Ortega homestead last night."

"I sent men over to the homestead last night, sure. But it was because some of their sheep had strayed onto my land. That's all."

"Not to burn the homestead?"

"No. Not at all."

Kennedy nodded. "Not what our friend here says?"

"Who are you going to believe, Ben?" Conker demanded. "Me or this murdering saddle tramp?"

"Why did you have two well-known outlaws on your payroll, Conker?" Buck asked.

"What?"

"The Carters. Jack and Joe Carter."

"Never heard of them."

"These two dead men here. I shot them last night

when your men came onto Ortega land with torches."

"I never knew their names. They just came looking for work, so I hired them."

"Just like that?"

"Just like that."

"What about the torches?" the deputy asked.

"It's dark riding at night. Maybe my men were—" he stopped. Then, "Who the hell do you think you are asking me questions?"

"You're a liar, Conker," Buck said.

The rancher's eyes narrowed. "Prove it."

"Maybe I will."

"Arrest him, damn it, Ben," Conker snarled. "You're the sheriff, do your job."

Kennedy's hand moved towards his six-gun. Buck noticed it and shook his head. "You're making a mistake, Sheriff," he cautioned him.

"The only one making a mistake here is you, stranger," Kennedy growled.

"Don't say you weren't warned."

Ignoring the words, the sheriff began drawing his weapon.

The Winchester snaked out of the saddle boot with speed and ease, taking the sheriff by surprise. The weapon roared a fraction before the six-gun came level. The bullet raced from the rifle and burned a furrow across the sheriff's gun arm and his six-gun fell from numb fingers to the wooden boards with a loud thud. Buck levered another round into the Winchester and swung it around to cover Conker and his men who were stunned by the suddenness of what had transpired.

"You men just hold still. Anyone making a move towards a gun will wind up in the dirt beside these other dead fellers."

"You've done it now, Mister," Conker seethed. "You just shot a lawman. You'll hang for sure. I'll see to it myself."

"He was warned," Buck said.

"Do you think you're above the law?" the rancher snapped.

Buck peeled the lapel of his jacket back to reveal the star of a united states deputy marshal pinned to his shirt. "I am the law. Buck Chaney, deputy marshal."

Conker's mouth opened and closed as he tried to respond but nothing was forthcoming. Eventually he was able to speak. "What are you doing here?"

"I was looking for the Carters. Killed three but there's still one I need to clean up."

"He's dead," Kennedy said through gritted teeth as pain climbed his arm.

"There," said Conker. "There's no need for you to stay. You can leave Blanco County now."

"Might stick around for a while. Seems to me there's trouble brewing."

"It has nothing to do with you, Chaney. Our sheriff can take care of things."

"Maybe. But we'll see," Buck said. He moved and climbed onto his horse after untying the reins. "Guess I'll be seeing you. Oh, I'll be back for those horses after."

Cradling the Winchester across his thighs he turned his horse around and noticed the crowd that was still gathered and watching intently. He pointed the bay towards them and stopped not far from a man with spectacles and a suit. "Where's the telegraph office?"

"On Holt Street. Go back down along Main and turn left."

The deputy touched the brim of his hat. "Thanks."

"Where did he go?" Conker asked one of his men.

"To the telegraph office."

"Wait until he's gone and tell me. I'm going to send a wire to Perdition."

"To Coleman?" Gilbert asked.

"Yes, to Coleman."

"Killing a United States Deputy Marshal is bound to attract trouble."

"I don't care. If he causes us trouble, then I want him gone."

"Just leave him to me," Kennedy growled. "I'll kill the son of a bitch for free."

Conker snorted derisively. "You can't even arrest him."

"The next time he won't even see me coming."

"I tell you what," the rancher said. "You take your chance. If you get it done before Coleman gets here, then all good. If not, you turn your damned badge in, and I'll give it to someone I can rely on. In the meantime, Max, send someone for the others. It's time we had another meeting."

Brenham, Texas

Lance sat across from Lily at a table in the small café run by a thin, petite woman named Mary Ellison. His face was lined and showing the stress of his job and little sleep as he sat there deep in thought. "Good morning, Lance," she said, trying to gain his attention.

When he remained unresponsive, she gave him a small kick under the table. He jumped and looked up. "What was that for?"

"Oh, you are here. I was beginning to think I was all on my own."

He gave her a sheepish look and said, "Sorry, I was miles away."

"Don't I know it. What do you have planned today?"

"I thought I might go and see the editor of the Brenham Times. See if I can dig up something useful. What about you?"

"I'm going to go down to the saloon and start work."

"Sorry, I forgot," Lance apologized.

"That's OK. You've a lot on your mind."

The door opened and Lance saw the telegrapher, Burns enter holding a piece of paper. Upon seeing the two of them sitting at the table, he hurried across. "Sorry to disturb your breakfast, Sheriff."

"It's fine, we were just about finished. Lily, this is Mister Burns, the telegrapher for Western Union."

"Ma'am."

"Mister Burns."

Lance pushed his almost empty plate of bacon and eggs away from him. "What is it? I presume you're looking for me."

"This telegram came for you via Barlow," he replied handing the piece of paper over to the sheriff.

Lance gave him a coin for his trouble and before the telegrapher could leave, he told him to wait just in case he needed to reply.

The message was simple. It was Buck telling him he was having some trouble and would appreciate some help. "What is it?" Lily asked.

"Buck needs some help. He's in Bell, Blanco County seat."

"How far away is that?"

"About a week's ride."

"Are you leaving straight away?" Lily asked.

Lance shook his head. "No. I'm needed here. I can't go but I might know someone who can."

"Hardy?"

"Yes," he replied before turning his gaze to Burns. "Send back that I'm organizing some help for him."

"Yes, sir."

The sheriff reached into his pocket and took out another coin. "Will this cover it?"

"Yes, sir."

"Thank you."

Burns took his leave and Lance removed more money from his pocket to cover their meals and tip. He placed it on the table and said, "I'm sorry, my dear, but I have to get to work."

Lily gave him a smile and said, "It's OK. Why don't you come by the saloon after and I'll buy you a drink?"

"I'll do that." He walked around the table and kissed her on the cheek. "I'll see you then."

Outside, the sunburned brightly in the sky and the air was fresh. Lance breathed in deeply before turning left to walk the short distance along the boardwalk then crossing over the rutted street to the jail. When he opened the door and stepped inside, he was surprised to find someone waiting for his return.

"Sheriff," Hardy Walsh greeted him. "Look who decided to pay us a visit this morning."

Holt Carmody stood near the desk, sipping a mug of coffee. He nodded curtly. "Sheriff."

"Does this mean what I think it does, Holt?"

"Yes, sir."

"Has Hardy filled you in on what's been happening?"

"Yes, sir."

"Good. Now forget about it. Do you feel like a ride?"

Carmody frowned. "I guess so."

"It's outside of our bounds, Holt. You ever heard of a place called Bell?"

"I know it."

"My brother has had some trouble over there, and I got a wire from him asking for some help. I can't go because of what's happening here."

The new deputy nodded. "I can go. Any idea of what I'm riding into?"

"No. Just that he holed up at a place owned by someone named Ortega. It'll probably take you a week to get there."

"I'll throw some things together and leave right away."

"How about I swear you in first?"

"Might be an idea," Carmody replied with a wry smile.

Once it was done, Lance said, "Get anything you need and bill it to the county. Come see me before you go."

A few minutes after Carmody had left the office, Walsh asked, "What do you want me to do this morning?"

"Find out if the stage is running. And if it is, get our prisoner on it. I'm going to see the Brenham Times editor and ask him a few questions. I'll see you after."

The Brenham Times was further north on Main Street next to the Brenham Cattleman's Trust and Loan. The editor's name was Maddox Hurst, a nuggety man with wire-framed spectacles, who wore suits and string ties. When Lance entered the office, he was struck by the overpowering smell of printing ink that pervaded the air.

Looking up from what he was writing at his desk, Maddox smiled at his visitor. "Sheriff, I'm glad you stopped by, I was going to come see you this morning."

"Why's that?"

Hurst came to his feet and approached the sheriff. He held out his hand. "I'm sorry. Let me introduce myself properly. I'm Maddox Hurst, editor. And you are Lance Chaney. Former major of Union Cavalry, marshal of Barlow, now our county sheriff."

"Do you know what I had for breakfast this morning, Hurst?"

"Sorry. It's a habit I have. I must know everything."

"Why were you coming to see me?" Lance asked.

"To ask some questions about the murders that are happening, of course. Why are you here?"

"I was going to ask you some questions. Except, what I ask you, I'd better not read about on the front page of your paper, understand?"

"But news is news. People—"

"I know all that stuff. But if I tell you not to print things I don't want printed, then they stay that way. Then we might be able to come to some kind of arrangement on other things. However, if you break our deal then I'll fall on you. Hard."

Hurst could tell by the expression on the sheriff's face that he meant every word. He nodded. "I can work with that."

"Good. Let's talk. You go first."

"Do you have any idea who might be responsible?"

Lance shook his head. "No idea."

"Are they – did the same person do it?"

Lance shrugged. "I don't know. It is strange that they both were friends—"

"Not anymore," Hurst said.

"Pardon?"

"Not anymore," Hurst repeated. "When they came back from the war they were changed."

"You knew them before the war?" Lance asked.

"I knew a lot of them before the war."

"Do you know why they changed?"

The editor shook his head. "No."

"I heard they went together. Is that true?" the sheriff asked.

"They went with Denham. He gathered all who were willing to fight, and they rode out of here in early sixty-two."

"How many?"

"Thirty men. Mostly boys, actually."

"How many of them came back?"

"Five came back. Denham, Ferguson, Lane Trevor, Stinky Smith—"

"Stinky Smith?" Lance inquired.

"He's the local drunk and has been that way since he returned. Got off his horse outside Manny's Cantina, went inside and got drunk. Been that way ever since."

"What about the fifth man?"

"Doug Wellings, works out on the Rafter K."

Lance nodded and thought about what he'd been told. "Where's that?"

"North of town. You ride the trail until you reach the fork. Take the left one, cross Ford Creek and keep going until you see the ranch house." Hurst paused and then asked, "You think they are connected, don't you?"

"Truthfully, I don't know, but something tells me that they are. There's something in their past that could be the reason they are now being killed. And if I read that in your paper I—"

"I know, I know."

"Before I go, what happened to Denham's son?"

"Why?"

"Just curious. I heard last night that he died in the war."

"He died a hero, so they say. No one has ever really said how. Just that he died a hero."

"Thanks," the sheriff said. "If you can think of anything else, let me know."

"I will."

Perdition, Texas

Jim Coleman's Colt leaped into his hand as he heard the board outside his room door squeak with a footfall. He thumbed the hammer back and waited a few heartbeats before taking up the slack on the trigger. The hammer was about to fall on the loaded chamber when a tentative knock came.

"Mister Coleman? Are you there, sir?"

The killer let the hammer down and said, "Yes, I'm here. What do you want?"

"I have a telegram for you."

"Slide it under the door."

There was a shuffle outside in the hall and the paper slipped under the locked door. Footsteps receded and Coleman walked over and picked it up.

There was a moan from the killer's bed and a black-haired woman sat up. The sheet fell away and revealed small, round breasts. "What's the noise?"

"The telegrapher just brought a message for me."

"Oh," the woman moaned and slumped back down. Then, just as she touched the pillow, she shot back up. "Oh! It's morning?"

"Sure is, sweetheart."

"Good Lord, he'll kill me," she blurted out referring to her husband.

"Well, darling, get the hell out of here," Coleman guffawed.

"Don't you laugh at me, you son of a bitch," she snapped. "You know what he's like."

The killer did. Alana Trent's husband was the Perdition blacksmith and was a mean brute of a man who was ugly as sin and bigger than a barn. Should he find out that Coleman was bedding his pretty wife, he'd kill her and then come after him.

"Tell him the truth," the killer said. "Tell him you've been slipping out of a night to come and roll in the sheets with me."

"Do you want him on your tail?" Alana asked, incredulous, throwing a disbelieving look his way as she pulled her pantaloons on.

"It'll save a lot of problems," Coleman allowed. "I'll kill him, and you and I can poke whenever we want."

"As much fun as that sounds, Jim, I won't be part of you murdering him."

The killer shrugged. "It was just a thought."

Coleman went back to the note. He read it and looked over at Alana who was buttoning her dress. "I'm going away for a while. I have work to do."

"You mean you're going to kill someone again."

"It's what I do."

"How long?"

"I'm not sure."

"Then be careful. I'm not sure I could replace you with anyone else in this town."

"If you don't get going you won't need to."

Her eyes widened. "Damn it." Alana swept across the room, planted a kiss on the killer's lips, and then disappeared out the door.

Coleman grabbed his valise, tossing in some spare clothes before collecting his rifle and heading for the door. He locked it behind him and walked along the hallway carpet runner and stomped down the stairs. Behind the gleaming counter was a gray-haired lady who looked up and said, "Going somewhere, Mister Coleman?"

"Yes, Missus Granger, as a matter of fact, I am. I'll be back. I'm just not sure when."

"We can only hold your room for a month, sir."

He nodded. "If I'm going to be longer, I'll send word to let you know."

The lady smiled sweetly. "Thank you, Mister Coleman, that would be much appreciated."

He touched the brim of his hat and stepped outside onto the boardwalk and turned left, going to collect his horse at the livery which stood at the far end of town.

"Coleman you son of a bitch!"

The killer's steps slowed and eventually stopped. He cursed under his breath as he placed his valise on the ground, leaning the rifle against it. Alana had obviously spilled all to her husband. Coleman turned and tucked the flap of his suit coat behind his six-gun.

Hoss Trent stood well over six feet in his stockinged feet, and it had been said that was short of a horse in his top paddock thanks to a Minié ball while fighting at Harper's Ferry.

Coleman's gaze was drawn to the Henry rifle in Trent's hands and knew what was coming. "What can I do for you, Hoss?"

"I'm goin' to blow your pecker off for pokin' my

wife with it, and then I'm goin' to use it to kill you with."

"Just turn around and go home, Hoss. I have no desire to kill you today."

"Too late for that, Coleman. You shouldn't a been diddlin' my wife."

The killer could see there was no swaying Hoss from his undeniable need for reparation. He stepped out onto the street and smiled at the big man. "She was a mighty fine poke, Hoss. Mighty fine."

With a snarl the big man swung the rifle up to kill the man who had cuckolded him. Before he could bring the weapon into line, Coleman's weapon cleared leather and the first bullet exploded from its barrel.

The slug hurtled across thirty feet and slapped hard into the big man's chest. He staggered under the impact but didn't go down. Coleman shot him in the chest again and again the blacksmith refused to fall.

"You have to be kidding," the killer growled.

"Going to kill you, Coleman," Hoss managed and took a step toward him.

Coleman shot him again. This time the blacksmith fell like a tree, bullet in his head.

"Not today you ain't," the killer grunted.

"No!" The shriek ripped along the main street as Alana pushed through the crowd on the boardwalk, rushing toward her fallen husband. Coleman noticed the streaks of blood on her face and realized what had happened. She fell to her knees beside the dead man, shaking him, willing him to get up. When she realized it wasn't going to happen, she looked up and stared at Coleman. "You murdered him, you son of a bitch. Murderer!"

The killer casually replaced the spent cartridge in his six-gun and holstered it. Then he turned away and retrieved his valise. And with Alana's shouts ringing in his ears, headed to the livery to collect his horse.

Bell, Texas

"I've sent for Coleman," Conker told the committee. "I'm hoping he'll be here within the week. Any objections?"

"Killing a federal lawman isn't a smart move, Hank," Red Samson said from the opposite side of the table.

"Neither is having him hanging around asking questions, Red. We've got too much invested in this."

"Kill one marshal and we'll sprout another," Harv Wilson pointed out.

"By the time that happens, Kennedy will have investigated the matter and the case will be closed. The marshal will have been shot by some passing drifter. We have to make sure that Coleman understands that there are to be no witnesses so we can supply our own. Sure, the marshals will investigate but they'll find nothing."

"If you say so, Hank," Samson said accepting the explanation.

"What about you others?" the rancher asked Peters and Wilson.

They both nodded unconvincingly.

"That still leaves us with the other problem of Ortega and his stinking sheep," Conker growled.

"You want to try something with the marshal still above ground?" Peters asked.

"I want that grass. So, yes, I'm willing to keep going. But this time we'll go after the sheep."

"You want more of our men, Hank?" Wilson asked.

"No, I'll use my own. They'll do it tonight."

CHAPTER 8

Rafter K, Brenham, Texas

Lance took the trail north out of Brenham, and upon reaching the fork he took the left arm as instructed by Hurst. From there he followed the trail across the undulating landscape until he found Ford Creek. The trail dropped down to a narrow crossing, wide enough for a wagon and no more. He found the ranch house three miles further on.

It was one of the larger ones the sheriff had seen and bespoke of Kent's prolonged presence in this part of Texas.

As he rode into the yard, a man emerged from a large, double-doored barn to greet him. Lance hauled back on his reins and eased his horse to a stop. The man before him was tall and thinly built. His eyes caught the badge pinned to Lance's chest. "You the new sheriff?"

"Lance Chaney," he replied with a nod.

"You here to see Mister Kent?"

"In a way."

"Uh huh. I'm Chuck Rivers, Rafter K Foreman."

"Pleased to meet you," Lance said and started to dismount.

"Ain't said you could get down, lawman. You just

wait there, and we'll see what Mister Kent says."

The sheriff's eyes narrowed revealing his irritation. If the foreman saw it, he gave no indication, instead he turned away and walked toward the house. Lance sat there for several minutes, waiting as the hot Texas sun beat down on him from the cloudless sky above. Two men and a woman appeared on the porch from inside. Rivers was one and Lance assumed the gray-haired man beside him was Kent.

"Ride on up here, Sheriff," he called out. "Getting too hot to be standing around in the sun."

Lance edged his horse forward until he was adjacent to where they were standing. "Get down. Rivers will take care of your horse."

The sheriff climbed out of the saddle and handed the reins over to the foreman. He stepped up onto the porch and the rancher stuck out a thorny hand. "I'm Lorimer Kent. This is my wife, Faye. I got two full growed kids around here somewhere; only God knows what they're up to."

Lance looked at the thin, middle-aged woman. "Ma'am. Lance Chaney, at your service."

Faye smiled. "My, a gentleman out here. Take note, Lorimer."

"Huh," the rancher grunted. "What can I do for you, Sheriff?"

"I'm here to see one of your hands, actually. Doug Wellings."

"He's out on the north range somewhere checking for strays. We shifted the herd east of here two days ago where the grass was more plentiful. What do you want to see him for anyway? Is he in trouble?"

Lance shook his head. "No, I just need to ask him a few questions. I'm actually hoping he'll be able to help me with something."

"I'll have Rivers saddle me a horse and we'll ride out there together."

"Appreciate it."

Lance waited while the horse was readied and then was surprised by seeing Rivers had a horse too. Kent noticed Lance's expression. "I don't go much anywhere without Rivers these days. My reflexes ain't what they used to be."

They rode out of the yard and headed north over open range. An hour after leaving the house they came into sight of a small herd of cows gathered near a creek. There was, however, no sign of Wellings.

"There," Rivers said pointing at a horse a couple of hundred yards beyond the cattle which stood cropping grass.

Immediately Lance was on edge. He leaned forward and took his Henry from the saddle boot. "Wait here, Mister Kent," he said and rode ahead.

There was a noise behind him, and he turned his head. Rivers was trailing him. "Shouldn't you be looking out for your boss?"

"I do what I'm told," Rivers replied. "Just not by you."

"Uh huh. Keep your eyes peeled. I have a feeling we'll find ourselves a dead man beside that horse."

Lance was right. Wellings had been shot in the back. By the looks of the tracks and bent over grass he'd been moving a cow towards the main group when he'd been shot. The sheriff glanced about and saw a clump of rocks from the direction of where he figured the shot came from. He climbed back onto his horse and rode the hundred and fifty yards to where they were and dismounted again. A quick look around confirmed his suspicions. "This was where the bushwhacker holed up," Lance pointed out to Rivers. "Going by the sign he was here a while."

"Waiting for Wellings to come back," Rivers said.

"That would be my guess," the sheriff replied. He pointed to the east. "He went that way? What's over there?"

"The north trail and eventually the rail line," Rivers said.

"Go tell your boss to head back to the ranch and send some men out for the body. Then you and I are going to take a little ride and see if we can track down this shooter."

"He's got at least a couple hours start on us," Rivers pointed out.

"Then we'd best not waste time then, should we?"

After some loud protests from Kent, he was finally convinced to return to the ranch. River rode back up to where Lance waited, watching the rancher ride away. "Stubborn man?"

"And then some," Rivers allowed.

The sheriff nodded. "Let's go find us a killer."

They followed the trail for an hour before losing it on the edge of Ford Creek, which cut its way through the ranch from the north. They each rode in opposite directions in the hope of finding some sign but came up empty. When they met back up Rivers said, "I got nothing. It's like the killer just disappeared."

"I found nothing either. You're right, whoever it was, knew how to cover their tracks."

"What now?"

"Do you know anything about what Wellings did in the war?"

"No. He never talked about it."

"Not to anyone?" Lance asked.

"Not as far as I know," Rivers replied.

Lance thought about it for a moment. With Wellings dead that made three of the five who came home from the war, Denham included, who'd been killed. It was too much to be a coincidence. He needed to see Denham to at least warn him that his life was in danger.

"I need to get over to the Circle D and see Denham. Let Lorimer know what we found."

"I'll do that."

Then Lance kneed his mount forward and set a course to the Denham ranch.

Circle D, Brenham, Texas

"Good to see you, Sheriff Chaney," Denham greeted Lance when he arrived at the Circle D. "Is this a social call or business?"

"Law business, Clive," the sheriff informed him. He looked about at the rancher's wife and daughter who stood in the yard with them. "Would you mind if we had a word in private? What I have to say might distress the ladies some."

Denham nodded. "Come over to the corral, Sheriff. We can talk there."

They walked over to the corral and stood near the rails. "OK, they can't hear now."

"Doug Wellings was shot in the back this morning on Rafter K land," Lance told him.

"Is he dead?" the rancher asked.

Lance nodded. "Yes."

"Good Lord. Any idea who did it?"

The sheriff shook his head.

"Damn it," Denham cursed. "First Ferguson, then Lane, and now Wellings."

"They all served under you in the war, Didn't they?"

"Yes. They were the only ones who made it back home with me. Apart from that damned drunk of course."

"The drunk?" Lance asked knowing who he meant.

"Clint Smith. They call him Stinky."

"I'm starting to think that the killings are all connected, Clive," Lance explained.

"Why would you—yes now I see. And you think that I could be a target too, don't you?"

Lance said, "What I think is that there is something tying all of these killings together and I'd like to know if you have any idea what it is?"

Denham spread his arms in a display of helplessness. "What can I say? I've no idea."

"Ferguson and Lane Trevor were friends before the war. What happened to destroy that?"

"The war," Denham replied. "The war destroyed everything."

"Did anything specific happen that would cause someone to reach out from the past, hellbent on revenge?"

"You were a Major, am I right?" the rancher asked.

"I was."

"Then you know what goes on."

"I do. War is terrible."

"Amen to that."

"Can you think of anything that might have happened? From my experience, people tend to have a reason that makes them kill another. But killing three, I think that reason is pretty strong for them to go that far."

"You're assuming that they are connected, Sheriff. What if they're not?" Denham asked.

"Believe me, Clive, these killings are connected. If I were you, should you need to go anywhere, keep a man close just in case."

Denham nodded. "I will. What about Clint?"

"I'll have a talk to him. See if he can think of anything."

"Good luck. Once I'd believe whatever he told me, now, I wouldn't believe a damned thing. The war really messed him up."

"Stay safe, Clive."

"Thanks for the warning."

Lance walked over to his horse and climbed aboard. Mary Denham approached him and asked, "How's Hardy, Sheriff?"

"He's fine, Mary."

"Could you tell him I have to come to town tomorrow? Please."

Lance smiled. "I'll do that for you."

"Thank you."

The sheriff turned his horse around and rode out of the yard.

"Are you coming in for afternoon tea, Clive?" Mary called to her husband.

"I'll be in shortly, Mary," he replied. "Pour, I won't be long."

"Don't be, it'll go cold."

Denham muttered something under his breath and walked towards the large barn. He went inside and the scent of fresh hay and the stench of horse-shit assailed his nostrils. "You still here?" he asked the empty building.

A man emerged from one of the stalls, his face masked by the shadows. He was dressed in range clothes and looked just like one of the cowhands that worked on the Circle D. "I'm still here, Colonel."

"You have to get this fixed up tonight. The sheriff can't be allowed to talk to Smith," Denham growled.

"Haven't let you down yet, have I?"

"Get it done. If he talks to Smith, then it's over."

"It's only over if he lives to do something about it," the man surmised.

"I don't want it to come to that. The sheriff's brother is a deputy marshal. The last thing I want is him sniffing around."

"Pa—"

"Don't call me that. I don't have a son. Get out of here before your mother or sister see you. Kill Smith and then leave Brenham and don't come back."

"What about the money?"

"I'll get it to you over at Wichita Rocks. Don't ever come here again. What if the sheriff or your ma had seen you? To them you're dead. Damn well stay that way."

The young man stepped forward. His hair was long and unkempt, his face unshaven and his clothes stained and dirty. His blue eyes flared. "I'm only your son when you want something, Pa? Is that it?"

"I already told you I don't have a son. You came to me, remember?"

"That's right, Colonel, I did. But instead of helping me, you had me kill for you."

Denham felt his anger rise. "This is your mess, Christopher. If you want more money, clean it up."

"Pa, are you in there?" Mary called out as she approached the barn.

"Get out of here, Christopher," Denham hissed. "Fix your mess."

The younger Denham melted back into the shadows and his father turned and hurried towards the open doors. "I'm here, Mary."

"Who were you talking to?"

"Just myself," he lied. "What is it you want?"

"Ma said to tell you the tea is getting cold."

"Well we'd better not keep her waiting any longer. Let's go."

Brenham, Texas

It was almost dark when Lance arrived back in Brenham, He caught up with Walsh at the jail and told him everything about what had happened.

"So, the rider just up and vanished?"

Lance nodded. "It all has something to do with the war, I'm sure of it. It's the only thing that glues it all together. I need to find Stinky Smith and talk to him."

"If you go to Manny's, he won't be far away."

"How'd you get on with our prisoner? Did the stage get off all right?"

"The stage left this morning and our slimy friend was on it," Walsh stated.

"Good. Oh, I almost forgot, a certain Mary Denham asked me to tell you that she would be in town tomorrow."

"What's she coming to town for?"

"If I had to guess, I'd say to see you."

"Can I—"

"You can have an hour off while she's in town," Lance told him before he'd finished.

Walsh grinned. "Thanks, Lance."

"Don't thank me. You can buy me a drink. I want to see how Lily is getting on at the Railway before I go and find Smith."

"I'll stand you two."

"Shoot, no need to get a man drunk," Lance grinned.

Walsh slapped him on the shoulder. "The second one will be for the next time."

"You're fired!"

"You can't do that," the man with the slicked-back hair blustered. "I'm the best dealer you have."

Lily held the man's hot stare. "You're also the slickest bottom dealer I've ever seen."

Lance and Walsh stopped in their tracks as the words tumbled from Lily's mouth. She was calling one of her dealers a cheat in front of everyone in the bar. This was not going to end well, even if she was a woman.

The dealer reached under his coat. "No one calls me a cheat. Not even a woman."

Lance's hand dropped to his Colt, but before he could draw it someone else intervened, which stayed his hand. A big man, no, a giant with dark beard and lightning reflexes grabbed hold of the dealer's arm and squeezed. The hideout gun held by the dealer fell to the floor as he cried out in pain.

The giant gave a mighty swipe of his right fist and the dealer seemed to fly as he landed in a heap six feet from where he'd been standing. The giant lumbered forward and picked the semi-conscious dealer up with his left hand and shaped to hit the man again.

"Milt, leave it. Help him out."
The man known as Milt nodded. "Yes, ma'am."
Lance and Walsh watched as he half dragged the dealer towards the doors. "I didn't think mountains could walk," Lance observed.
"Obviously they can," Walsh replied.
They paced across a clean floor, the sheriff noticing immediately that the sawdust was gone. He stopped near Lily who was occupied apologizing to the cardplayers. When she turned around and saw him standing there her eyes lit up and a broad smile split her face. "Having a busy day, I see," he said.
"Just straightening things out," she replied and wrapped her arms around him and kissed his cheek. "Ooh, you smell like a horse."
"I should, I've been riding most of the day."
"Would you both like a drink?" Lily asked.
"Sure do. Hardy is buying."
Lily shook her head. "No, I'm buying. Go to the table over near the far wall."
"Yours?" Lance asked.
"It is now."
The two men crossed to the table that Lily had indicated, and she soon joined them with a bottle and three glasses. Lance looked at her dress, it was emerald green and matched her eyes. "Nice dress."
"Thank you."
"Who was the man-mountain?"
She smiled. "That was Milt. I found him today. He's taking care of security for me."
Lance frowned. "What do you mean found?"
"I was over at the slaughter yards today talking to the manager about supplying me with meat."
"What for?"
"For when I put the new kitchen in. Nothing like a hungry drunk."
"What's wrong with the butcher?" Lance asked.
"It's cheaper if you go straight to the source and buy in bulk," Lily told him. "Anyway, Milt was

there, and I asked him if he wanted to come and work for me. And he agreed."

"You might want to consider putting in bigger doorways," Walsh said. "Before he knocks himself out on one."

"I'll talk to the carpenter tomorrow," she replied.

Lance stopped pouring the drinks. "What carpenter?"

Lily chuckled. "The one who is going to build on out the back. That way we'll have our own room, the kitchen, plus some extra rooms."

"Don't you have enough rooms for your girls?"

"Not for them, for travelers, customers. At the moment there is only a few at the top of the hallway."

"Good Lord, woman," Lance said. "You don't do things by half."

"That's only the start. I've ordered a new chandelier and mirror. Spittoons, and a footrail to replace the one that's there. New lamps for the walls to lighten the place up a little and it looks like I'll have to hire a new dealer."

"What was the go there?" Walsh asked as he sipped his whiskey.

"He was dealing from the bottom. Thought he could get away with it."

Lance looked across at Walsh who nodded. "I got it. The next stage."

"Make sure he's on it."

The sheriff finished his drink and poured himself another. "How's Posey handling a woman as his boss?"

"He's quite good, actually. Knows his stuff. I met another of the barkeeps earlier too; his name is Tyson Bald. Do you know him, Hardy?"

"Yes, ma'am. He'll work for you."

"How are your girls working out?" Lance asked redirecting his gaze to a table where a pretty whore with long black hair and low-cut blue dress sat with a cowboy.

"That's Peggy," Lily informed him. "She seems nice. Her parents died a few years back and she took the only work that she could find to survive at the time."

"Familiar story."

Lily sighed. "Yes. Are you going back to the hotel after you've left here? Maybe take a bath?"

"After I leave here I'm going over to Manny's Cantina. There's someone there that I have to see."

"Then you'll have a bath?"

"Yes, then I'll have a bath."

"Good, because you aren't sharing a bed with me smelling like that."

Lance finished his drink and stood up. "I'll see you later tonight."

"I'll be late," Lily replied.

"So, what else is new?"

"I'd best take a turn around town," Walsh informed his boss.

Lily reached out and touched Lance's arm. "Oh, what happened about Buck?"

"I sent my new deputy to help him out."

"New deputy?"

"I'll tell you later."

The two men left the saloon and walked out into the night.

The cry of abject terror was followed immediately by the sound of two gunshots. Lance drew his Colt and jogged along the street past Celestine Sparks' House of Joy which was on the corner opposite Manny's Cantina.

He turned the corner just in time to see a man fire two more shots at a figure lumbering along the street, fleeing for his life. One of the shots obviously struck home because the runner threw up his arms and fell to the ground.

"Hey!" Lance shouted and fired two shots. He

cursed instantly because he knew that they'd both missed. The shooter disappeared behind the cantina.

Customers started to emerge from within the adobe-built building to see what the ruckus was about. "What's going on?" Lance heard one man shout. The sheriff knelt beside the fallen man. He was breathing but only just. Lance looked up at one of the men standing over him. "Get the doctor, now. And one of you find Hardy Walsh. Go!"

The sheriff rose from his crouch, holding his Colt out in front of himself. He hurried towards the corner of the cantina and peered around. He could see nothing in the gloom of the shadows. He walked forward, keeping his back in contact with the rough building wall. When he cleared the back of the cantina the moonlight lit the landscape with a pale silver glow. Sporadic structures were scattered about, mainly houses. He heard a dog bark and moved towards the sound.

Lance crept around an outhouse and saw a shadow duck behind a woodpile. Got you. He raised his gun and was about to take another step when the shadow reappeared and fired.

The bullet made a cracking sound ad it hit the outhouse to Lance's right. The sheriff dropped to a knee and fired back. The Colt roared three times and he saw the shooter take refuge once more behind the woodpile.

Then whoever it was popped up again and fired, this time only twice. Once to get Lance to take cover and the second to keep the sheriff's head down to enable him time to change position.

Lance fired again just as the shooter disappeared. He came to his feet and started forward slowly, cautiously, not wanting to run headlong into a bullet. Then the sound of retreating hoofbeats reached his ears. The shooter was riding away.

The sheriff ran out into the open and saw the

shadow laying low on his horse as he made his getaway. The Colt came up and Lance blasted off a couple of shots at the receding horse and rider. Then he cursed out loud before turning and hurrying back towards the street where the man had been shot.

He pushed his way through the crowd and looked down at the man on the ground. "Who is it?"

"Stinky Smith," a man said.

The answer brought a sigh of resignation from the sheriff. It was his fault. Maybe if he'd come to see the man before— "What's he saying?" Lance asked as he realized the drunk was mumbling.

"Probably that he wants another drink," a bystander said bringing a chuckle from the crowd.

The sheriff whirled on them and growled, "If you ain't here to help then get the hell away from him. Go on, get! Now!"

The crowd started to disburse, some returning to their positions inside the cantina. Then Doc Harding appeared with Walsh. "Who's the patient, Sheriff?" the doctor asked.

"Stinky Smith. The shooter got away."

Walsh gave his boss a sharp look. "It looks like you were right."

"Yes. I was right and too slow in acting upon it. This is on me."

"Don't be too hard on yourself, Sheriff. If the shooter wanted to get Stinky, he would have done eventually. Whether you warned him or not."

Stinky was still mumbling even though Harding was still working on him. "What's he saying, Doc?"

"Something about a ghost. That he saw a ghost."

"What do you make of it?"

"Delusions of a dying man," Harding surmised.

"He's dying?" Lance asked just to confirm what the doctor had just said.

"Yes. He'll be lucky to make it back to my surgery."

"Can he hear me, Doc?"
"I doubt it."
Lance crouched down beside the dying man. "Stinky, what did you see?"
"He's—he's dead."
"What?"
"Gh—ghost."
"Who's a ghost, Stinky?"
"De—dead."
"Stinky, who's dead?" Lance tried again.
The drunk whispered something and the sheriff leaned in closer. "What did you say, Clint? Tell me again."
Smith's mouth open and closed and only a faint whisper came out. "Chris Denham."
The town drunk sighed and then died without saying any more. Lance climbed to his feet.
"What do you suppose he meant talking about a ghost?" Walsh asked.
"I don't know," Lance lied. His mind reeled. Christopher Denham was supposed to be dead. This meant he needed to find this killer more than ever. "In the morning I'm going to see if I can follow the track of this killer once more."
"You want me to come with you?" Walsh asked. "We could get a posse together."
Lance shook his head. "No, it's only one man. I'll go myself. Besides, you'll have a visitor."
"Oh, I forgot. It's not important."
"Stay," the sheriff insisted. "I'll be fine."
"Well then," Walsh said. "You go, I'll finish up here."
Suddenly feeling tired, Lance said, "Yes, maybe I will. I'll see you in the morning before I leave."
Lance turned away from the scene of the killing and walked along South Street, his mind trying to fill in pieces of a puzzle he had no idea of where they fit. He had to find the killer and see if whether the words spoken by the dying man were true.

CHAPTER 9

Ortega Homestead, Texas

Buck was dreaming about the war. Although they were receding with the passage of time, every now and then one would rear its ugly head and torment his sleep. Like the one gripping him now.

Trevilian Station. This one he'd had before. His horse had been shot out from under him and Buck staggered to his feet. He raised his six-gun in his right hand as the Union cavalry approached. Feeling a burning pain in his right leg, he looked down to see a bullet wound in it. Blood was staining the pants leg of his britches.

Then another appeared, this time in Buck's right leg. More burning pain scorched up into his brain. He cried out, lifted his head and stared at the riders in Union blue. The Colt in his hand bucked, powder momentarily blocking his vision of the scene before him.

A breeze sprang up, whipping the smoke away so he could see that the charging line was still intact. Beside him a Reb soldier appeared, and Buck shouted at him, "Where's your horse?"

"I don't have a horse."

"Yes, you do, where is it?"

The young man in the bloodstained butternut uniform turned and stared at Buck through sightless eyes, a black hole in the middle of his forehead just below his campaign hat. "No, I don't. I'm infantry."

Buck recoiled in horror, staggered, and nearly fell. He turned back to face the oncoming cavalry charge and saw they were almost upon him.

He fired his gun again and again, and again. Still they came on. Now he could see their faces, horrible smiling faces that looked more like bare skulls. The horses, hooves thundering across the churned-up earth screeched as though they were in pain. Their eyes, orange in color, rolled in their heads, foam snorting from their nostrils.

Buck cried out in fear and shot at them again, but his six-gun was empty. He tried again and nothing happened. Again. Again. Again—

"Senor Buck, wake up!" the voice was urgent.

Buck shot up in his bunk. "What is it?"

"Can you hear it?" Eduardo asked.

"Hear what?" he asked still half asleep.

"Listen."

Buck listened intently, holding his breath for the added silence. At first, there was nothing then the faint pop-pop-pop of gunfire could be heard. He stared at the Mexican shepherd who'd just lit a lantern. "You heard it, yes?"

"I heard it. Gunfire."

"Si, gunfire."

"But where's it coming from?"

The deputy marshal climbed from the bunk and hurried across to the door and opened it. The cool night air rushed inside. Buck stood in the doorway and the sound became much clearer. It only took him a few heartbeats before he realized what was happening.

"They're shooting the sheep. Damn it, wake Antonio up and then wake up Manuel. I'll start saddling the horses. Bring your new rifles."

Buck dressed quickly, pulling on his boots before rushing out to the corral to start saddling the horses. A few minutes later the others joined him.

"What is happening?" Ortega asked.

"I think they're shooting your sheep," Buck told him.

"But why? Why would they do that? They hurt no one."

"Because the sheep are eating the grass they want," Buck told him as he climbed into the saddle. "That's reason enough. Now, come on."

He heeled his horse forward and before the animal was out of the yard it was galloping hard while behind him, the others were still getting mounted up.

Buck brought his horse to a stop as he topped a low rise and looked out across the depression before him. In the pale moonlight, he could make out the lumps laying on the ground unmoving. "Son of a bitch," he cursed.

Behind him he could hear the approach of the others, the hoofbeats of their galloping horses growing louder the closer they came. When Ortega reined in beside him, he heard the Mexican give out an audible gasp. "Madre de Dios."

"Why?" Eduardo muttered. "Why?"

"Where is Perro?" Antonio asked using the word for dog.

With the Winchester cocked and laid across his thighs, Buck started his horse forward. Even in the dark the scene as they rode through was distressing. At a rough count he figured there were at least forty sheep dead, and then there were those that weren't and would have to be shot. He turned in the saddle and said to the others, "Start shooting the wounded sheep. I'm going to see what I can find further on."

He rode along up out of the depression and found the main flock a mile or so away from the others. They were skittish and took flight as soon as they saw the man and horse. It would take the shepherds on foot to calm them. Someone familiar.

The deputy was about to ride back to the others when he heard the deep growl. He turned in the saddle and saw the faint outline of the dog. It was laying on the ground. In the moonlight, he could see the dark patch on its white fur. Buck climbed down.

"It's all right, Perro," he said. "I'm a friend."

He slowly approached and knelt beside the wounded animal. He stroked its fur and whispered softly to the animal. "We're going to have to get you back to the homestead, boy. Carmella can take care of you there."

Buck picked the dog up and put him over the front of his horse while he mounted up behind it. He rode slowly back to the others who were just finishing up shooting the wounded sheep. In the east the sky had just begun to lighten and turn pink; heralding the beginning of a new day.

"The dog has been shot. I need to get him back so your wife can take care of him, Manuel. Then I'm going to town to see the sheriff."

"He will do nothing."

"Maybe not, but I'm going anyway."

"I will come with you."

"OK then."

Ortega turned to the others. "Finish here then find the sheep. Bring them closer to the house."

"They're back that way," Buck told them. "You might need to do it on foot. They're a bit wary of riders."

The two shepherds nodded and then went back to what they were doing while Buck and Ortega rode back to the homestead.

Buck held the dog down while Carmella did her best to remove the bullet. He had bound rawhide strings around the dog's muzzle to prevent him from biting them as they tried to save the animal's life. Eventually, the lead came free and Carmella sighed with relief. "I have it."

"Let's get him patched up," Buck said, stroking the animal to keep him calm.

Twenty minutes later they were finished, and the dog was placed by the fire in the living room on a rug. "Keep an eye on him," Buck told her. "He's a tough dog."

"He is a big baby when it comes to the family. But if you do something to his sheep, he becomes a big oso," she said using the Spanish for bear.

"I'm going to town to see the sheriff. I think Manuel is going to ride with me."

"But Manuel rode out not long after you came back," Carmella said concern in her eyes. "I thought he was going to see to the sheep. You do not think that he would go to town and try something on his own?"

"No, maybe you're right. Maybe he's gone back out to the sheep." Buck knew it was a lie and he hoped the Mexican wasn't about to do something stupid.

Bell, Texas

Manuel Ortega was good and mad, and not thinking straight when he rode into Bell, clutching the Henry rifle in his right hand. As the horse picked its way along the main street a morning storm rumbled its way across the landscape to the north, its clouds of leaden gray ominous, maybe even foreboding.

On the boardwalk either side of Main Street the townsfolk stopped and stared as the Mexican rode, staring straight ahead, seemingly in a trance.

It was the first time any of them had seen him bring a weapon to town and their thoughts immediately turned to trouble.

Up ahead Ortega saw the horses outside the Stockman's Saloon. He turned his horse toward the rail outside of the Gunsmith shop, dismounted and tied off the reins before stepping up onto the boardwalk.

From inside his business, Robert Hollings was looking through the front window and saw him arrive, hurrying outside to meet him. "Don't go up there, Manuel," he cautioned. "Get back on your horse and ride out of town."

"Do you know what they did?" Ortega snapped, anger in his voice.

The gunsmith nodded. "I heard. They were laughing about it when they came in."

"I have to prove to them that I will not be driven off my rancho. We will stay."

"If you go up there you will die, Manuel. Then who will take care of your family?"

"I am not a coward. If I do nothing that is what they will think, and they will come back again and again until there is nothing left of my flock."

"All I'm saying is think about it," Hollings urged him. "Go to the sheriff."

Ortega spat on the boardwalk. "The sheriff is one of them. He will do nothing. No, I must do this."

The Mexican kept walking and left the gunsmith shaking his head in disbelief. As he progressed along the boardwalk, Ortega noted how loud his boots sounded on the dry boards. With each step, the clunk of his heel reminded him of the tick of a clock. Maybe this one was counting down to something he'd rather not consider. Maybe this was a bad idea. And maybe Hollings was right.

Ortega stopped, his emotions awhirl, thoughts no longer focused on the ones who'd killed his sheep, but on those who mattered most. Carmella and Louisa. He turned and began walking back the way he had come.

Behind the Mexican, the batwing doors on the Stockman's Saloon swung open and six cowboys emerged led by Max Gilbert. They saw Ortega and stopped. Gilbert watched the Mexican for a moment and then said, "Well, well. Lookee here. It's the damned Mex. Can smell the sheep stink on him from here."

Ortega kept walking, ignoring the words that were designed to get a reaction from him. But then another of the cowboys went, "Baa."

Ortega stopped. Behind him, the cowboys chuckled and then the one who'd done it before, went Baa again. And this time the Mexican turned to face them.

"Ooh," Gilbert said feigning fear. "The sheep lover looks mad."

The Mexican's hand gripped the rifle tighter, his knuckles turning white. His ire was rekindled and starting to build again. Across the street, Hank Conker and the others of the cattleman's committee emerged to watch the proceedings with great interest.

"Wolf got your tongue, Ortega?" the Broken C foreman sneered.

"Maybe he can't," cackled one of the other cowboys. "Maybe he's like his sheep and can't."

That was all it took. Those words coupled with the images of his dead and wounded animals. The latter bleating in pain right before they were put out of their misery. Tipping point was reached.

The Henry started to come up in Ortega's hands as he leveled it at the men before him. A loud snarl escaped his lips which resembled a cry of anguish. His finger began tightening on the trigger and the hammer was about to fall when the first bullet slammed into his chest a little left of center.

He staggered to his right, his face a mask of pain

as he fought to bring the Henry back level and shoot. Gilbert's six-gun crashed again, and Manuel Ortega was knocked off the boardwalk and onto the street to fall face-first into the dust.

The Broken C foreman stared at the corpse and then looked across at his boss. Conker nodded and then turned away, returning inside to the comforts of the Association lounge.

Within minutes Sheriff Ben Kennedy appeared. He took one look at the dead Mexican and asked, "What happened?"

"He bit off more than he could chew," Gilbert replied. "He threw down on us, so I shot him."

"Why'd he throw down on you?"

"Maybe he had a bad night," one of the other cowboys said and caused the others to chuckle.

"What have you done?" Kennedy asked.

"Nothing at all," the Broken C foreman said. "Just killed a man who tried to kill me."

"You've got witnesses who'll swear to that of course?"

"How many do you want?"

The thunder of hoofbeats coming along the street drew their attention and they saw Buck Chaney riding hell for leather towards them. He came out of the saddle before the horse could pull up. Stopping in his tracks when he saw Manuel Ortega's body still lying on the street, he could tell instantly that the Mexican was dead.

Anger coursed through him like a swollen river. Rage threatened to spill over. His hot gaze settled on Kennedy and he asked, "What the hell happened?"

"He threw down on these Broken C men. Tried to gun them down right here. They had to defend their selves."

"He barely knew how to handle a damned gun. He wouldn't just throw down on men like this. No, there was more to it than that."

"There's witnesses who will swear to that fact," Kennedy explained.

"Who? These cow turds?"

"Watch your mouth, Chaney," Gilbert said harshly. "Just because you're wearing a badge don't mean you can walk all over us."

Buck took the words as an invitation to prove the Broken C foreman wrong and was about to do just that when he glanced down at Ortega once again. He shook his head. "This isn't done with yet. Count on it."

"I won't be too hard to locate," Gilbert grinned. "Now how about you get the sheep stink out of our fine town."

With a couple of guffaws, the Broken C riders mounted their horses and rode out of town.

Buck picked up the dead Mexican and looked around to see the gunsmith leading Ortega's horse toward him. "I tried to stop him, but he wouldn't listen."

Buck nodded. "Did you see what happened?" he asked as he lay the dead man over the saddle.

"Yes. He walked up towards the saloon, and for some reason he stopped. He even turned around and started to walk away. But then the Broken C riders came out. I don't know what was said but it ended with Manuel trying to shoot them and Gilbert killed him. He didn't stand a chance. It'll kill his wife."

"Yeah."

Buck climbed up onto his horse and looked at the gunsmith. "The name's Buck Chaney. Deputy Federal Marshal out of Van Buren. But I actually live in Barlow."

"Robert Hollings, gunsmith."

"Thanks for your help, Gunsmith."

"I didn't do much," he replied.

"You did enough. I'll be seeing you." Buck wheeled the horse around leading the one Ortega had ridden into town.

Suddenly he stopped and stared at the window in the Cattleman's Association building across the street. Standing there looking out was Hank Conker. For a moment the deputy thought he saw a smile on the rancher's face and contemplated putting a bullet through the window and into that smug face. Instead, he set his bay in motion and rode out of town trailing the horse carrying the body of the man who'd saved his life.

Comanche County, Texas

For some reason the shooter had made no attempt to hide his tracks, making Lance's job of following him that much easier. They circled to the north and then cut across the northern trail and the rail line as they headed east. At one point they crossed the Willow Creek trail, a ranch owned by Garvey Power, a middle-aged rancher with a wife and two kids. Both girls. Once on the other side of the trail the tracks headed east through some brush, across a slow-moving creek and out onto some flat country where they arrowed towards a large crop of rocks and boulders.

Lance eased the horse down to a walk as he approached the stand of rocks. The tracks went directly to them, and he had no desire to ride headlong into an ambush. It was late morning and the sun was reasonably high but still the glare made his eyes narrow as he searched for anything that would confirm his suspicions.

The shot when it came sounded like a whipcrack. The horse beneath Lance grunted and then moaned as it started to go down. The sheriff kicked free of the stirrups and dragged his Henry from the saddle boot as he leaped clear.

When he hit the ground, he rolled and came up on one knee. Lance looked for a target but saw nothing. The bushwhacker fired again, and the bullet drove into the ground beside the sheriff. Lance fired a hurried shot at a puff of gun smoke and then was up and running for the only piece of cover around. The rocks where the shooter was holed up.

Small dirt geysers kicked up around his running legs as bullet after bullet plowed into the earth. Lance launched himself at the nearest rock and took shelter behind it. A slug cracked into its hard surface and then screamed off into oblivion as it ricocheted away. The sheriff levered a round into the Henry and fired a hasty shot back at his attacker.

The shooter fired again, and Lance could see he'd shifted position amongst the rocks. Maybe he was trying to circle around and come at the sheriff from a different angle. Lance levered another round into the weapon's chamber and then, instead of firing, he drew back and started to circle around in a wider arc than he figured the shooter was going to make.

The Comanche County sheriff squeezed between two large round boulders and then climbed over a lower jagged one. A few minutes later, Lance stopped and listened. Silence hung heavily in the air. He moved forward, making his way carefully around another large gray boulder and happened upon the shooter. Belly own on a flat rock waiting for his quarry to appear. Only this hunter had now become the hunted.

Lance inched forward as quietly as he could. He needed to take this man alive for two reasons. The first to find out why he'd killed the three men and the second he needed to know whether he was indeed Christopher Denham.

Once he was close enough, the sheriff's voice rang out full of authority. "Just hold it there, Mister. I got you covered."

With a cry of alarm, Chris Denham whirled and brought his rifle sweeping around in an attempt to kill. Lance fired his rifle and the ground erupted between Denham's feet. "Drop it!" he roared.

The killer froze, dropping the rifle at his feet.

"Now the six-gun. Thumb and finger."

Chris did as he was ordered.

Lance closed the gap between himself and the killer so he could get a better look at him. He was dirty, had long unkempt hair, unshaven and his cheeks were sunken. All the hallmarks of a man who'd been on the run for a long time.

"Who are you, Mister?" the sheriff asked.

Nothing.

"I asked you a question?"

Still silence.

"You don't want to talk, that's fine with me. Start walking."

Chris did as he was ordered, and Lance started to follow him. When he reached Denham's weapons, he called out, "Stop."

The sheriff bent down and scooped up the six-gun, tucked it inside his waistband. Next, he picked up the rifle and then said, "Keep moving. Where's your horse."

No answer.

"Shoot. I'll find it."

When they came upon the killer's horse, a chestnut, it was obvious that the mount had fared no better than its owner. Their next stop was Lance's dead mount where he removed his saddle and bridle. Then, with the saddle in hand, he walked over to his prisoner and thrust it at him. "You shot my horse, you carry this."

"You can't make me do that?" Chris growled.

"So, you can speak. Going to tell me your name now?" Lance asked.

The question was met with more stony silence.

"Get walking."

Brenham, Texas

When Lance reached the jail with his prisoner, word spread quickly along the main street and a crowd began to form. By the time he locked the cell door, they were gathered on the street outside the jail, and voices were becoming raised. "Sheriff!

Sheriff Chaney! Get out here!"

Lance looked across at Walsh and said, "The mob gathers."

"Uh, huh. Like hounds baying for blood."

"Let's go and see if we can calm them down."

Once outside on the boardwalk, they were faced with an angry mob. Not overly large, but big enough to be a problem should they wish to take action. And at their head was the mayor, Fellows.

"Have you got the killer in there, Sheriff?" he demanded.

"I have a prisoner, yes, Mayor."

"Is he the one?"

"I'm not sure."

"Sure he's sure," a voice called out from within the crowd. "Bring him out and we'll give him a taste of Brenham Law."

"The only law in Brenham is my law," Lance said firmly. "Should there be any trouble, I'll lock whoever causes it."

"Well, Sheriff," Fellows said, "Is he the one?"

"He could be. But he'll stand trial for it and be judged by a jury of his peers."

"Hell, I'll be on that jury," another man called out. "He'll get justice all right."

"All right, break it up," Lance barked. "Everyone get about your business, go back to whatever it was you were doing before you came along here and decided to cause trouble."

There were a few angry mutters from the crowd but they gradually began to disburse until the mayor was the only one left standing there. "Is there something I can do for you, Mayor?" Lance asked.

The round man shook his head. "No, I'm just trying to decide on something."

"What would that be?"

"Whose side you're on."

Before Lance could respond to the remark Fellows turned and walked off.

"I'd like to put a bullet in his fat ass," Lance growled.

"Don't let me stop you," Walsh told him.

"I'm tempted. Damned goose he is."

"Looks like we're about to have more visitors, Lance," Walsh said, indicating two men walking toward them along the boardwalk.

"The doc and the judge," Lance surmised. "I wonder what they want."

"Word has it you've got your man," Dyson said by way of greeting.

"Maybe, Judge. You should both come in, there's something we need to discuss."

They followed the two lawmen in and halted in the main office. "Well, what's it all about?" Dyson asked.

"Any of you men know Christopher Denham?"

The judge shook his head. "No, not really."

"Doc?"

"I knew the boy," Harding confirmed.

"What about you, Hardy?"

"Some," the deputy allowed.

"Remember last night when Smith was talking about a ghost?"

Walsh nodded. "I do."

"Doc?"

"Yes, sure," the doctor replied with a frown.

"Well just before he died, he told me that the ghost was Christopher Denham," Lance explained.

"Surely not," Harding said skeptically.

Lance just nodded. "I think I have him back there in my jail."

CHAPTER 10

Brenham, Texas

"Good Lord, it is him," the doctor said in disbelief.

"Are you sure?" asked Dyson.

"As sure as I can be," Harding replied.

"What about you, Hardy?" Lance asked his deputy. "Now you've seen him up close."

"It's possible, I guess. The way he's dressed and all the dirt and such he sure looks like he's just crawled out of the grave."

"I'm reasonably sure he's been putting men in there recently. The question is why?" Lance said.

"Christopher?" the doctor said. "It's you, isn't it?"

The prisoner said nothing, just sat on the bunk in silence.

"Can I go in there and examine him, Sheriff?" Harding asked.

With a shake of his head, Lance said, "Not now, Doc. I'm not sure which way he's going to jump. Maybe give it a day or so."

"What are you going to do now, Lance?" Dyson asked when they reentered the main office.

"I'm going out to the Denham place and talk to Clive. See if he'll come and take a look at our prisoner," the sheriff replied.

"Sounds good," replied the judge.

"The other thing that worries me, Judge, is him getting a fair trial here in Brenham. The jury is going to be heavily biased."

"You want the trial moved if we get that far?" Dyson asked.

Lance nodded. "I was thinking down to Barlow. The jury would be impartial."

"I can see your concerns, Sheriff, but—"

"We have a responsibility to give the prisoner a fair trial, Judge. Even if he is guilty. There's no way he'll get it here. You saw what happened out there."

After a pause for thought the judge said with a curt nod, "All right, we'll move it to Barlow if we have to."

"Good. Thanks, Judge, I'll have Hardy take him down there tomorrow. Is that OK with you, Hardy?"

"Sure. I can do that."

"Good. Now I need to get out to the Circle D and back before dark."

Circle D, Brenham, Texas

Lance eased the horse to a halt in the Circle D ranch yard and was met by the foreman, an Irishman named Liam O'Connor. "What do you want, Sheriff?"

"I need to talk to Denham. Is he around?"

The Irishman eyed him suspiciously. "I'll see."

He went inside the ranch house and then reappeared with the Circle D owner. "What can I do for you, Sheriff?"

Lance looked at the foreman and then back at Denham. "I'd like a word to you without the audience."

Denham nodded at his man and O'Connor walked away. "There you are, Chaney. I must say these one on one talks are becoming a habit."

"Tell me how your son died," Lance said in a mirthless voice.

Denham's stare hardened. "Why?"

"Because I want to know. You tell me first and I'll say my piece."

Denham didn't like it and the expression on his face said as much. "We were in Missouri. Our numbers had been whittled down a heap over the years and the regiment I commanded was little more than a raiding force. We'd been out on a mission to hit a Yankee supply depot. I lost ten men on that raid. More than I could afford."

"Sorry Mister Denham but weren't you a mite old to be out conducting raids on Union positions?"

The rancher smiled. "Most likely. But at the time the south needed all the men in the field she could muster. And I wasn't one to sit back and let others fight for me."

Lance nodded. "OK. Go on."

"Well, we were on patrol. We were about out of food and I sent out a forage party under the command of Christopher. He was a lieutenant at the time."

"So, what happened?"

"They were caught in a Union cavalry ambush while they were gone. Christopher was killed right off and the others managed to get away."

"So how do you know he was dead?"

"Because I saw his body."

"How?"

"I went back. I had Ferguson take me," Denham replied.

"Ferguson?" Lance queried.

"That's right."

"The very same Ferguson who was killed?"

"Yes."

"Who else was on that forage detail?" Lance all but demanded.

"Ferguson, Clint Smith—"

"Lane Trevor, and Doug Wellings," Lance finished.

Denham nodded. "That's right."

"And now they're all dead. What happened on that forage detail, Denham?"

"I told you," the rancher replied.

"Something must have happened, Denham."

"Not that I know of."

"What if your son wasn't dead?"

"Don't be ridiculous."

"I have a man in my jail I believe is your son. I'd like you to accompany me back to town to identify him."

Denham's reaction was one of stunned silence.

"Mister Denham?"

"What?"

"I want you to come to town to identify him."

The rancher composed himself and said, "I don't need to. My son is dead. I saw it with my own eyes."

"Before Clint Smith died—"

"What? Clint Smith is dead?"

"That's right. The man I have in jail killed him last night outside Manny's Cantina. I tracked him this morning and found him on Willow Creek range holed up amongst a bunch of rocks. He shot my horse out from under me."

"You said Smith said something. What was it?"

"He said that he'd seen a ghost. When I pressed him before he died, he said it was your son. When I brought the killer back to town, I have two more people who say that it's Chris."

"It can't be him."

"Then come back and prove me wrong."

Denham considered his options for a moment and then nodded. "All right then. I will come into town tomorrow and see for myself."

"I would have preferred you to come back with me today. You'd best make it early. I'm sending him to Barlow."

The news seemed to surprise Denham. "Barlow? Why?"

"Because I don't think he can get a fair trial here. Plus, the townsfolk are getting pretty worked up, and there's no telling what sort of trouble they will instigate the longer he's kept in my jail."

"I'll come in early then."

"Fine, I'll be expecting you."

"It's still a waste of time. My son is dead. I saw it myself."

Lance walked back to his mount and climbed aboard, tipping his hat briefly before turning his horse back toward town. Once the sheriff was out of sight, Denham went in search of his foreman who was in the barn. "Liam, are you in here?"

"Down in the end stall, boss."

When the rancher found him the foreman asked, "What did the sheriff want?"

Denham's eyes narrowed as he said, "Liam, I have a very important job for you. And I need it done tonight."

Brenham, Texas

Lance joined Lily for dinner that evening in Ma's Café just across the street from the Cactus Flower Saloon. It was owned by a large jovial woman who looked as though she enjoyed her own cooking as much as her customers did. While Lance ate steak and vegetables, Ma had also provided chicken for Lily.

"You're quiet this evening," Lily noted.

"Sorry," he apologized. "It's just there's a lot going on at the moment and I'm trying to get it all straight in my head."

"Tell me about it," she said.

"You don't want to hear," he replied.

"Sure, I do. It might do you good to talk."

He stared at her for a moment and realized that

she was indeed serious. He began laying out everything that he knew.

"Do you think that the man in the jail is Denham's son?" she asked.

"There's a good chance that he is. The doc seems to think so, and so does Hardy. And so did Clint Smith."

"It is strange that everyone on that forage party is now dead. What if something happened and this is some kind of revenge? A vendetta if you like?"

"That's what I'm thinking. Something happened on that forage party and now Chris Denham has come back from the dead to exact retribution on the others."

"That would make Denham a liar," Lily pointed out.

"Then there's that. He said he saw his son's body. And if he is lying that means he knows what happened on the forage party."

"Then why didn't his son come home with him if he knew he was alive?"

"Who knows?"

"What do you think?"

"I think that I need to get that man in my jail to talk," Lance said. "It's the only way I'm going to get answers. Something isn't right and I need to know what it is."

"What if..."

Lily stopped and piqued Lance's interest. "What is it?"

"Well, Denham is running for governor, right?"

"That's right."

"Say that he knew what happened and everyone else knew too. The ones who returned home with him that is. And now he's running for governor, something in his past, bad enough to stop him from getting elected, just happens to be looming, waiting to come to light."

"Are you saying that he is responsible?" Lance asked.

"I'm not saying anything, but it is strange that all of his men are dead and he's the only one left. He's the only one who knows what happened in the war and he's still alive. There are now no witnesses left to stand in his way."

Lance reached out and took her hand. "You are in the wrong job, my dear."

"You think I could be right?"

"I think that anything could be possible."

Lance stood up from the table. "Come on, I'll walk you back to the saloon."

"Will you be late tonight?" Lily asked.

"I don't know."

"It doesn't matter, I have Maggie for company."

"How is she doing?" the sheriff asked.

"She has work at the school helping out with the children," Lily replied getting to her feet.

"Good. At least that will take her mind off Buck."

"No more news?"

"No."

They walked outside and were greeted by the cool night air and the noise coming from across the street at the Cactus Flower saloon. "That sounds ominous," Lily said.

"Yes, it does. Do you think..."

She nodded understanding. "I can find my own way back."

"Thanks, I'll see you later tonight. I might come in for a drink."

"I'll be expecting you."

Lily leaned in and kissed him on the cheek and then started off along the boardwalk.

Lance watched her for a moment before his attention was once more drawn across the street to the saloon. He stepped down onto the thoroughfare, walked across the ruts before making his way up onto the walk on the other side.

The noise filtered out through the open doorway which got closed off by locked shutters of a night. He stood there momentarily, running his gaze over the room. It was full of cowboys and townsfolk.

Lance stepped into the room and walked up to the bar where he stopped, peering into the mirror which gave him a clear view of everything.

Everything went quiet and he guessed straight away what had been happening. The bartender came along and asked, “What do you want, Sheriff?”

“Beer.”

The man poured a beer and sat it in front of Lance who made no move for money. Instead, he asked, “Where’s Jacobs?”

“Not here,” the barkeep said staring back at the sheriff with tired eyes.

“Who’s buying the alcohol?”

“What?”

“Come on mule head, I know what’s going on. Who is buying the alcohol?”

“Still don’t know what you mean.”

From behind Lance, a voice called, “Hey Sheriff, why don’t you join us for a drink. Then we can go down to your jail and conduct business.”

There was a chorus of cheers and laughter. Someone else said, “We already got a rope.”

Lance turned slowly until he was facing the crowd. He dropped his hand to his Colt and spoke in a low voice, “I suggest you all go home and sleep it off.”

“We’s only just getting started, Chaney,” another customer said.

“Maybe you need to get finished. If I see any of you around my jail tonight, I’ll lock you up and you’ll go before the judge.”

“Says you.”

The sheriff’s eyes narrowed. “Yes, says me.”

With that, he started towards the door. With each step the noise grew, and he knew that his words hadn't achieved anything. He could expect to see them again tonight, probably a bit worse for wear the way the alcohol was flowing freely, and they would pay for their indiscretions. He had no intention of losing a prisoner to a lynch mob, no matter what the crime.

Lance walked into the jail and took down a sawn-off shotgun from the rack, breaking it open. Hardy Walsh sat back with his coffee, watching him cross to the desk and open the top drawer looking for shells.

"You expecting trouble?" the deputy asked.

"Maybe," Lance replied. "Someone is supplying free alcohol to the men at The Cactus Flower and riling them up."

"Lynch mob?"

"Maybe. But we need to be prepared for them if they do, because I'm not losing a prisoner to a bunch of murderous drunks."

An anxious couple of hours passed by before the sound of distant voices filtered through the office door. "Here we go," Lance said.

The din grew steadily louder until they figured the mob was directly outside the jail. They picked up their weapons before opening the door and stepping out. The crowd was larger than the one that had accompanied the mayor earlier, and many carried torches, and someone had a rope this time.

"I did warn you people when I was in the saloon what would happen, didn't I?" Lance said loud enough for his voice to reach the ones at the rear of the crowd.

"We figure," a big man dressed in range clothes at the front said with a liquor-laden voice said, "that you might want to hand your prisoner over so we can save the court the time."

"Who are you?" the sheriff asked.

"Trigg."

"Trigg?"

"That's right."

Walsh said in a low voice, "Local troublemaker."

"I see," Lance said with a nod. "What if I don't want to give him to you?"

"Well. We'll just take him."

"How about you all go home and sleep off some of that drink in your bellies?"

"Maybe after we finish what we set out to do?"

Lance sighed as he looked out across the lynch mob. Almost every face held the determination that was needed to carry out the Devil's work that they intended to do this night.

"All right, you've got me," Lance said. "You know I'm not going to open fire with this shotgun and kill four or five of you."

"See," Trigg gloated. "I told you they wouldn't risk getting shot full of holes just for a low-down skunk."

"Instead of shooting you, I'll let four of you come into the office and escort the prisoner out."

Trigg stepped forward and turned to the crowd. "Who's coming with me?"

Three more stepped forward and started to follow the mob leader up the steps. When he reached the boardwalk, the cut-down shotgun in Lance's hands swept out and up, taking the man just under the jaw. Teeth shattered and blood spurted from his mouth. His eyes rolled back in his head and he fell like a tree. The men behind him stopped, confused at the sudden violence, their alcohol-soaked brains a little slow to process what they were witnessing.

The sheriff came down to meet them, the butt of the shotgun sweeping left and right. Within moments four men were down, two out cold while the other two lay moaning and bleeding into the dirt.

Lance looked up at the stunned crowd, his eyes narrowed, and his voice grew a hard edge. "Get this through your damned skulls. If any of you try something like this again, I'm not going to go so easy on you. Now, get these pieces of trash out of here."

Suddenly a shot came from inside the jail. Lance and Walsh looked at each other and then ran inside.

When they got to the room that contained the cells, they found their prisoner slumped on the floor. "Get the doc," Lance ordered Walsh as he raced back out to get the keys to the cells. Once he had the door open, he rushed to the fallen prisoner's side. It was plainly obvious that he'd been shot in the back and that the bullet had come from the barred window at the rear of the cell. Lance rolled him over. Chris Denham's eyes fluttered open.

"Hang in there, the doc is on his way," Lance said.

"Grand Valley," Chris whispered weakly. "Grand Valley."

"Grand Valley what?"

"I—I guess he killed me."

"Who?" Lance asked. "Who killed you?"

"Fath—" Chris coughed, a wet wracking cough that brought blood to his lips. "Father."

"Your father did this?" the sheriff asked.

Silence.

"Who's your father?" Lance asked him, shaking him by the shoulders. "Hey, talk to me. Who's your father? What's your name?"

"Chris—"

"Chris? Chris who?"

But Chris Denham was beyond talking. He was dead.

"Damn it," the sheriff cursed as he climbed to his feet. He looked over at the barred window. It was the only way the killer could get a shot at the prisoner without going in the front door, because when the jail was built there had been no rear door put in.

Lance crossed to the window and looked out. It was dark and the shooter would have had no trouble slipping into place without being seen. One of the many questions that Lance wanted answered was whether the shooter was the one that had supplied the free alcohol, or did they make the most of the opportunity when it arose? Then there was the third one. Was the killer coming anyway?

The sheriff walked out into the office and met Doc Harding and Walsh coming in. "Don't rush, Doc. He's dead."

The doctor stopped. "What happened?"

"He was shot through the back window," Lance explained. "Killer got away."

"Any idea who it was? Did he say anything before he died?"

"I got out of him that his name was Chris and he said that it was his father who killed him."

"So, he is Denham's son?"

"I don't know. He said it was his father but there is no way he could have seen who it was. Plus, he said his name was Chris and there is any amount of Chrises out there."

"But we told you who he was," Harding said.

"And I believe you, but a jury needs more. He did say one other thing. Grand Valley."

"Grand Valley?" asked Walsh not sure he'd heard right.

Lance nodded. "The only Grand Valley I can think of is in Missouri."

"But what did he mean by it?" Harding asked.

"I won't know until I go there and ask questions."

"You're going to Grand Valley?" Walsh asked.

"Yes. I'll take the train, day after tomorrow. I'll be gone probably four days. But I need to try and find out what this is all about and Grand Valley might just be the place to do that."

"What about Denham. He's coming in tomorrow."

"I'll talk to him before I go. There's something he's hiding, and I want to shake his tree and see what happens."

"Careful," Walsh told his boss. "Sometimes when you shake trees, big things fall on you."

"He's dead." Lance's voice was blunt and straight to the point, and he studied the face of the man opposite.

"I beg your pardon," Denham said.

"Your son. He's dead."

"I already told you that," Denham replied. "He died in the war."

"No, he didn't. He died last night when someone shot him through the back window of the jail."

The rancher was unflustered. "I don't know who you had in your jail, Sheriff, but it wasn't my son."

With a nod of his head, Lance said, "You could be right. Before he died though he said something to me that I'm not quite sure on. Maybe you could help me out?"

"I don't see how."

"He said Grand Valley. The only one I can think of is in Missouri. Does that mean anything to you?"

Denham's face was impassive. "Should it?"

"I don't know, you tell me."

Denham sighed. "Sheriff, you seem to be under some illusion that I can help you, which I can't."

With a shrug of his shoulders, Lance said, "I was hoping you could. Now I'm going to have to catch the train tomorrow and head up there myself. Oh well, not to worry, thanks anyway, Clive. Sorry about your son."

"He wasn't my son."

Lance watched him walk away and was soon joined by Hardy Walsh. "What do you make of it?" the deputy asked.

"He's lying. I'm now more convinced than ever that he's hiding something."

"I was afraid of that," Walsh said morosely.

"I'm sorry, Hardy. It won't do your cause any

good if we have to arrest Mary's father."

"The law is the law, Lance, and nobody's beyond it. It's what I signed up for."

Circle D, Brenham, Texas

"Liam, where the hell are you?" Denham roared as he stood in the middle of the ranch yard, trembling with rage.

"I'm here," the Irishman said.

Denham turned to see him over near the corral. Stomping over to him he said, "I've another damned job for you."

"What is it?"

"The sheriff is leaving for Grand Valley on the train tomorrow. I don't want him to return to Brenham. Understood?"

"Yes, sir."

"Find someone to make it happen."

CHAPTER 11

Bell, Texas

The wagon rattling along the main street of Bell brought people out to watch its passage and stare at its passengers. Louisa Ortega sat between her mother Carmella and Buck who held the reins for the team. The previous day, they'd buried Manuel out at the homestead under a cottonwood the Louisa had picked out. The reason for her choice was so that her father could have nice shade in the hot summer.

Carmella had spoken little since Buck had returned the body of her husband draped over the back of his horse, until that morning when she'd told the deputy marshal she needed to go to town for some supplies.

He eased the wagon to a stop outside of the store and climbed down. He helped Carmella and then Louisa to the street. They climbed the steps onto the boardwalk together and entered the store.

A small bell attached to the jamb announced their entry. At the counter, they were met by a somber-faced man who was fast losing his hair. "Hello, Carmella," he said in a pitiful voice. "I'm sorry about Manuel."

"Thank you," Carmella replied solemnly as she handed over the list of things she needed.

The store owner, whose name was Percy, looked at the list and hesitated. "What is wrong, Mister Percy?" Carmella asked.

"I—" he stopped and glanced at Buck. "I can't give you these things, Carmella, I'm sorry."

Buck looked over at the counter from where he'd been flicking through a catalog. He frowned, "Why's that, storekeeper?"

"It's not me, understand. I'm only doing as I was told."

"By who?"

The man looked sheepish and his head bowed.

"Who, storekeeper?"

"The Cattleman's Association," Percy mumbled.

"Well, I'm telling you to fill the order," Buck growled.

"I can't. They—"

"They have no right to stop you from filling the order. There is no law to say that."

"Please, Marshal. I have to live here."

"So does the lady. You either fill the order or I'll do it myself."

Percy nodded. "Ok, I'll do it."

The entry bell jingled its metallic sound once more as the door was opened to admit three cowboys who stepped inside. Immediately Percy's demeanor changed, and he became nervous and licked dry lips. The leader of the three, a man with red hair, said, "I hope you ain't serving this Mex bitch, Percy. You know what will happen if you do. Fires have a bad way of just happening."

"Please," the storekeeper pleaded. "It can't hurt."

"It can you," the redhead said.

The storekeeper's shoulders dropped even lower and he shook his head. He turned away and started to fill the order anyway. "You were warned, Percy. Don't say you weren't."

Without a backward glance, the three men turned and walked out of the store, leaving a tense and heavy silence behind them. Carmella broke it when she asked, "Did they mean what they said?"

The storekeeper nodded. "I think so."

She turned to look at Buck. "Can you do something?"

"Like what?"

"You're the law, aren't you?" Carmella snapped.

"They ain't broke any real laws yet. Not federal anyway."

She glared at him.

Buck nodded and then walked toward the door. On his way out he stopped at a barrel filled with pick handles and pulled one free, hefting it in his hand, checking its weight. It would be perfect for working out some of his frustrations.

The deputy followed the trio out onto the street and called out, "Hey!"

They stopped and turned. "What do you want?" the redhead asked with a sneer.

"I figure that you boys might need a lesson in respect," Buck replied as he strode toward them.

"Who's going to give that? You?"

The deputy never broke stride as he snarled, "Yes!" and then swung the pick handle around in a vicious arc.

The hickory shaft smashed into the man's face, splitting lips and dislodging teeth. He reeled away but Buck followed him. Another savage blow and the redhead went down in a heap. But it didn't end there as Buck rounded on the nearest cowhand with a two-handed swing that knocked the stunned man out on his feet.

The third man had the sense, good or bad, to go for his six-gun in the hope of protecting himself. But he was pitifully slow, and he followed his two friends on the train to darkness. Maybe now they would think about their actions and the Cattleman's association would get the message.

Buck looked up and saw the gathering of townsfolk who had stood and witnessed the brutal spectacle. He swung his gaze around and saw Conker standing outside the Cattleman's Association office. Beside him was Gilbert, and for a fleeting moment, Buck wished he would try something. Instead, they both stood stoic, fixing him with their granite stares.

The deputy turned and walked back to the store. Once inside he saw Carmella watching him. "What? You asked me to do something. I did it. What good it will do, I've no idea."

"Did you have to do that? Hasn't there been enough violence?"

"If you stay, there's going to be a lot more," Buck pointed out. "But even if you decide to leave, I'm staying long enough to bring some law to this place."

"They already have a sheriff," Carmella pointed out.

"That sheriff was once an outlaw. Ben Kennedy was wanted in more than one state before he took root here. Not unusual, however, there's more than one outlaw sheriff across the west. Some actually make good lawmen and walk a straight line. However, Kennedy doesn't figure to be one of them."

Suddenly the expression on Carmella Ortega's face changed. Hardened. "I'm not leaving, Marshal Chaney. My husband died for our land and is buried on it. If you are staying, then I would like you to do something for me."

"What's that, ma'am?"

"I want you to hire me some men."

"You already have men."

"No, Eduardo and Antonio are shepherds, nothing more. I want men who are able to defend and protect my land from the Cattleman's Association."

Buck considered the request for a moment. Hiring guns was inviting a war, but the war had already started. "How many?"

"Two, just to keep me and Louisa safe and do some work around the yard."

"Trying to find someone who wants to work on a ranch that runs sheep will be damned near impossible."

"But you will try?"

"Sure."

"Thank you."

Buck turned to the storekeeper. "You almost done with that list?"

"Ah—nearly."

"When it's done put it in the wagon out front. I'll be back soon, Carmella."

"Where are you going?"

"You wanted men. I'm going to find them. Storekeeper, what's the roughest saloon in Bell?"

"The Yards," he replied. "It's—"

"I'll find it," Buck cut him off and left the store.

Outside, the men to whom he'd shown the error of their ways were being helped to their feet. Standing across the street was Sheriff Kennedy with Conker and Gilbert. They stared in his direction, talked some more before Kennedy stepped down onto the street and started heading toward him.

"I want to talk to you, Chaney," he called out.

"I don't want to talk to you, Kennedy."

"Well, too bad. I'm the law and when I say we talk, we talk. Right now I'm deciding whether or not to arrest you for assault."

"Go away," Buck said abruptly. "You're not a lawman. You're a damned outlaw. Bought and paid for by the big cattlemen."

"That's a load of—"

"It's the truth. I sent a wire the other day to the marshal's office in Van Buren asking about you. You're a wanted man."

The shock was evident on the sheriff's face but before he could say anything, Buck continued. "I'll give you one hour to get out of Bell, Kennedy. If you're still here then, I'll come after you. Understand?"

When he said nothing, Buck turned away and started to walk along the street toward the edge of town where he knew the cathouse to be and the stockyards.

"Turn around, Chaney," Kennedy growled. There was ice in the sheriff's voice and there was no mistaking what was coming next.

Buck turned, his hand lingering near his Colt. "There's been enough blood spilled today, Kennedy. Don't push me."

"I'm pushing you, Marshal. You see, this is my town and there's not enough room in it for you and me both."

The deputy sighed. "All right, have it your way. But don't say you weren't warned when you're lying on the street toes up."

With a hiss of air, Kennedy went for his gun. He was fast. His hand blurred and came up with his weapon clutched in his hand. His thumb curled the hammer back and then he died. Two slugs in his chest punched his ticket on the Hell Express.

He staggered under the blows and for a moment Buck figured there was a need to shoot him a third time, but eventually, his legs could support him no more and he hit the hard-packed earth of the rutted street with a thud.

The deputy marshal shifted his gaze from the fallen sheriff to the men on the boardwalk. "Guess you'll need a new lawman, Conker."

The rancher just stood grinding his teeth, the ire on his face plain to see. He turned and said something to his foreman and they disappeared into the building.

Buck thought about sending someone for the undertaker then dismissed the idea. Let them sort it out. He had things he had to do.

"I'll get us a new lawman by damn," Conker snarled and kicked the chair hard enough for it to splinter and fall apart on the plank floor. "And then this damned town will know the meaning of what real law is."

Max Gilbert stared at his boss. "Who are you going to get?"

"The best-damned lawman in Texas," the rancher growled. "And I know for a fact he's no more than three days' ride away."

"Who?"

"Troop Quinn."

"And his regulators?"

Conker nodded. "That's right. I heard the other day he was in Tucker cleaning it out. I'm sure if I offer him enough, he'll take over here and then help rid us of this damned sheep scourge."

"What about the marshal?"

"With a little luck, he'll be dead by the time Quinn arrives. Coleman will have taken care of the problem."

"I hope you're right," the foreman said sounding somewhat skeptical.

"Having doubts, Max?" the rancher asked.

"As you've just seen, this lawman is going to prove hard to kill. What if he kills Coleman instead?"

"Then he'll become Troop Quinn's problem."

The door to the office opened and Groves, the telegrapher, entered with a folded piece of paper in his hand. "I have a message for you, Mister Conker."

"Give it here and then get out," the rancher snapped.

Groves gave it to him and then departed, not waiting for a coin he knew would never come. Conker unfolded the telegram and read it. He looked up and smiled at Gilbert. "A week."

"What's a week?" Gilbert inquired.

"The lumber will be here, and I'll dam the creek where they water them."

"They won't take that laying down. They'll try to stop it as soon as we put it up."

"We'll put guards on it, and if they try to do just that, they'll be in for a shock."

The yards saloon was like many rundown single-room bars in many frontier towns that Buck had seen before. The counter wasn't much more than boards on trestles and the whores were barely attired, in underwear and corsets that were faded and stained. He was sure if they smiled most would be missing a tooth or two. From where he stood it looked like this was where whores went to die.

The building itself was a one-level affair, poorly lit with two canvas walls that ran off the false front. From a darkened corner a high-pitched yipping sound drew his attention and he saw one of the prostitutes bouncing up and down on the lap of a man with his head buried between her enormous breasts.

"You the marshal?" a female voice asked him.

Buck turned and saw a grimy-faced woman with dark hair standing there, pale breasts thrusting up and threatening to spill out over the top of her corset. She smiled at him and as expected, he saw she was missing a front tooth. He figured she was maybe in her late twenties, but the hard life she'd been living made her look almost fifty.

"I'm him," Buck allowed.

"You wanna poke?" she asked tracing a finger down his arm.

"No, thank you."

"I'm clean," she told him as though it would make a difference.

"No."

"I'll use my hand then. Tickle your cowbells with the other. Make it feel good."

"I said no."

"Cow turd," the woman hissed and walked off to find someone else to poke.

Buck walked toward the bar. As he stepped up to it an unshaven man with stained clothes greeted him with a gap-toothed smile. Christ, not another one, Buck thought.

"What can I do for you, Marshal?" the man asked.

Suddenly the loud yip of the woman in the corner grew to a howl of passion. The deputy said, "Don't you have rooms for that sort of thing?"

"Sure, I got two of them. Both in use."

"Of course, they are," Buck muttered. "I'm looking for two capable men."

"They are all capable," the barkeep said. "Of what, I'm not sure, and some more than others."

"Someone who won't slit my throat for two dollars as soon as I go to sleep."

"There are a few."

"Maybe men who fought in the war," Buck added.

The man nodded. "There are three. Tully, Graham, and Ringo."

"Where are they?"

"Tully and Graham are over at the table by the window."

Buck looked in their direction. The so-called table was a crate with three or four boards hammered to the top of it. The men looked like cowhands with the ass out of their duds. Unshaven and dirty.

"Uh-huh," Buck said.

"Ringo is the one under Felicity in the corner."

The deputy shook his head. "He would be. Give me a bottle."

The barkeep reached down and took a bottle from a crate at his feet. He put it on the counter and Buck gave him some money. When he walked across to where Tully and Graham sat, he asked, "You fellers want a top-up?" showing them the full bottle.

"Won't say no if you're buying, Mister."

"It's marshal, actually," Buck told them as he sat down. "Buck Chaney."

"So, you're the one who has the town buzzing," Tully said. "I'm Bert Tully and my friend is Jim Graham."

"Pleased to meet you both."

"So, what brings you to our table?"

"I am offering you both work, if you're interested," he told them as he filled their glasses from the bottle he'd bought. "That's if you need it."

Graham nodded. "Could always stand to earn money."

"You may not say that once you find out what it is. Before I tell you though, I need to know that I can rely on you. Can I?"

"You can," Tully asserted.

"You heard about Manuel Ortega being killed and leaving a wife and kid?"

"Yes."

"She needs two men like yourselves to help out on her place," Buck informed them.

"She already has two," Tully pointed out.

"They're shepherds. Put a gun in their hands and they're liable to shoot themselves in the foot."

"Are you trying to hire our guns, Marshal?" Graham asked. "If you are, then we're not your men."

"Not as such," Buck replied. "You'll be working for the widow. Ranch work. You'll not go looking for trouble. But if some comes, you'll be expected to keep the woman and girl safe to the best of your ability. If that means shooting, then so be it."

The two men looked at each other before nodding. "All right, you've got yourself some men."

Buck reached into his pocket and took out his billfold. He peeled a couple of notes off it and put them on the table. "Get yourselves some new clothes and a bath. You have horses and weapons I assume?"

"We do."

"I'll expect you out at the Ortega place tomorrow. Any questions?"

Both men shook their heads. "Good, I'll see you then."

"I've found you two men," Buck told Carmella. "They'll be out at the homestead tomorrow morning.

"What are they like?" the woman asked.

"They're good men," he told her. "Reliable."

"And you know this from one meeting?"

"There are certain things you can sense in men."

"OK then. I'll take your word for it."

The deputy pointed at the wagon. "Have you finished?"

"Yes. We can go home now."

They all climbed onto the wagon, Louisa between them. She looked up at Buck and asked him, "Did you hear the shooting?"

Alarm spread through Buck and he looked over at Carmella. Surely, she knew what had happened. If she did, she showed no sign of it. He looked back at the girl and said, "Yes, I did as a matter of fact."

"Do you know what happened?"

"I've no idea," he lied and flicked the reins across the backs of the two-horse team. They lunged in the traces and the wagon jolted forward.

Tucker, Texas

Troop Quinn watched on as the man who was sentenced to die pissed himself on the gallows. The stinking liquid poured onto the boards, splattering the man's leather boots. There was a low mewling sound escaping from the man's lips beneath the black hood that had been slipped over his head. The man had been fine until the first trapdoor had been tripped.

"Shut your bawling," Quinn growled at him. "Hang like a goddam man."

His words did nothing the calm the condemned man. Beside him, the third man who was to hang started to go the same way as the one beside him and it made the boss regulator good and mad. "Damn blithering sons of bitches," Quinn snarled and pulled both levers at the same time.

The blubbering stopped immediately as the ropes snapped taught and the men's necks broke like thin twigs. The crowd gasped at the unexpected end to the spectacle and then started to move away. Quinn turned to Bo Randall and said, "Get the undertaker to cut them down and—"

"Mister Quinn?" a thin, aging man called out.

Quinn turned and glared at the man, upset with the interruption. "What?"

"I want to talk to you about this—this abomination you just conducted in my town."

"It was called a hanging, Mayor," Quinn said as he walked down the steps of the gallows. He stopped in front of the mayor and at six-four, the regulator stood over him by a good half a head. He was much wider across the shoulders too, and where the mayor was gray, Quinn had black hair as well as a large black mustache.

"They were men, not animals, Mister Quinn. They deserved to be treated with some dignity."

"They were horse thieves. When I was a ranger before the war, we wouldn't even give them a trial. We'd just string them up from the nearest tree and let them dangle until they stopped kicking. Waste of time a trial. They were guilty as hell."

"Well I think it's time that you and your men moved on, Mister Quinn. Law such as you provide, Tucker can do without."

The regulator bit his tongue before he lost control of his temper. If they wanted him gone then so be it. "We have money coming, Mayor."

The thin man reached into his pocket and took out a large roll of notes. "I think you'll find it all there."

Quinn took it and swept back the left side of his black coat and slipped the money into his pocket. "Thank you, Mayor, we'll be gone inside an hour."

Quinn walked back to the jail and found Bodie there keeping an eye on their prisoners. Four men known as the Hollow Creek Gang. A band of ruffians led by a snake of a man named Underhill. They'd been hitting stages in the county for the past three months and were part of the reason Quinn and his men had been hired. They were to go to trial in the coming days.

Quinn looked at the burly Bodie, a half breed Comanche in his late twenties with long dark hair, who looked more like his mother's people than his father's. Go and tell the others we're leaving. Get your horses and any supplies you need. The town is paying for them."

"You serious, Troop?"

"Sure, I'm serious."

"What about the prisoners?"

"I'll take care of them, now get to it."

As Bodie left, another man entered. "Marshal Quinn I have a message for you."

"Bring it here."

The man hurried across, passed the message over, then turned and left. Quinn opened the note and read it. Then he tucked it into his breast pocket. "I guess we're going back to work."

Quinn reached down and took his Colt from its holster and checked its loads. Satisfied that all was good he walked into the back room where the two cells were. A broad-shouldered man rose from one of the bunks in the cells. There were two outlaws in each cell. "What do you want, Quinn?" Underhill asked.

"I have some good news for you boys. There's not going to be a trial."

"What do you mean?" asked the outlaw boss.

"Just that. No trial."

"You're letting us go?" one of the other outlaws asked.

Quinn shook his head. "Didn't say that, either."

A cold smile touched the regulator's lips as he brought his six-gun up and started shooting.

When the rest of the regulators returned later with all the horses with them, Quinn was standing outside of the jail on the boardwalk, reloading his Colt. He looked at the four of them. Bodie, Randall, Poulson, and Crocker. Each man had been with him since the end of the war. When they'd arrived back in Texas the state had been a seething bed of lawlessness. Quinn and his men became the remedy for it. "We've got more work," he told them.

"Where we headed?" Randall asked.

"Place called Bell."

"How much does it pay?" Crocker inquired.

"Enough to keep us in women and alcohol," he replied.

"That'll do me."

"What about the rest of you?"

"What do we have to do?"

"Preside over a sheep war."

Paulson spat on the ground. "Hell, I'm in."

Quinn slid his six-gun into his holster and said, "What are we waiting for? Let's go."

CHAPTER 12

Brenham, Texas

The train whistle blew for the second time and Lance gave Lily one last kiss. "You watch yourself while you're gone," she chided him. "And make sure you come back to me."

"I'll be gone four, maybe five days. What can happen in that time?"

She rolled her eyes. "I've known you long enough Lance Chaney to know how you and trouble get along."

He gave her a wry smile. "You're getting me mixed up with my brother, Buck."

He bent down and picked up his valise and then looked at Hardy Walsh. "While I'm gone keep a lid on this place."

"Do be careful, Lance," Lily said as he turned and walked toward the train."

"I'm always careful."

He climbed aboard the train along with a number of other passengers traveling the same direction, and moved along the car until finding a vacancy about midway along. He sat down on the seat closest to the window and looked out to see Lily had followed him along. She waved to him and he waved back. Then suddenly the train gave a lurch and they were moving.

Apart from the locomotive, there was a baggage car, two passenger cars, and the caboose at the rear. The train picked up speed and it was soon rocking as it clacked a steady rhythm along the rails.

The conductor came through the passenger cars and checked tickets. When he reached Lance he said, "Welcome aboard, Sheriff. Going far?"

"Grand Valley in Missouri," Lance replied.

"Should be there the day after tomorrow."

Lance frowned. "I thought these things were meant to be fast?"

"They are. They just don't have wings."

The sheriff nodded, annoyed he would be away so long. "I guess it is what it is," he grumbled.

"It'll be good to have the law along on this trip anyway," the man said.

"Why's that?"

"We're carrying a money shipment."

This was news to Lance. "How much?"

The conductor looked around to ensure that no one could overhear. He leaned closer and said, "Ten thousand dollars."

"Where from?" Lance asked.

He shrugged. "I don't know, they don't tell me these things. I only know that it's in the caboose in a safe."

"So, how do you know about it?"

"The station master told me when it was loaded. Told me it was a secret shipment."

"It's not a secret anymore, is it?"

The conductor frowned for a moment and then saw what the sheriff was saying. "I guess you're right about that."

"Keep an eye on my valise, would you?"

"Sure, sure."

Lance came free of his seat and walked along the aisle to the rear of the passenger car. He opened the door and walked between the car and the caboose. Before he opened the door, he looked through the window in it. He could see two men sitting in relaxed positions, chatting with each other. He opened the door and the men's heads swiveled in his direction as they brought weapons around. "Relax, gentlemen. I'm Lance Chaney, Comanche County sheriff."

"What can we do for you, Sheriff?" one of the guards, an average built man with a beard, asked.

"Just wanted to tell you that your secret shipment of money isn't so secret anymore. You might want to be on your toes."

"Damn it," the guard who'd spoken to Lance cursed. "How on earth did you find out?"

"The only 'how' you need to figure out is how many," the sheriff told them. "Because if enough people know, then the wrong people know. And if they know, then you're in a heap of trouble."

"Are you going to help us?" the second man asked.

"Maybe. If you need it. What're your names?"

"Ralph and Sam," the man with the beard said. "I'm Ralph."

The sheriff nodded. "If something happens, I'll take a seat at the table. Just be ready for it."

"Thanks, Sheriff."

Lance went back to his seat and sat looking out at the scenery as it flickered by. It was all well and good to have a seat at the window on this side, but what if someone came from the other side? As it was, he needn't have worried.

Palmyra Junction, Arkansas

Palmyra Junction wasn't exactly a Junction as such. It was a water and wood stop for the train, as well as a telegraph station and that was it. The train would stop there long enough for a comfort break and allow the passengers to stretch their legs. Water was normally taken on, as well as restocking their wood supply. The junction was manned by three men. The telegrapher, and two others who took care of the railroad side of things. All shared the accommodations provided which comprised a long bunkhouse. But right now, those three men were toes up looking at the moon with unblinking gazes. They'd been shot multiple times through the chest by the outlaws who now awaited the arrival of the train and the ten thousand dollars it carried.

Big John Maddox replaced the cartridges in his Navy Colt and stuffed it into his holster. The scar-faced outlaw turned to one of his four men and growled, "Don't just damned well stand there, Hickory, get this fly bait out of here before the train comes."

Hickory Wells mumbled something and then started to drag the first corpse into the brush out of plain sight. Maddox looked around for his other men, Bob Kentrell, Price Graham, and Chick Saddler, but they were nowhere to be seen. Then he heard the scream from the bunkhouse and knew what they were up to.

Palmyra Junction was close to Indian Territory and along the trail, they'd come across a Choctaw man and woman. The man they'd disposed of already, but the woman... His men hadn't had any fun for a good while and they'd asked if they could keep her for a little longer. Against his better judgment, Maddox had agreed. Now his doubts were coming to fruition.

"Lousy bastards," he growled and stomped across to the bunkhouse. He flung the door back and in the dim lantern light saw the three of them standing in a compact triangle with the woman trapped at the center. Her shirt was torn open and her firm breasts were visible as she tried to fend the animals off. They were moving in to rip her skirt when Maddox shouted. "What the hell do you sons of bitches think you're doing?!"

They whirled to face their irate leader. "We're just having some fun," Kentrell whined.

"You ain't got time for fun," Maddox snapped. "The train will be here soon."

"But you said—"

"That was then."

"Damn it, Maddox," Saddler groaned.

"Shut up and get outside," he snapped before looking at the woman. "You stay in here. You try anything and I'll let them have you."

The outlaw leader followed his men outside. "Get ready. Have your minds on the job at hand. If any of you wreck this, I'll shoot you myself."

"Are we even sure the money is on the train?"

"I was told so," he growled.

"By who?" Graham inquired.

"You don't need to know. Help Hickory get rid of the bodies," Maddox said and stormed off.

Lance was sleeping when the train rolled into Palmyra Junction. As it slowed the cars bumped and jerked until the locomotive pulled to a stop. The conductor came through the carriages and said, "Palmyra Junction folks. Here's your chance to have a break if you need it."

He stopped near Lance. "How about you, Sheriff?"

"I'm comfortable here," Lance told him and tipped his hat further forward across his face.

"As you wish," the man said and kept walking. He called back over his shoulder. "We'll be leaving in thirty minutes."

The sheriff raised his hand in acknowledgment and then settled back down.

His solitude lasted all of five minutes. That was all the time it took for Maddox and his men to get into the caboose and crack the safe open, shooting the guards they had surprised.

The gunfire, though distant in Lance's mind, was enough to bring him out of his slumber with a jerk. He tipped his hat back and listened, trying to make sure he hadn't dreamt it during his nap. Shouts of alarm were followed by more gunshots and the sheriff leaped from his seat and drew his Colt.

Lance ran along the aisle towards the rear of the car and threw the door open. He stepped across the linkage gap between the carriages and threw his shoulder against the door into the caboose. His eyes dropped to the floor and he took in the bodies of the two guards, both dead, shot through and through. "Damn it," he cursed and ran for the door at the other end past the open safe.

Out on the rear platform, the shouts grew louder. Lance caught sight of the conductor. He pointed towards the bunkhouse. "Sheriff, they went that way."

Lance looked towards the bunkhouse and leaped down from the rear of the train. He heard the shriek of a horse and then the thunder of hooves.

Five riders appeared from behind the building, throwing up dust in their wake, yelling at their horses to spur them on. The sheriff raised his six-gun and fired at the closest rider. He heard his target cry out and then the outlaw toppled from the saddle. Lance shifted his aim and fired three more times. This rider stiffened but remained in the saddle as the outlaws disappeared into the darkness.

He hurried across the rough ground to check on the fallen rider. The outlaw was dead. If the bullet hadn't killed him then the fall from the horse had because his neck was broken.

"You got one of them, Sheriff," the conductor said as he hurried over to where Lance was crouched over the dead man.

"Maybe so, but they got away with the money and killed the two guards."

"They also shot Mister Travers," the conductor told him. "He had a gun and tried to stop them, but it didn't do him any good."

The sheriff came to his feet and started reloading the Colt. "Does anybody know who they were?"

"It was John Maddox."

He looked to his left and saw an Indian woman, disheveled, blouse torn enough for her to be forced to cover herself. "Who are you?" Lance asked.

"I am Quiet Stream. My husband was Henry Lone Elk of the Choctaw Tribe."

"Was?"

"Those men killed him and took me with them."

"I'm sorry for your loss. Do you know where they were going? Did they say?"

"They have a hideout in the Ouachita Mountains."

"Are you OK?"

"I will live," she said sadly and sank to her knees.

"Conductor look after her."

"Yes, sir."

Lance looked around and saw the dead outlaw's horse which had stopped shortly after having lost its rider. He hurried across to it and looked it over. It seemed to be in reasonably good condition, and there was a Henry Rifle in the saddle boot. There was also a canteen tied to the saddle horn.

For just a moment he considered that this was nothing to do with him. Hell, it wasn't even his state, let alone his county. "Damn it," he hissed and climbed aboard the bay horse.

The animal skittered sideways, unused to the strange rider. Lance called out, "Conductor, make sure my Valise gets off at Van Buren. Leave it with Chief Marshal Mike Dodge. Tell him what I'm doing."

And without waiting for an answer, he heeled the horse forward and disappeared into the night, after the fleeing outlaws.

Ouachita Mountains, Arkansas

The terrain became rougher and more rugged the further he rode but at some point, during the night it had rained and the tracks in the damp earth were easy enough to follow. The trees were thick on either side of the narrow trail and branches often reached out like arms to touch each other above Lance's head; a giant green umbrella.

Ahead the trail wove between slabs of granite with clinging patches of pale-green and gray lichen. Past that it cut down a slight rise and across a narrow rocky stream before climbing a steeper bank on the other side and opening out into a long narrow meadow at the bottom of the valley.

Lance drew rein and stopped the horse at the edge of the tree line. His eyes darted left and right before coming back to the saddled horse around three-hundred yards in front of where he sat.

"Now what do you suppose is going on here?" the sheriff asked out loud.

The horse snorted and changed its stance. Then it snorted again. Lance reached down and took the Henry from the scabbard and checked to see that there was a round in the breech. "Let's go and have a look, shall we?"

The horse moved forward out of the tree line at a slow pace. Its hooves made a dull sound on the damp grass. The sheriff's eyes continued scanning left and right, trying to ascertain the likelihood of riding into an ambush. But the closer he got to the horse in front of him the easier he felt. That was until he saw the lump move in the grass next to it.

Lance brought the horse to a halt once more and then dismounted. He walked slowly forward until he stood over the wounded man on the ground. The outlaw's ashen face was etched with pain. "Who are you?" he grated.

"Name's Chaney. You?"
"Bob Kentrell. You gotta help me."
"You part of the gang that hit the train?"
"No."
"Liar," Lance snapped. "I put the bullet in you."
"All right, yeah. I was part of it. But I'm dying. You gotta help me."
"No, I don't. You're almost dead."
"Pl—Please Chaney," the man gasped a plea. "You—"
"Maddox leave you, huh? Slowing him down too much?"
Kentrell gave a slight nod. "Son of a bitch he is."
"That makes two of you," the sheriff growled. "How far ahead is he?"
"I don't know."
"How far, damn it?"
Kentrell coughed. "Couple of hours."
Lance turned and walked away."
"Hey. Are—are you going to help me?"
"You've got a gun. Help yourself."

Price Graham and Chick Saddler grew more nervous with every passing hour. They'd lost Hickory Wells in the holdup and Maddox had just left Kentrell to die. Now they were starting to question which one of them would be next.

Night had draped a dark blanket across the mountains and stars were starting to dot the clear sky overhead. A screech owl's call echoed through the trees.

"You think he's going to kill one of us next?" Graham asked Saddler as he poked at the fire with a small stick.

"Will you keep it down?" the outlaw hissed. "He'll hear you. Besides, he didn't kill anyone."

"He as good as killed Kentrell. Maybe he wants to keep all the money for himself."

"Shut up," Saddler snapped in a low voice.

"What are you two prairie dogs whispering about?" Maddox asked as he came back into the firelight, buttoning his flies.

"Nothing," Graham said avoiding the outlaw's gaze.

"Well, how about one of you fix us something to eat. We still got some beans left?"

Saddler stood up and moved around getting what he needed to get the food cooking, keeping a furtive eye on Maddox in case he decided to kill them before they ate. Once he was done, he scooped the steaming beans out onto three tin plates which they'd each retrieved from their saddlebags. While they ate, Maddox said, "Well, you men will get an extra share of the loot. Split three ways."

The others kept silent, forking food into their mouths.

"Nothing to say?" Maddox asked.

They grunted like pigs with their noses in a trough but nothing more. "Fine, I'll keep it for myself."

The comment was designed to elicit a response, even if it was in protest. And if the outlaw boss was expecting something, he was sadly mistaken. All he got was silence and the cool of the chilled night air.

"Hello the camp?"

Plates were dropped and guns slid free of leather. The three outlaws came to their feet and whirled in the direction the voice had come from. "Come on in, stranger. Just keep your hands where we can see them."

A figure materialized out of the darkness, hands out to the sides. "Smelled your food. Thought you might have some spare. Haven't eaten since yesterday."

"Who are you, Mister?" Maddox growled.

"Name's Lance Cooper," Lance said.

"Who are you, Lance Cooper?"

"Nobody. Just drifting. Thought I might head west and see what it's all about?"

"You wanted?" Maddox asked.

"Why? Are you some kind of law?" Lance asked dropping his hand to his six-gun.

Graham chuckled. "Are we, hell? If we are, we're in the wrong game."

"Where's your horse?" Maddox asked.

"Back there," the sheriff said indicating over his shoulder.

"What're you running from?"

"Listen," Lance growled. "If I have to answer all these questions just to get something to eat then I'll just keep riding."

"Just hold hard there, Cooper," Maddox said. "I was just making sure of who you are. Matter of fact I might just have a proposition for you."

"Do tell."

"Get yourself some beans and we'll talk. Take Saddler's plate. He looks like he's finished."

"That's mighty friendly of you. What's your name anyway? You seem to have me at a disadvantage."

"I'm John Maddox. These hombres are Price Graham and Chick Saddler."

"Are you that Maddox that robbed Hurstville bank last year over in Kansas?"

"What if I am?"

"Just want to make sure I'm shooting the right man is all," Lance said and drew his six-gun.

Stunned, Maddox and his men were slow in moving. By the time the boss outlaw started to draw his weapon, it was too late.

Lance targeted Maddox first. He was the main threat. Take him and the others might even throw their weapons down. The first shot punched into the killer's chest and he staggered back. A pained snarl erupted from his lips as he willed himself to kill the man before him.

The sheriff fired again, the sound of the shot,

rolling into the night. The bullet struck no more than a palm's width from the first. The bullet hammered into Maddox's chest and he fell like a stone.

Lance turned at the hips and brought the Colt around as he searched for a second target. His foresight settled on Saddler. The outlaw had his gun clear of its holster and was coming up to the firing position. The six-gun in Lance's fist roared once more and Saddler was flung back, the gun in his hand falling from lifeless fingers.

Now there was only Graham left to deal with. He found the outlaw staring at him, uncertainty on his face, his six-gun drawn but down at his thigh. When he realized that he was about to die he dropped the gun and threw his hands up into the air. "Don't shoot!"

Lance's finger was stayed from squeezing the trigger, but only just. He said, "Where's the money?"

"In Maddox's saddlebags."

Lance tied him up and moved to check the saddlebags. He found the money and left it where it was. He turned back to the outlaw and said, "Get some sleep. We've got a long ride tomorrow."

"Where we headed?"

"Van Buren."

Gentleman Jim Coleman made good time to Bell. He arrived a day earlier than expected and set himself up in a room at the Stockman's Saloon overlooking the street. Once he was unpacked and refreshed from the journey, he went down to the lobby and stopped at the counter where the clerk was tallying numbers. "Where can I find Mister Conker at this time of day?"

The man behind the desk looked up with tired eyes. "If he's not at the association building then he's out at his ranch."

Coleman nodded his thanks and went outside.

He stopped on the boardwalk and allowed a rider to pass by, taking notice of the dark stubble on his square jaw and hair to match. The man moved easily with the horse's gait as though they were one. Something a man picked up after years in the saddle. The rider kept going and Coleman stepped down onto the street. He crossed the dusty thoroughfare and then stepped up onto the boardwalk on the far side.

He looked up at the façade of the Association building, unimpressed by the showy trappings of big money that had obviously been poured into the place. He tried the doorknob and it turned easily. Pushing the door open into the cool interior, he stepped inside, allowing his eyes to adjust to the dim surroundings. I see you made it," Conker said.

"Always do."

"You want a drink?"

"No."

"Suit yourself."

"What do you want?" Coleman asked the rancher.

"I need you to kill a man."

"That's what I usually do."

"He's a deputy marshal," Conker told him.

The killer nodded. "That will be extra."

"How much?"

"Five Thousand."

Conker winced. "I can get it for you."

"Half upfront."

"I'll have it delivered to you."

"Where will I find him?"

"Out at the Ortega place. He won't be as easy as the last one," the rancher explained.

"I'll work it out."

"I'll have your money in a couple of hours."

"Thank you. I'd appreciate that."

There was something about the man Holt Carmody had seen on the boardwalk outside of the hotel that stayed in his mind. It would bug him until he figured it out, but first he needed to find out where Buck Chaney was at so he could get the lay of the land. And the best place to do that was at the local jail.

He rode up to the rail out front and noted that it was next to the courthouse. He climbed down from his horse and walked up the steps, across the boardwalk and found the door locked.

"No one there," a voice said.

Carmody turned to his right and saw a man dressed in wool pants and a flannel shirt. "Know where I can find him?"

"Cemetery."

"Cemetery?"

The man nodded. "Yeah, sure. He's dead. The marshal killed him a couple days ago."

"You know where I can find the marshal?"

The man studied him for a moment and said, "He's out at the Ortega place, I expect."

"Where's that?"

The man stared at him in stony silence.

"I asked you a question, Mister."

The man spat on the boardwalk, looked down his nose, then turned and walked away.

Carmody frowned. He decided to try the courthouse and walked next door. The interior was dark and dreary. He could smell the cedar which was the main construction material for the place. The cool air was a welcome break from the heat of the day. The quiet was almost deafening. "Hello?"

A man appeared from the backroom and Carmody figured he was the judge. "What can I help you with, young man?"

The closer he got to the deputy sheriff the more he could see that the man had aged hard and his face was weathered. "I'm looking for the Ortega place."

"I wouldn't go shouting that too loud around here, young man if I were you. Not if you don't want to get run out on a rail."

"That bad?"

"Sheep."

Carmody sighed. "Bad enough."

"You're right there. Already been two killings."

"Two?"

"MacDonald and Ortega. Cattlemen are responsible. They're a law unto themselves around here. Now that the marshal showed up, things might be different. Especially after he shot the cattlemen's sheriff. Although I've been hearing whispers."

"About what?" Carmody asked.

"About the cattlemen sending for Troop Quinn to take over the law in the town. You might want to warn him."

"What about you? Aren't you the law?"

The judge chuckled. "Son, around here Judge Lemuel Bates is as useless as those sheep. I haven't held court in nigh on six months. Like I said, the only law around here is the cattlemen. Funny thing is, when the marshal showed up, I thought someone might have sent for him. Guess I was wrong."

"Who's Troop Quinn?"

"Badman. Law for hire. Runs a band of regulators. There's normal law then there's their law."

"Tell me where to find the Ortega place, Judge, and I'll be on my way."

Five minutes later Carmody was on his horse and headed back along the main street under the watchful gaze of the citizens of Bell. When he reached the Stockman's Saloon, he recognized the man he'd spoken to when he'd first ridden into town. He was with three other men standing on the boardwalk. Cowhands by the looks of them. He pointed at Carmody and the three men stared in his direction.

"Hey, Stranger," one of them called out. "Where you think you're going?"

Carmody eased his hand down to his six-gun as he kept riding. The man stepped down onto the street to block his path. "I asked you a question, Mister."

"I guess I figure that's my business," Carmody replied as he studied the man's face.

"Know what I heard, Mister. I heard you was a stinking sheep lover."

"Whoever told you that was misinformed," Carmody replied. "Now let me past."

"Or what?" the man sneered. He glanced at his friends on the boardwalk. The man that Carmody had seen earlier had reappeared and was watching events with interest.

"Or I'll ride right over you," Carmody said in a low voice.

The man's face hardened. His mirthless smile gone. "Mister, if you want to get out of this town in one piece then I suggest you head back to where you came from."

"Is that your last word?"

The man nodded. "It is."

For some reason, Carmody felt the need to call over to the man on the boardwalk he'd seen earlier. "You in this?"

The man shook his head. "No. Nothing to do with me."

"HYEAAH!" Carmody shouted and kicked his horse. The animal leaped forward and its deep chest barreled into the man standing before it with a sickening thud. The man cried out in pain as the animal trampled over the top of him. As the horse did its damage, Carmody dragged his six-gun from its holster and pointed it at the men on the boardwalk who stood there stunned.

Hauling back on his reins he brought the animal to a halt. "He was warned. All I wanted to do was leave town, but he wouldn't let it go. He may live, might die, I don't really know, nor do I much care, if I'm honest. But I'll tell you one thing for sure. The next man who tries to stop me from riding out of here, I'll kill."

"That was uncalled for, Mister," one of the cowboys on the boardwalk called out.

Carmody looked down at the writhing form. "That's what happens when you try to bully your betters," he growled.

The cowboy grumbled something else but Carmody didn't catch it. Instead, he glanced at the man on the boardwalk who hadn't moved. Then it came to him. Gentleman Jim Coleman. If he was in town, things were about to get worse.

Coleman nodded at the rider and the deputy nodded back before turning his horseback along the street and kept riding.

CHAPTER 13

Van Buren, Arkansas

At the same time, Carmody was riding out of Bell in Texas, Lance Chaney was riding into Van Buren Arkansas with his prisoner and his macabre loads on the two other animals, drawing more than one curious gaze.

"What are they staring at?" Graham asked bitterly.

"A dead man most likely," Lance replied.

They kept riding along the dry, dusty street until they found the marshal's office. He pulled up at the hitch rail and tied his horse to it. "Get down."

Graham slid from the saddle and stood beside the horse.

"What's all this then?"

Lance looked up at the deputy marshal who stood on the boardwalk outside of the office. He said, "Prisoner's name is Graham. Other fellers are Saddler and Maddox. The other two of the gang are dead. Or at least one is," Lance said remembering Kentrell.

"Who are you?"

"Sheriff Lance Chaney. Comanche County, Texas."

"Little off your range ain't you?" the deputy asked.

"That was my thinking," Graham said. "Does he have any authority here in Arkansas?"

"You shut up," the deputy snapped.

"He has all the authority I say he has," Chief Marshal Mike Dodge said as he walked out the door. "Howdy, Chaney. You seen that Reb brother of yours?"

"Howdy, Mike. I heard from him. Ran into some trouble in Bell, Texas. I had to send someone to help him out."

Dodge nodded at the corpses. "Seems like it runs in the family. You seem to attract trouble."

Lance said, "I thought once the war ended then the killing would stop. Guess I was wrong."

"Who is it?"

Lance told him.

"Big John Maddox. Couldn't happen to a nicer outlaw. At least we've got one to hang."

The sheriff sighed. "You get my valise from the train?"

Dodge nodded. "Yeah. Got it inside. Let Cramer take care of this, and come inside."

"Why me?" the deputy complained.

"Because you're here, Big Ears," the marshal replied. "Come on, Lance."

Once inside the office, Dodge offered him a seat and a coffee. Both of which Lance took with gratefully. "Where you headed, Lance?" the marshal asked.

"Grand Valley in Missouri."

"None of my business, but can I ask why? It's a long way from Barlow."

"I'm the sheriff of Comanche County now. Living in Brenham," he informed the deputy. "Headed up there on law business."

Lance went on to tell him what had happened in Brenham. "Sounds like you could be on the right track to me."

"I need to find out what happened, if anything at all."

"Well, there's another train tomorrow. How about I stand you a meal tonight and a drink and we can catch up on things."

With a weary smile, the sheriff said, "I could use one of them. Probably both."

"Good. Go get yourself cleaned up and I'll see you after."

Circle D, Brenham, Texas

"He wasn't on the train," O'Connor told Denham.

"What do you mean he wasn't on the train?"

"I don't know. The man I sent word to said he wasn't on it."

"Well tell him to wait, damn it," the rancher growled. "Chaney will be there. Damned if he won't. That kind always has to know things. Wish he'd just stay the hell out of it. I wouldn't be in this fix if Christopher hadn't done what he did in Grand Valley."

The rancher caught sight of his daughter walking toward the corral, dressed in pants and a shirt. "Where are you going, Girl?" he called out to her.

Mary stopped and looked at her father. "I'm going to town."

"Why?"

"I thought I might go and see Hardy."

"I'll talk to you later, Liam," Denham said in a low voice. Then loud enough for his daughter to hear, "I don't think you should see that young Walsh anymore, Mary."

"Why not?" she asked with a frown.

"Because."

"You're not giving me a reason, Pa."

"I said, that's why," he said firmly.

"I'm going, Pa." The words were spoken with defiant determination.

"I forbid it!" he snapped pulling her up short as she turned away.

Mary faced her father, her eyes sparkled as her anger, inherited from her father, ignited. "You forbid me?"

"Yes."

"You…forbid…me?"

"I just said so, didn't I?"

"Hate to tell you this, Pa. But I'm a grown woman and your days of forbidding me to do things are well behind us."

"Don't you speak to me that way, young lady," he chided her. "I'm still your father."

"Goodbye, Pa."

Mary turned away and walked towards the corral where she would cut out her horse, Brandy. "If you go to town, Mary, don't bother coming home," he yelled at her.

"Maybe I won't."

Suddenly Martha Denham appeared on the ranch house porch. "What's all the yelling?" she demanded.

"Your damned daughter is what," the ranched growled. "She won't listen to a damned thing I say."

"I think that makes her your daughter, Clive," his wife replied. "What seems to be the problem?"

"I damned well forbid her to go to town and see that blasted deputy."

"Hardy Walsh?"

"That's the one."

"Looks like she listened to you."

"You talk to her, Martha. I'm done."

"I like the young man, Clive so I'll not interfere. Besides, she's a grown woman."

"She's my daughter."

"Oh, shut your caterwauling. Leave the girl alone."

"It'll end in tears. Mark my words."

Ten minutes later Denham watched his daughter ride from the ranch yard. In a low voice, he said, "Mark my words."

Ortega Homestead, Texas

"Rider coming in," Ralph called over his shoulder from the woodpile.

Buck looked up from where he was dozing on the porch. He tipped his hat back and watched the rider come into the yard. The deputy marshal swung his feet around and stood up. Not far from where he had been sitting Louisa Ortega appeared in the doorway. "You go back inside little girl," Buck told her.

"I want to see."

"Not this time."

"But—"

"Now," Carmella Ortega snapped from behind her daughter and guided her back inside.

Buck stepped down from the porch as the rider drew rein. "Looking for Buck Chaney if this is the Ortega place."

"It is and I am," Buck replied. "Who might you be?"

"Name's Holt Carmody. I'm your brother's new deputy. He sent me here to give you a hand. From what I've seen you're going to need it."

"Pleased to meet you, Carmody. Step down and we'll talk." The deputy sheriff dismounted his horse and stretched his back before Buck asked, "You've been to town then?"

"Yes. Saw a feller there that I hadn't seen in a while. Gentleman Jim Coleman. You heard of him?"

Buck shook his head. "Can't say as I have."

"Killer for hire. If he's here, then you can bet he's getting paid for it."

"I'm not surprised. I'd say he's been brought in by the cattlemen."

"Had a run-in with some cowboy in town thought he could stop a horse," Carmody explained. "He figured wrong."

"You make friends real fast."

"Not hard when you mention the word sheep."

Buck nodded and turned to Carmella. "Carmella, this is Holt Carmody. My brother sent him."

The woman stepped out into the yard. "Thank you for coming, Mister Carmody."

"Call me Holt, ma'am."

"Then you call me Carmella."

"I'll do that," Carmody said with a smile.

"I'll introduce you to the others directly," the deputy marshal said. "Come inside and I'll fill you in on what's been going on. Ralph, take care of the horse, can you?"

"On it, Marshal."

They went inside and Carmody saw Louisa who'd been watching from the doorway. "Who's this pretty little desert flower?"

"I'm Louisa."

"Pleased to meet you, Louisa,"

"Louisa, sweetie, would you go outside and play while the adults talk. Maybe see if you can find Perro."

"He will be with the sheep," she said.

"No, I think I saw him by the barn," Buck said. "He's not strong enough yet."

"Who's Perro?" Carmody asked.

"The dog," Buck said.

"Oh."

Once the little girl was gone Buck started from the beginning and caught Carmody up.

"So, the town is wide open?"

The deputy marshal nodded. "Yes."

"You thought about going in and taking over the law yourself?"

"I have but they've got me outgunned. Right now, it's all about protecting the homestead. However, with you here, things could change."

"I say let them come to you," Carmody surmised. "Whittle them down that way."

Buck nodded. "Could be dangerous with a man like Coleman on the prod."

"Maybe."

The deputy marshal came erect.

"Come on, Holt, let's go for a ride. I'll find you a fresh horse."

"Where we going?"

"Town."

"Buck, no!" Carmella gasped.

"Better this way, ma'am," Carmody explained. "At least this way he'll be in front rather than behind."

Bell, Texas

The two men rode slowly along the street, crossed over Yard Street and continued riding until they eventually reached Law Street. As they rode past the Stockman's Saloon, Buck noticed a man who'd been outside watching their progress suddenly disappeared within. They brought their horses to a halt and tied them at the hitch rail outside the jail. "You know how I said I was going to wait for them to come to me?"

"I think I was the one who suggested that," Carmody replied.

"Well, I guess I'm not that good on waiting."

Buck stomped up the steps and kicked the door open on the jail. The door flew back, and the pair walked inside. Even though the office had been vacant only a matter of days, there was still a thin veneer of dust on the desk and other surfaces. "Check the weapons on the gun rack, Holt."

Carmody did as requested while Buck looked over the desk and through the drawers. He found a couple of spare badges as well as some wanted dodgers. The keys for the cells were there too.

"The weapons look to be fine, Buck."

The deputy marshal nodded. "Hold up your hand."

"What?"

"Hold up your hand, I need to swear you in as a deputy marshal."

"But I'm already a deputy sheriff," Carmody pointed out.

"Not here. You can be a deputy marshal anywhere."

"I'm starting to think that getting tangled up with you and your brother might not have been the smartest idea. Probably even go so far as to call it a health hazard," he said to Buck.

The deputy marshal smiled. "We have that effect on folks."

"What now?" Carmody asked.

"If I'm right, and judging by the looks we were getting on the way through town, we should find out right about—"

"What the hell are you doing in here, Marshal?"

"—now."

Buck and Carmody turned to face Conker and Gilbert who were standing just inside the doorway. Buck said, "We're just looking around. Seeing as it wasn't getting much use, we thought we'd use it ourselves."

"Don't get too comfortable. There'll be a new sheriff in a couple of days," Conker rumbled.

"Really? I didn't know. I hope whoever it is, is better than the last one."

The rancher glared at Buck and said, "I'm sure they will be."

The deputy marshal was curious. "They?"

"Troop Quinn."

"Forgot to tell you about that," Carmody said.

Buck's eyes grew hard. He'd heard of Quinn. Heard of his methods. "You let Quinn know that when he arrives if he treats this town like the others he's sheriffed in, then he'll be on the inside looking out of these cells."

"Just be gone when he gets here," Conker snapped.

"You don't scare me, Conker. Understand that."

"Understand this, lawman. Within the week I'll be damming along Rocky Creek to keep those stinking sheep out of it before they poison the water."

Buck's blood ran cold. A dam meant that the sheep would have access to only a shallow creek on the east side of the property for water because the dam would back the water up on Conker's land. In summer he'd been told it ran dry and Rocky Creek was the only one that ran all year round. The other thing was that the creek was also the boundary between the Ortega spread and the open range which some of the ranchers used through the summer when their water dried up too.

"You'd best rethink that idea, Conker. You can't dam the creek. What about the water for the open range?"

"The other ranchers will have access to it because it will border the open range."

"You put it up and you'll be told to take it down. Be a pure waste of time, money and effort on your part."

The rancher reached into his pocket and took out a piece of paper. He threw it at Buck and said, "Before you get all high and mighty, Mister Lawman, you might want to read this."

Buck fought the urge to shoot the rancher and bent double to retrieve the slip of paper. He unfolded it and read through the writing. He raised his gaze and then passed the paper to Carmody before saying, "There's nothing wrong with them sheep and you know it."

"I say there is and so does the association committee, hence that piece of paper which tells me that I can dam the creek and keep the diseased animals away from the water that the cattlemen use."

Carmody looked up after he'd finished. "This can't be legal."

"The judge signed it," Conker gloated. "That's all the legal we need."

"I advise you not to build the dam, Conker," Buck said again.

"The dam is going up and there's nothing you can do about it, Mister," Gilbert snapped.

The deputy marshal focused his gaze on the foreman. "Don't think I've forgotten about you, killer."

"I hope not, Marshal."

The two men walked out of the office leaving Buck and Carmody staring at each other. "What are we going to do, Buck?"

"One thing at a time," he replied. "Let's get back out to the homestead."

"I thought this was meant to draw out Coleman."

"It was but I guess we drew out Conker instead. Now we know his plan we can make one of our own."

They left the dusty sheriff's office, closing the door behind them, the broken lock not preventing it from shutting reasonably well. "Wait a moment, Buck," Carmody said and turned to his left. He started along the boardwalk towards the courthouse.

"Where are you going?"

"I have a feeling," he called back over his shoulder.

Buck sighed and started to follow. Their boots making a loud clunk on the dried boards. They entered the courthouse and found the judge sitting on one of the pews in his courtroom.

"Judge, you got a minute?" Carmody asked

The man turned to face them and straight away the deputy sheriff could see what had happened. "When did they do it?"

"After you left. They wanted me to sign a paper. I said I wouldn't do it, so they beat me until I did."

"Son of a bitch," Buck hissed. "Judge that land on the other side of the creek. Is it actually open range?"

"Yes."

"So, the creek is open range?"

"Yes."

"That means they can't dam it. So when they try I'll pull it down. Legally."

"The dam isn't going to be on open Range. Besides, all that will do is lead to a full-blown shooting war," the judge said.

"Look around you, Judge," Buck said. "It's already started. The cattlemen are bringing in Troop Quinn, Gentleman Jim Coleman is in town, Ortega and MacDonald are dead, and now the ranchers are trying to dam the creek. Diplomacy is long gone, Judge. It's time to let the guns do the negotiating."

"I wish you luck, Marshal. You're going to need it."

They left the courthouse and gathered their horses. On their way out of town, when they rode past the saloon, Coleman was sitting on a seat out the front. Carmody pointed him out and Buck stared long and hard at the killer as they rode by. There was no reaction from Coleman.

It would be two days before the killer acted. And when it came, the action wasn't against Buck. The killer did something else to draw the deputy marshal out.

Two days...two days before the rider-less horse came into the yard with blood on its saddle.

CHAPTER 14

Bell, Texas

It was a Thursday. It was the commencement of three events that would be talked about and remembered for many years by the residents of Bell who would never be the same again. It was the bloody beginning of what would worsen substantially before the final bloody end. The catalyst was the arrival of Troop Quinn and his regulators.

The five horsemen rode into town, disheveled and dirty from many days on the trail. One would later compare them to the four horsemen of the apocalypse, except there were five. They rode up to the jail, tied their horses to the hitch rail, and then went inside. They'd not even had a chance to sit down before Max Gilbert arrived. "I take it you're Troop Quinn and his men?"

Quinn stared at the foreman. "That's right. Who are you?"

"Max Gilbert. Foreman for Mister Conker."

"The feller who hired us."

"That's him. He said for you to come out to the ranch when you get here. He's expecting you."

"Tell your boss that if he wants to see me, then come to town. Me and my men have a thirst that needs addressing."

"But the saloon ain't open yet."

"Then we'll open it. Now, go away."

"Yeah," said Bodie. "Go away."

Angry, but not stupid, Gilbert returned outside and was about to step down onto the street when a man called out to him. "Max, I had six wagon loads of lumber come in early this morning. What does your boss want done with them?"

"They down at the freight yards?"

"Sure are."

"Leave them there until later. I'll come back with some men and get it."

"OK."

Gilbert found his horse at the livery and rode out of town. At the ranch, Conker was far from amused about Quinn's response to his expectations. With his usual choice words, the rancher ordered his horse saddled, and he accompanied Gilbert back to town along with six of his other hands to drive the wagons of lumber back to the ranch. They found the regulators at the Stockyard Saloon, drinking by themselves.

"I don't like being dictated too," Conker stated upon seeing Quinn.

"That makes two of us so how about we start afresh," Quinn replied.

"All right."

"You men find yourself another table while me and Mister Conker talk."

The four men got up and moved while Conker sat down. "Why do you need us?" Quinn asked.

"Our sheriff was killed, and we have a problem that needs resolving."

"Such as?"

"Sheep farmers. I want them gone and I need a lawman who sees things my way."

Quinn smiled. "You pay me enough and I'll see it any way you want."

"I stated how much I was willing to pay."

Quinn nodded. "I did. The amount was a little confusing. No one offers that much without a reason. What's your reason, Mister Conker?"

"A United States Deputy Marshal by the name of Buck Chaney."

"Can't say I've heard of him."

"He's moved in on the side of the sheep farmer. I've hired a man to take care of him, but should that fail, I'd expect you to maybe see to the problem. Also, I plan on damming a creek that borders the free-range. I have a letter saying I can legally do it but a couple of your men watching over its construction would help."

Quinn thought for a moment. Killing a lawman wasn't ideal but it wouldn't be the first one he'd buried. "I guess we can accommodate you, Mister Conker."

"You guess? Well, I guess I will have to accept that. We start stringing tomorrow."

"Who's the gun you hired?"

"Jim Coleman."

"Gentleman Jim?"

"That's him," said Conker. "I've used him before."

"OK. I'll keep an eye out for him."

The rancher was curious. "You know him?"

"Let's just say our paths have crossed before."

"Is there going to be a problem?"

Quinn shook his head. "No issue from me there won't."

"And from him?"

"You'll have to ask him that."

"I will, next time I see him."

Ortega Homestead, Texas

"Buck, you better come out here," Carmody said poking his head in through the barn door.

The deputy marshal walked outside into the

bright sunlight and blinked several times to allow his vision to adjust to the glare. Then he saw the horse standing in the middle of the yard. It was Sam's horse. Buck had sent him out earlier to check on the shepherds and the sheep. He walked over to it, Carmody beside him. "How long has it been back?"

"I'm not sure. I only just noticed it."

"Where's Ralph?"

"Out back, chopping firewood."

There was blood on the saddle. Buck reached out and dabbed at it with a finger. It was still tacky. "Something is wrong. I need my horse."

"You're going to need the wagon too," Carmody pointed out. "If he's wounded or in bad shape, you'll need to bring him back."

"OK, hitch up a team."

Carmella stepped out onto the porch, having seen the horse from where she'd been watching out of the homestead windows. "What is wrong? Where is Sam?"

"We don't know. Tell Ralph to keep his rifle close and have an eye open for trouble," Buck told her.

She nodded tentatively and then disappeared around the back of the house. Ten minutes later the men had the team hitched and Buck's horse was saddled. The wagon rattled out of the yard with Buck riding beside it. Once they were clear of it, Buck heeled his horse into a canter and left Carmody and the wagon falling quickly behind.

Sam was dead. He lay on his back, eyes wide, and a single fly crawled in and out of his mouth. His chest was a mass of deep red blood that had stained his shirt and was beginning to dry. Buck shook his head and spat on the ground in disgust. "Bastard," he hissed.

Behind him, he could hear the wagon coming.

Carmody drew it to a halt and stared down at the corpse. "I guess we know what happened now."

The deputy marshal grunted. "He was murdered."

"I hate to point this out, but I can hear the sheep from here which means that Eduardo and Antonio should have heard the shot that killed him."

"You're right," Buck allowed and climbed back onto his horse. "I'll go and check it out."

He found them lying together. Both Eduardo and Antonio had been shot through the chest; but unlike Eduardo, by some miracle, Antonio had survived. His eyes fluttered open and he looked up at the man standing over him. "He—he shot us."

"Who? Who shot you?"

"Man, never seen him before."

Buck stood erect and fired his six-gun twice into the air. "Hang in there, Antonio. We'll get you to a doctor."

"I am dying, senor."

"Not if I can help it."

Carmody already had Sam on the wagon when he arrived and when he saw the other two, a curse escaped his lips. "Antonio is still alive. We need to get him into town. Help me get him loaded on the wagon."

Once both were on, Buck tied his horse to the tailgate and climbed in. He rode in the back while Carmody drove. The trip was slow, tedious. But eventually, the wagon rattled across the bridge into town. The first person they came across, a slim young man outside the livery, Carmody asked, "Where's the sawbones?"

"You got a hurt man in there?" the man asked in a slow type of voice.

Buck held up bloody hands and said, "What do you think, horse's ass?"

"Oh, right. If you go further along the street to Settlement which is on your left and Doc Walker's place is the third one on your right."

"Thank you."

"He won't be there though."

"What?"

The young man kicked at the dirt he stood on and said, "He'll be at the saloon this time of the day."

Buck rolled his eyes. "Get us moving, Holt."

The wagon lurched forward and rumbled on. Buck looked down at Antonio whose condition appeared to be worsening. His face was ashen and his cheeks sunken. Blood lay pooled on the bed of the wagon and the deputy marshal was surprised that a thin man like the Mexican had so much in him.

Carmody pulled back on the reins outside of the saloon and he helped Buck get Antonio out of the wagon.

Buck carried him up the steps of the boardwalk and Carmody held the doors open to give unfettered access. Once inside, Buck glanced around the room and shouted, "Where's the damned doctor?"

Many pairs of eyes turned and stared at the spectacle. A hushed whisper resonated around the room until Doc Walker stood up. "I'm here."

Buck started towards him. "Put some tables together. Now!"

By the time he reached the doctor, two tables had been pushed together, the chairs moved out of the way, and he was able to put the dying Mexican on them. Buck stepped back and wiped his hands on his pants.

"Hey, you can't—"

Carmody's six-shooter leaped into his hand and the cold hard barrel pressed up under the speaker's jaw. He leaned in close and said, "Don't try telling us what we can and can't do. Just go about your business or I'll plaster your brains all over this saloon. Make no mistake, we're not in the mood for your horseshit."

The man slunk off quietly through the crowd

which had gathered to get a look at Antonio.

"What happened?" the doctor asked.

"He was shot down by some yellow skunk," Buck told him.

"Where?" he asked, cutting away the shirt. Before the deputy marshal could answer he continued, "You're just lucky I'd been out on a call and had my bag with me."

"Lucky? Tell that to the other two dead men we have in the back of the wagon."

Walker's gaze flicked up. "Two more?"

"Yes."

"I thought all this might end after Manuel died, but it's only getting worse. You're the law, why don't you do something?"

"Just save his damned life, Doc, instead of lecturing me."

Walker kept working on Antonio who moaned as he dug for the bullet.

"Hey!" someone called. "It's one of them sheepherders. Let the stinking Mexican die, Doc."

Buck turned to face the speaker. His glare was hot, face red. "Mister, you've got until yesterday to get out of here."

"Or what?" the man sneered.

Carmody had made his way through the crowd to within a few feet of the talker. His right arm flashed up; hand filled with six-gun. There was an audible crack as the hard barrel crashed into the talker's face, who collapsed like a poleaxed steer, bleeding from more than one place.

"Hey! You can't do that," another cowhand protested as he took a step forward.

Again, the six-gun flashed, and another body joined the bigmouth on the floor. "Anyone else?" Carmody asked. "My arm ain't tired yet."

No one moved.

"Good, now shut up and stay out of the way."

"What if I don't want to?"

The crowd separated, and standing there as though he was Moses parting the Red Sea, was Jim Coleman.

Both Buck and Carmody studied the killer but it was Carmody who replied to the question. "I already asked once, Coleman. I ain't going to repeat myself again."

"Do I know you?"

"I expect you do. The Name is Holt Carmody."

"You the same Holt Carmody who killed Frank Gallagher out of Kansas?"

The deputy nodded. "I heard tell that was me. Didn't know his name at the time."

Buck studied the pair. So Carmody had a reputation. First he'd heard of it.

"They say he was good with a gun," Coleman said.

"Obviously not good enough."

"I'd like to talk some more but it's actually the marshal I'm here to see."

Buck straightened and wiped his hands on his pants. "I was wondering when you'd get around to it, Coleman."

"I'm ready when you are."

"How about we take it outside. No sense in anyone getting killed that shouldn't," Buck suggested.

The killer stared at him thoughtfully for a moment before giving a sharp nod. "Let's."

They walked towards the doors and Walker called after them, "Hasn't there been enough killing?"

"It's either kill him or arrest him for murder, Doc," Buck replied. "And I don't think he's up for being arrested."

The crowd followed them outside, a buzz of excitement dragging along with them. The two men stepped down onto the street and backed away from each other until there was twenty feet between them. "That far enough for you, killer?" Buck asked.

Coleman nodded.

"What the hell is going on here?" a voice rumbled.

Buck looked over his shoulder and saw five men marching up the street towards them, all armed with rifles.

Upon the boardwalk, Carmody rested his hand on his six-shooter in case things went awry.

"I asked a question," the man at the center of the group snarled. "I'll not have gunfights in my town."

Troop Quinn.

"Back off, Quinn, this has nothing to do with you," Coleman ordered. "I can accommodate you next if you want."

"Still the same Coleman. Always holding a grudge."

"You should know. Just give me a moment while I kill the marshal here."

Quinn's eyes flicked to Buck. "You the marshal I've been hearing about?"

"Could well be."

"Well hell, don't let me interfere. Go for it." His smile was cold.

"How about it, Marshal? You ready to die?"

"You talk too much, Coleman," Buck growled, and his hand slashed for his Colt.

Coleman was taken by surprise at the lawman's speed, and struggled to catch up with his draw. For a moment he thought he was going to make it and excitement flashed through him at the thought of another man going down before his gun. But ecstasy turned to agony as the first slug burned deep into his chest. He staggered back then gathered himself. A bloody grin of triumph split Coleman's lips as he started to bring his six-gun up. It came level and the killer tried to squeeze the trigger but found out he couldn't. It was taking all his strength just to keep the damn thing elevated.

Buck shot him again. The bullet plowed into the killer's chest, removing the last vestiges of light from his eyes. His legs gave out and he collapsed into the dust of the main street.

A heavy silence hung over the town once the echo of that final shot had rolled away. Not even an excited murmur emanated from the crowd. It was Quinn who broke it. "I guess that's it then," he said loudly. "Coleman's dead. I'll take your gun, Marshal."

Buck glared at the regulator. "You what?"

Quinn's gaze hardened. "I said, I'll have your gun. Can't have people shooting out their problems on the street of my town. There'll be a hearing."

"The hell you say. I'm a federal deputy."

"I don't much care. My town, my rules. You may well get off as self-defense, but the principle of the matter is, a precedence needs to be set, and it starts here."

Buck glanced at Carmody who gave a slight shake of his head. Then he noticed the stance that Quinn's men had taken either side of the regulator and he knew that should he try anything, they would burn him down.

"How long am I in jail for, Quinn?" Buck asked feeling ridiculous.

"Just until the hearing is held with the judge."

Buck holstered his Colt and unbuckled his gun belt and passed it over to Carmody. He took it and stepped back. Quinn frowned. "Who are you?"

"The name's Holt Carmody."

"And what do you do, Holt Carmody?"

"I'm his deputy."

"I see. All right Chaney, start walking."

"What do you want me to do, Buck?" Carmody asked.

"Nothing yet, Holt. We'll just see how this plays out."

Brenham, Texas

It was like an itch she couldn't scratch. A feeling that something wasn't right, and she'd had it ever since the two cowboys had entered her saloon. One was big and broad while the other was thin, whip-like. She studied them from her table as they crossed the room towards the bar. She garnered Milt's attention and he came over to her. "Who are the two men who just came in?"

"The ones up at the bar, Miss Lilly?"

"That's them."

"The big feller is Monk Lawson. The thin feller Razor Evans. Not the nicest men you'll meet," Milt explained.

"Do tell."

"I heard it said that they're both wanted in Ohio. I'm not sure if it's true or not but it's said that Razor cut up a cowboy after he cut in on a whore he was drinking with. The man's friends thought they'd help the cowboy out, but Monk pulled iron and shot two of them."

"Nice," Lily said with a grunt. "Keep an eye on them."

"Yes, ma'am."

After he left, Lily picked up the deck of cards she kept on the table and started playing Solitaire.

All the time she kept an eye on the new arrivals. Watched them drink. Watched them play cards and watched them both take one of her girls upstairs. Peggy and another called Sally. She sighed. Maybe her feeling about them was wrong.

Then again, maybe it wasn't.

The screams echoed through the saloon as the girl named Sally, who had been in the room with Razor Evans appeared at the top of the stairs, blood streaming from her cheek. An expression of abject fear etched on her face amidst the bloody mess.

Lily looked up and her blood ran cold. She grabbed a customer from near her table and snapped, "Get the deputy."

Milt came away from the wall where he stood, scooping up his sawn-off shotgun and started towards the stairs. Behind the whore, a shirtless Evans appeared with a six-gun in his hand. He looked down over the balcony as he grabbed the woman by the hair. He saw Milt with the shotgun and fired at him, hitting the big man low down on the left side.

Milt buckled and fell to the floor, writhing in pain. A man next to him dropped to the floor beside the big man and checked him over. On the landing meanwhile, Sally struggled to free herself but Evans had a firm grip and wasn't about to let her go. "The bitch stole from me. Something like that don't go unpunished."

He dragged her back out of sight, Sally screaming as she went. Lily looked at the men gathered staring up at the vacant space. "Don't just stand there," she pleaded. "Help her."

They all turned to look at her. One man said, "If she stole, she deserves what she gets. Besides, she's only a whore."

The others nodded and murmured their agreements and Lily shook her head in disgust. "Spineless sons of bitches," she snarled and hurried across to where Milt lay writhing in pain. She scooped up the shotgun and walked purposefully towards the stairs.

"Where you going?" someone asked her.

"To do what you gutless assholes won't," she threw back at him and stomped up the steps.

By the time Lily reached the landing, she was already trembling. She gripped the shotgun so tight that her knuckles turned white from the pressure. She stopped, rethinking her choice to do this alone, and then decided that having come this far she should keep going.

The first step along the hallway was the hardest. The second, a little less so. By the time Lily took her third, there was no going back.

The first few doors on the left and right were closed, guest rooms. The ones the girls used were the four at the back. Two were closed and two were open. She checked the open ones first. The first room contained the girl who'd gone upstairs with Monk. She sat on the bed trembling with fear, her cheeks stained with tears. "Are they in the next room?"

The whore said nothing, not even looking up at Lily.

"Peggy. Are they in the next room?" Lily whispered harshly.

Peggy finally looked at Lily and said, "N—no. They left. He did something to Sally and left out the b—back stairs."

Thank God she hadn't started building the rear rooms yet. "Wait here."

Lily walked along the hall to the next room and stood in the doorway. For a moment she couldn't decide whether to scream or faint. In the end, she did both.

Hardy walsh came back into the Railway Saloon and walked across to where Lily sat with Maggie and sat down. "I've taken care of everything and Hathaway will get her ready for burial."

Lily stared at him. "I'll pay for it."

He nodded. "I'll let him know."

"I—I can't believe he would do that to her," Lily stammered.

"I'll get him. How's Milt?"

"The doctor says he might make it. Might not either."

Walsh looked around at the empty saloon then climbed to his feet. "I'll go now."

"Be careful, Hardy," Lily told him. "Take someone with you. A posse."

"I'll be fine. I'll be gone no more than a couple of days."

"Are you sure they left town?" Maggie asked.

He nodded. "They were seen leaving and their horses are gone from the livery. They headed west."

"Into Comanche country," Lily observed. "You can't go alone."

Walsh sighed. "I tell you what. If it makes you feel better, I'll take Chick Roberts with me."

Lily frowned. "Who's Chick Roberts?"

"He's an old scout for the army. Been out a while but he'll be good company."

"Fine. But still, be careful."

10 Miles West Of Brenham, Texas

The trail was easy to follow. It was cut deep into the landscape and tufts of grass were churned over from the hoofmarks. They rode towards the setting sun until coming across a stream in the lee of a steep low ridge. It snaked for a mile before cutting through the same ridge lined with brush either side.

By this time the sun was low in the sky. "We'll camp here," Walsh said to the gray-bearded man who rode on his right.

Chick Roberts drew rein on his horse. The man had done it all. Scouted for the army, driven freight wagons, ridden shotgun on a stage run from El Paso to Wichita Falls, and ridden night herd on many a ranch. Not to mention ridden into Mexico after rustlers who'd slipped across the Rio to steal Longhorns.

"I figure we ain't that far behind them, Hardy," Roberts said. "Couple of hours. There is a chance that the varmints might keep riding through the night."

"Well, I ain't," Walsh said, a finality in his voice. "The last thing we need is one of our horses to step in a hole and break a leg out here in Comanche country. Even if we are ten or so miles from Brenham."

"There's Comanch around?" Roberts asked.

"Few days ago, one of the freighters who'd been running supplies over to Fort Granger near the Comanche Trail said he saw some. Only at a distance, mind."

"But that's still fifty miles west of here," Roberts pointed out.

"Only a days' ride," the deputy pointed out.

"'Spose you're right. I'll hunt us up some dried wood. Unless you're intending us having a cold camp?"

"No."

They set up a small camp withing reach of the creek but back from it in the brush in a small clearing. Once they were done, they ate and drank coffee. "What's the new sheriff like?" Roberts asked.

Walsh lowered his mug. "Good man. Served as a major in the war."

"Johnny Reb, huh?"

The deputy shook his head. "Nope. Yank."

"Man had some sense."

With a nod, Walsh said, "Strange thing is, his brother rode with the south."

"Lot of that went around at the time."

"Sure did."

"Where's his brother now?"

"He's a deputy marshal for the Arkansas district out of Van Buren. Currently over in Bell working on something."

"But Bell is in Texas," the old scout pointed out scratching at his head through his gray hair.

"That's right."

"How—forget it."

"They used to be marshals down in Barlow.

When Deke died, the judge asked Lance to come up to Brenham and take over the county duties."

"Why not you?" Roberts asked.

"I'm happy doing what I am."

"Each to his own, I guess."

Walsh finished his coffee then climbed to his feet. He scooped up the Henry rifle from where it lay against his saddle and said, "I'll be back."

Roberts looked up at the sky. It was dark and the stars were starting to appear overhead. "Where you going?"

"Thought I might climb this ridge and see if I can spot a campfire."

"I'll come with you," Roberts said and got up.

They ascended the rough shale slope scattered with low brush. At the top, they crouched down low to prevent sky-lining themselves against the rapidly lightening heavens as the moon rose in the east. For a tense minute, their eyes scanned the country before them. At first there was nothing, and then Walsh picked out the faint pinprick glow in the distance further to the west. "I can see a campfire."

"Where?" asked Roberts.

"Straight out about two fingers below the horizon."

There was a brief silence before the old scout said, "I see it. About four or so miles out."

"I figure that too."

"The other one is smaller but closer."

Confused, Walsh asked, "What other one?"

"Look to the left of the other fire and drop your eyes. It looks like a star."

Walsh did as Roberts said and picked up the glow. "It's closer but smaller."

"Uh, huh, that's what I said," the old scout agreed. "Know what that means, don't you?"

"Comanches."

Roberts spat on the ground. "Yes, Comanch."

"You figure they know about Monk and Razor?"

"More than likely. I guess we'll find out come morning."

"I guess we will."

Bell, Texas

"The doc saved your friend, by the way."

Buck looked up at Troop Quinn from where he lay. "That's good."

"You know, things would be a lot easier if you just rode out of here," Quinn said to Buck. "Easier all around if you ask me."

"Man don't operate that way when he takes an oath," the deputy pointed out. "You should know that."

"I do the law my way," Quinn stated. Then asked, "Who's that Carmody feller anyway?"

"My deputy but you already know that."

"Seems to be a confident man."

"I guess he knows how to take care of himself."

"So, why are you here anyway?" the regulator asked.

Buck sat up and swung his legs over the edge of the cot. "I was tracking the Carters. Had them cornered too, but one of them shot me. Ended up here on the Ortega place. They saved my life."

"I guess that's why you hung around?"

Buck nodded. "They needed help. The kind only the law could give them."

Quinn sighed. "You sure had the bull by the tail, Chaney. Throwing in with sheepherders."

"They're just trying to make a living like the rest of us."

"I heard tell you got the Carters," Quinn commented, changing the direction of the conversation.

"Yes, eventually," Buck said. Then he frowned and asked the regulator. "Why am I here, Troop? I think I can figure it out. The cattlemen need me out of the way, and you figure that instead of killing me it might be easier just to lock me away while they do it. Is that it?"

The regulator smiled. "Something like that. Mind, if you'd have resisted, we'd have shot you down."

"The hearing?"

"It'll still go ahead."

"So, what is it? What are the cattlemen doing?"

"As far as I know they're putting up a dam."

"They're going to go ahead with it," Buck commented. "Dam the creek off so the sheep can't get at it. Well, it won't stay up long. As soon as I get out of here it'll be coming down."

Quinn's gaze hardened. "I'd advise you to think long and hard before doing that, Chaney. The cattlemen won't take too kindly to it. And then they come to me. Then I don't take too kindly to that, which means I'll have to do something about it. Understand?"

Buck nodded. "I'll try to remember that."

"I'm trying to be nice here, Chaney. Kind of give you some friendly advice. The ranchers ain't going to stand for the sheep staying on the range. When you're let out of here just ride away and don't look back."

With a shake of his head, Buck gave Quinn an almost apologetic look. "Can't."

"Can't or won't?"

"Take it however it comes."

Quinn stared at Buck for a long time. He turned away and walked out of the room with the cells before returning a minute or so later. In his hand, he had the keys to the cells. He put one in the lock and opened the door. Buck looked suspiciously at him. "What's happening?"

"I'm letting you out."

"Why?"

"It ain't going to do any good by keeping you here. Even after what I said. So, I'm letting you go."

Buck walked out of the cell and followed the regulator out into the main office. Bodie was sitting behind the desk with his feet up. "Get the man his gun."

"You letting him go?"

"What does it look like?" Quinn growled. "Just do like I tell you."

Bodie dug Buck's gun belt out of a drawer and handed it over. The deputy marshal slipped it around his waist and buckled it on. He took the Colt out of its holster and checked it. "It ain't loaded."

"You don't think I'm giving you a loaded gun, do you?" Bodie asked.

"I guess not."

Buck raised his hand to the brim of his hat and touched it. "Be seeing you, Troop."

"Not if I see you first."

With that, Buck walked out of the jail and into the night.

CHAPTER 15

Ortega Homestead, Texas

"I'd think again before I climb down off that bronc you're forking Mister," the voice said from out of the shadows.

"Easy, Holt," Buck said. "It's only me."

"Buck?" Carmody asked confused. "What are you doing out of jail?"

"Troop Quinn let me go."

"Why? I mean what's he up to?"

"He realized that in or out of jail I wasn't going to stop what I was doing."

"So, he let you out to kill you?"

Buck nodded. "I guess you could put it that way. Wake everyone up. We need a plan and we need it yesterday."

Ten minutes later they were gathered in the kitchen. Buck, Carmella, Ralph, and Carmody.

"How is Antonio?" Carmella asked.

"He's alive. I don't know any more than that."

"That is something I guess but what is this about? Why have you dragged us from our beds?"

"Before dawn in the morning I want us all gone from here," Buck explained.

"What?" the woman asked surprised.

"We need to move the sheep and everyone somewhere that they can't find us. If we all stay here, then things are going to get worse."

"I am not leaving the home that my husband died for," Carmella said defiantly.

"Listen, Carmella. It's only for a short time. You'll be back. I promise."

"But where will we go?"

"I know of a place?" Ralph said.

All eyes focused on him. "Where?" Buck asked.

"There's a small valley back in the hill country. There's only one way in which one man could guard with a rifle. It's called Tejano's Canyon."

"What about water and shelter?"

"There's a spring and an old shack in there."

"How do you know it?" Buck asked.

"Let's just say that I wasn't always the man I am today."

Buck knew what he meant. "OK. Let's get ready. I want to be moving the sheep come sunup."

Comanche Territory, Texas

Walsh and Roberts were up at dawn, ate, saddled the horses, and were on the trail within the hour. Even though the terrain further west flattened out some they tried to follow the trail of the fugitives without sky lining themselves as much as possible. About an hour into the morning they cut sign of a Comanche war band.

"There's maybe fifteen, twenty of them. Extra horses," Roberts said. "Passed this way maybe two hours ago. They're headed north which means they'll cut our friends' trail."

Walsh nodded slowly as he stared at the mix of shod and unshod hoofprints. "Looks like they've been raiding."

"More than likely. What do you want to do?"

"Catch a killer. Let's follow the Comanches and

see what they do when they cut their sign."

"You're the boss," Roberts said as he urged his mount forward.

Twenty minutes later they found where the two trails intersected and when they did, they were surprised to see that the Comanche trail converged not only with those of the outlaws, but also with the deep ruts of a heavily-laden wagon.

"You figure that was the bigger fire we saw last evening?" Walsh asked his older companion.

"Makes sense. Only a fool or someone who's ignorant of the ways out here would do that."

"What would immigrants be doing out here? It's miles from any of the main trails except for the Comanche."

"I guess we'd better find out, Hardy, before anything befalls them."

After following the trail for five miles across the flat terrain, the going began to get rougher still. "Even the freighters don't come this way," Walsh pointed out.

Scattered rocks and shallow washes cut through the landscape. A rise further ahead of them gave way to deep gullies and some undulating ground. At one point they cut more Comanche sign which intersected the trail.

"All this Comanche sign has me worried," Roberts said. "That immigrant wagon is heavy. Maybe too heavy. And Monk and Razor are riding along with it way out here. The trail is headed just one way, directly west."

"What's your point?"

"I don't see that they're immigrants. Back there aways where the wagon stopped to rest the animals, all I saw were the tracks of heeled boots. If they was immigrants, they'd more than likely have a woman with them. I say they're out here selling rifles to the Comanches."

"You think they're Comancheros?" Walsh asked.

"Could be. The army ain't been able to stop them none."

"Makes sense, I guess. Being this far off a main trail and all."

The deputy sighed. That's all we need. Comanches and Comancheros together."

"You mean you're still going on?"

"Yes."

"You're crazy, son. There's at least four men where we're going, and Lord knows how many Comanches. They'll be liquored up to the eyeballs."

"That's what I'm counting on. If they are then we can get in there and do something to whatever they're carrying. With a little luck, they'll have gunpowder."

"I'll say it again. You're crazy, son."

Walsh set his horse in motion. "Come on, Chick. Can't live forever."

"Hell son, I ain't looking to die just yet, either."

Tejano's Canyon, Texas

The sheep bleated in protest as they were herded over the rough terrain. Behind them, the dog made sure that they kept moving. Louisa walked out front, leading so the sheep would follow her. The Texas sun beat down from a point in the sky some four hours after sunup. Buck looked over at Ralph. "How much further?"

Ralph pointed at the distant hills. "The cut in the hills yonder. That's where it is. Another couple of hours."

They pushed on amidst the dust, the flies and the heat. The hills in the distance grew steadily larger, and two hours later the cut between them came into view. On top of one was a large flat slab of rock where a guard could watch over the approaches.

The herd was pushed through the opening and

into the valley. It was actually more like a bowl-shaped depression in the earth surrounded by a large rock formation. It was lush with grass and had a stand of cottonwoods near the spring which the sheep would have full access to. There was only one problem. Someone was already in the shack.

Light smoke rose from the top of the chimney as it drifted up into the air. Buck looked across at Ralph and said, "You didn't say nothing about someone being here."

Ralph shrugged. "I don't know everything."

Buck reached down for his Winchester and Carmody did the same. He said, "I guess we'd better ride up there, slow and easy."

"Yeah," Buck replied. "Slow and easy."

They'd almost reached the rundown shack when a voice called out in a heavy Texas drawl. "That's far enough. Turn yourselves around and get gone. There's no room here for sheep rustlers."

"We ain't sheep rustlers," Buck called back. "Get out here so I can see you."

"I can see you fine from right here and—" The man paused. "Captain? Is that you?"

Buck frowned. "Who's in there?"

The door opened and two men tumbled out of the door and stood under the rickety-looking awning. "It's us, sir. Bert and Lonnie."

"Ackerman and Tucker?"

"That's us, sir," the thin Ackerman replied. He nudged his friend and said, "You remember Captain Chaney, Lonnie?"

The thickset Tucker nodded and smiled. "Sure do. Howdy, Captain."

Buck studied them for a moment then asked, "What are you boys doing here?"

"Nowhere else to go. You know—" once more Ackerman stopped. This time he was interrupted by his friend who pointed at Buck. "Is that a badge you're wearing, Captain?"

"It is," Buck replied. "I'm a deputy marshal these days. You boys wanted?"

"No, no, no," came the hurried response. "Not us, Captain. We was nowhere near Compton when that stage was held up."

Tucker gave his friend a nudge. "Shut up, Bert."

Buck knew they were lying but at that point in time realized that they were the lesser of two problems. The more he thought about them, the more he realized that he could use them. He'd ridden many patrols with these men and fought beside them in battle. And if there was something they were good at, it was fighting. "You men feel like earning some spending money?"

"Why sure?" Ackerman replied eagerly. "What we gots to do, Captain?"

"Whatever Ralph here tells you to. Got it?"

"We got it. You expecting trouble?" Tucker asked.

"Quite possibly."

"Then show us the way to the front. We're ready."

Grand Valley, Missouri

Lance Chaney rode into Grand Valley the way most strangers do. Under an eye of suspicion from the locals. The train from Van Buren had stopped in Bollinger Missouri and from there he'd hired a horse for the rest of the journey. He'd hoped to be on the way back to Brenham by now, but with everything that had happened…anyway, he'd send a wire from here.

He rode along the main street until he located the jail. He tied his horse to the rail and went inside where he found the county sheriff, a thin, gray-haired man by the name of Reynolds, using a broom to tidy his office. The oldster looked up and said, "Damned dust will get in everywhere if you leave it long enough."

Lance nodded. "It does."

The sheriff studied him with tired eyes. "Who are you, Mister?"

"Lance Chaney, Sheriff, Comanche County."

"Jim Rolston. Little out of your stomping ground ain't you?"

"Yes. Came up here looking for some information into a case I'm working."

Leaning the broom against the sidewall of the office, the sheriff walked behind his desk and sat down, indicating a chair to Lance.

He said, "You'd best tell me what it is all about. Been here for a while so I may be able to help."

"It would have happened during the war," Lance explained. "Maybe on a spread or farm outside of town."

The old man snorted. "You'll have to be more specific than that, Chaney. Lots happened around here during the war."

"I don't exactly know what," Lance replied. "Maybe you could name a few things and I'll see if it fits."

"All right. But I don't see how you'll know which one it is if you don't know yourself already."

"Let's try."

The sheriff came to his feet. "You want coffee?"

Lance nodded.

The man walked over to his potbellied stove, picked it up, and then cursed. "Damned empty."

"How about I stand you a beer?"

Rolston licked his lips. "All right. The Horseshoe is just down the street aways."

They walked outside onto the boardwalk. "You got a livery I can put my horse up?"

The sheriff grabbed a passing man. "Lem, take that horse there along to the livery. Tell Harlan the owner will be along shortly. Tell him I said."

Lance grabbed his valise from the horse before it was led away and said, "You mind if I leave this in your office?"

"Be my guest."

With the valise placed inside the door, the two men walked along to the saloon. The interior of the barroom was relatively quiet with very few customers and no girls in sight. They got their beers and walked over to a table near the front window. They sat down and Lance took a long pull of his beer. He looked up at Rolston. "That's not bad."

"It's why I drink here."

"You were going to tell me about what happened around here during the war."

"Bushwhackers, Jayhawkers, Quantrill, it was all around us."

"I need something specific if I am to work this out," Lance pressed.

Rolston thought for a moment. "We had Union troops come through here. Requisitioned food and animals at one time. One of the local farmers wasn't going to have any part of it and pulled a gun on the officer to protect his stock. He got himself shot."

"What else?"

"Quantrill came through raiding the outlying farms and stole horses and food for his men. Killed a few men who resisted," Rolston explained. "That was the first time. The second time he came through he was looking for slave runners."

"He find any?"

"There was only one family. Thompsons. He hung the menfolk."

"Anything else of note?"

"A bunch of Rebs came through, I forget when it was because they came through all the time like the Yanks. But this one particular time there was some trouble. A handful of them were sent over to a small farm to requisition some supplies. Things got out of hand. They hung the man and then raped the woman. Accused the man of being a Yankee lover so they tied him to a tree and made him watch while they did it. Then they left him hanging as they rode away. His wife trying to hold him up so he wouldn't die. When she was found he was dead, and she was sitting on the ground under his corpse with a bunch of Confederate money beside her."

"Where'd the money come from?" Lance asked leaning forward.

"I was told that the commanding officer came to her and threw it on the ground beside her."

"Why?"

"I don't know."

"Does that woman still live on the farm?" Lance asked, hopefully.

The sheriff gave him a curious look. "You think that might be the right incident?"

"Could be. It seems to fit."

"Fit what?"

"Fit what I need it to. Does she still live there?"

Rolston nodded. "Sure, but you won't get much out of her. She's not been right ever since it happened. She just walks about that farm doing the chores and doesn't speak to anyone. Just keeps it going on her own."

Lance got to his feet. "Where does she live? I need to see her."

"Just slow your roll, Stonewall Jackson, I—"

"I served with the Union. Major."

Rolston continued. "I'll come with you, OK?"

"Sure. Let's go."

Grand Valley, Missouri

The farm had seen better days. Slowly but surely, it was deteriorating to a point that it was beginning to fall down around the woman's ears. One of the doors was off the barn; the chicken coop was off-kilter, barely capable of keeping fowl; the porch needed fixing, the boards rotted and dangerous; and the split-rail fence was missing two rails. The woman was attired in a gray dress with the hems hanging on the ground, her hair partially up, partially down. When the riders rode into the yard, she looked up from splitting the wood to see who it was, glanced at the shotgun standing against the wall of the house, and then went back to work swinging the ax.

Lance and Rolston climbed down and walked across to where she worked. "Missus Willis?" the old sheriff said.

Eileen Willis picked up another piece of wood to be split, placed it down, swung the ax again.

"Missus Willis, this man would like to ask you a couple of questions. He's a sheriff from down Texas way."

Eileen looked Lance over and then went back to the wood.

The Comanche County sheriff stepped forward and started to speak. "Missus Willis, I'd like to ask you a couple of questions, if I may. My name is Lance Chaney."

Once again Eileen stopped and looked the man over. She just stared at them as if to say, "What are you waiting for?"

"It's about what happened to you during the war," Lance continued.

Her expression changed and for a moment the Comanche County sheriff thought she was about to hit him with the ax. She whirled and hit the wood with it instead. Then she hit the same piece again, and again, and again.

"Missus. Willis I don't want to talk about what happened. I just want to know if you heard any names?"

She ignored him.

"I think we should go, Chaney," Rolston said. "I think we've upset her enough."

Lance ignored him. "Does the name Christopher Denham mean anything to you?"

Her swing hesitated then continued.

"What about John Ferguson? Lane Trevor? Clive Denham?"

She whirled around, her knuckles white from where the gripped the ax handle. "I know their names, damn you," she snarled, the vehemence in her voice surprising both men. "Every last one of them. From the one who raped me to the ones who never did anything to stop it, to the ones who hung my husband."

"Was Christopher Denham one of them?"

"Yes. He was the one who raped me."

"If it's anything to you, ma'am, you should know he's dead. So are the others who were with him."

"All of them?"

Lance nodded. "All of them."

"Good, I hope they burn in hell."

"I'm sure they will."

"What about the old one?"

"What old one?"

"The one who thought money would fix everything for what his son did to me," Eileen spat.

"Clive Denham?"

"That was his name. He came to me long after Eric was dead, with money in his slimy fist. He told me his name and apologized for what his son had done to me. He blamed the war. Can you believe it? He blamed the war for his son doing what he did to me."

"If I arrest him will you come to Texas to testify against him?"

She shook her head. "No."

"But why?" Rolston asked. "It's your chance to—"

"To what?" Eileen demanded. "To have what was done to me dragged back up so people can point and whisper behind my back?"

"It's a chance for justice," Lance pointed out.

"No," she said again. "I won't do it."

Lance could tell there was no way the woman

would get up in court and testify. He nodded and said, "Thank you for your time, Missus Willis. I'll be in touch to let you know what happens."

"Don't bother."

Before he turned away, the Comanche County sheriff decided to give it one more try. "You know he's running for Texas governor?"

Eileen stared back at him as though contemplating her response. She said, "I'm not doing it."

Lance nodded. "Thanks again, ma'am."

They remounted and started to ride away. "I don't believe it," Rolston said. "After all this time that woman said more than one word."

"She's got a lot of hate and anger stored up."

"Ain't that the truth. I'm sure she'll breathe a little easier knowing that the ones who did it are dead."

"Not all of them. And her not testifying isn't going to help the case much."

The two lawmen rode in silence towards town, Lance mulling over what he knew, trying to work out how he was going to bring Denham in. He knew that it would only get as far as court and then be thrown out due to a lack of witnesses.

He was still deep in thought when a rifle whiplashed and he felt the hot air of the bullet that fanned his face. Both men gathered themselves and came clear of their saddles, Lance a little quicker than the older Rolston. The Comanche County sheriff took his Henry with him as he leaped clear and ran toward a large boulder at the side of the trail.

The bushwhacker fired again, and dirt erupted at Lance's feet from another miss. Lance's shoulder hit the boulder a solid blow as he took cover. A heartbeat later Rolston joined him. "One advantage of being so slow," he panted, "is you get to see where they're shooting at you from."

"Where's that?" Lance asked thumbing the hammer of his Henry back.

"There's a stand of trees about a hundred and

fifty yards out. He's in there."

The Comanche County sheriff leaned around the rock to look. The bushwhacker fired again, the bullets chipping rock shards and sending them into Lance's face. The misshapen hunk of lead screamed off into the Missouri day.

"I guess you're right," Lance told Rolston, as he wiped a trickle of blood from his burning face.

"I may be getting old but I'm not blind yet, son."

"Let's see if we can shake him up a bit."

They opened fire at the trees and bullets hammered into trunks, gouging furrows and chiseling out sharp splinters of wood. The bushwhacker returned fire, sending more bullets hammering into the rock.

"We could sit here and throw lead back and forward all day," Lance said to Rolston. "I'll draw his fire. You see if you can get a clear shot at him."

"How are you going to do that exactly?"

Lance looked around and saw another, smaller boulder fifty yards to their right. "I'll run for that rock. Whatever you do, don't miss."

Lance broke cover and began sprinting for cover that seemed impossibly far away now that he was in the open.

"Only said I wasn't blind," Rolston said bringing his gun up to his shoulder. "Never said I was a good shot."

The bushwhacker opened fire at the running target. Small geysers of dirt erupted around Lance's feet as the shooter missed time and again. Back behind the rock Rolston sighted along the barrel of the Henry and found the shooter next to the trunk of a large cottonwood.

In his eagerness to kill the running man the shooter had unwittingly emerged from his cover and left himself exposed.

Rolston curled his finger around the trigger and let out a long breath. The finger stroked the trigger and the Henry slammed back into the old man's shoulder. The weapon roared and the target disappeared behind a cloud of gun smoke.

A cry of pain reached the Grand Valley sheriff's ears and he gave a nod of satisfaction. "Damn son of a bitch."

He stepped out from the rock and called after Lance. "You can stop running now, son."

Lance stopped and stared back at Rolston. "You get him?"

"Now, would you be standing there if I didn't?"

"I guess not. Let's have a look at him."

They found the shooter where he'd fallen near the tree. The bullet had punched through the right side of his chest and traveled out the left, tearing apart all the vital organs in between. Lance said, "What did you shoot him with? A buffalo gun?"

The Grand Valley sheriff chuckled. "I have the local gunsmith load my shells with a few extra grains. I ain't as young as I used to be, so when I hit a man, I need to be sure he stays down."

"Well, he ain't about to get up in a hurry. You know him?"

Rolston stared at the dead shooter. He looked up at Lance and jerked his head. "I seen him before. He came to town a few days ago. Just hung around. You know him?"

Lance shook his head. "Never seen him before."

"Well, he knew you. You was the one he was trying to burn down."

"I kind of got that feeling."

"Well, if you don't know him, then why would he be gunning for you?"

"I have a feeling that I know why," the Comanche County sheriff said. "Help me find his horse and we'll take him back to your office. You got a bundle of dodgers there?"

"Always up to date," Rolston acknowledged.

"With a little luck, we might be able to find him in amongst them."

"He looks heavy."

"The dead always are."

"Ain't that the truth?"

Grand Valley, Missouri

"This is him," Rolston stated holding up a wanted dodger. "William Bent. AKA Willy The Killer. Says here he's wanted in Kansas, Ohio, Missouri, and Texas."

Lance held out his hand and took the creased piece of paper. It was him sure enough. The artist had captured his likeness rather well. It said the reward was five-hundred dollars for killing a shotgun guard in Kansas, and stage holdups in the other two states. But it was the Texas part that interested Lance. "You ever heard what he was wanted for down in Texas?"

"Nope, no idea."

"You got a telegraph in town?"

"Sure have."

"Good. Tell me where it is. I need to send a wire."

CHAPTER 16

Comanche Territory, Texas

The ground was becoming even more broken and harder for the wagon to traverse. Deep washes cut through the plain ahead of them and the long grass containing concealed rocks, creating a hazard for the horses. Hardy Walsh drew up on his horse and reached for his canteen. He unscrewed the cap and took a long pull at the water. Beside him, Chick Roberts did the same.

After replacing the cap Walsh looked up at the sky wishing for some cloud cover. "I figure we're about two hours behind them."

Roberts nodded. "I figure that myself. They're making good time over this here terrain."

The deputy looped the canteen's rawhide thong around the saddle horn and said, "We ain't going to catch them up by just sitting here then."

"You in a hurry to die, Hardy?"

"No. I just figure that if we push on, we'll catch them sooner."

"Not if them Comanches have any say in it."

"What Comanches?"

Roberts nodded in the direction of a low promontory to the north. "They're tucked in behind the tongue of land over there. I figure there's five of them. Just waiting there to cut an unsuspecting white man's guts open and dine on his warm liver."

"How long have they been there?"

"Not long."

"Waiting to ambush us."

"That would be my guess."

"Damn it."

"Look on the bright side, Hardy," Roberts said. "Could be twenty or thirty of them."

"Might as well be that many. We keep going then we'll wind up dead out here looking like a damned pair of porcupines full of blamed arrows."

"Then what do you propose we do?" Roberts asked.

"Turn back," Walsh said.

The old scout nodded. "Might be wise."

"Sticks in my damned craw that the son of a bitch is going to get away with it, you know," the deputy growled in a low voice.

"Live to fight another day, son. Live to fight another day. Your trails will cross again."

"What do I tell Lily?"

"The truth. Nothing but the truth."

"Let's get out of here."

They turned their horses and started to ride the miles back towards Brenham. "You figure they're going to follow us?" Walsh asked the old scout.

"Sure as it snows in winter," he replied.

The deputy glanced back over his shoulder. At first, he saw nothing, and then there they were. Except there wasn't five of them, there were ten at least. Riding hard on their ponies in the direction of the two riders.

"Looks like you were right and wrong, Chick," Walsh said.

"What?" he said and turned to look. "Damn it. Where'd they come from?"

Both men kicked their horses into a run in a desperate bid to outpace the Comanches. They'd gone a mile before Walsh looked back over his shoulder and noticed that the painted warriors were even closer than before. The Indians obviously had fresher horses.

Another mile slid by under the thundering hooves of the fleeing riders' horses. Walsh glanced back again and saw the Comanches even closer. He called across to Roberts. "We need to make a stand. They'll ride us down."

"Over there!" Roberts shouted as he pointed to a scar across the plain. "It's a wash."

They turned their mounts and pushed them hard to make it. The lip of the wash loomed up in front of them and fell away sharply. They reined in on their horses and let them find their own way to the bottom of the dry watercourse.

Walsh and Roberts came clear of their saddles, taking their rifles with them. They hugged the cut bank and slid their weapons into the firing position. Walsh was the first to fire. The rifle whiplashed and hammered back into his shoulder. His target disappeared behind a puff of smoke but then reappeared as the Comanche rolled back over his animal's rump. As he jacked another round into the weapon's breach, Roberts fired and another Indian fell from his racing animal.

The death of the second warrior elicited a cry of rage from the remaining Comanches who pulled up short. They milled around, ponies stomping and snorting. Walsh lowered his sights onto one of those waving his arms around. He squeezed the trigger and the warrior stopped and a dark patch appeared on his naked chest where the .44 Henry slug did its work. The Comanche slid sideways from the back of his pony and fell to the grass beneath it.

With a shout of anger, the rest of the warriors turned their horses and rode out of rifle range before stopping to take stock. "These sons of bitches been shot at before," Roberts observed.

Walsh studied them and then looked up at the sky. "Well, they've got us pinned down and they've not yet fired a shot."

"It'll be dark soon," the old scout said. "We should be able to slip out under the cover of it. Travel through the night and find somewhere to hole up in the morning."

More shouts of anger from the Indians reached out across the plain. Walsh settled down with his back against the cut bank. "I guess they won't be coming anytime soon."

Grand Valley, Missouri

Lance sent two wires and received two replies just before dusk. The telegrapher brought them to him as he sat in the saloon, drinking whiskey with Rolston. He slipped the man a coin and read the first one which was from Brenham. It appeared that Hardy was out chasing down a pair of desperadoes who'd murdered one of the girls in Lily's saloon. He stopped reading and thought of her, wishing he were there to be with her.

He lifted the second wire. This one came from Van Buren and Marshal Mike Dodge who had sent word to Lance about the incident in Texas he'd inquired about.

"You get the answer you were looking for?" Rolston asked.

Lance nodded. "Our bushwhacking friend was wanted for cattle rustling in Comanche County."

"Ain't that where you're from?"

Lance nodded. "I remember Deke telling me once a few years back that there was a rustling ring working around Brenham. One of them got away. That would be Bent, I guess. But Deke also mentioned that there was a ringleader. He never found out who it was."

"I'm guessing by the look on your face that you've got an idea?" Rolston surmised.

"I do. The problem is proving everything."

Comanche Territory, Texas

The two-legged coyote howled at the moon as it started to rise in the east. Walsh looked at Roberts through the darkness and said, "If we're going, it has to be now before the moon gets up any further. We can use the wash for a while and then climb out onto the plain."

"I'll lead," the old scout said. "Don't get lost, I ain't going looking for you in the dark."

"Let's go then."

The two men gathered their horses and started following the wash. It snaked towards the east and then cut south. Before they'd gone a mile, it shallowed, and the bank fell away so they could climb out. Once back on the plain the two mounted and pointed their horses towards Brenham once more.

They rode carefully throughout the night until the first pink vestiges of dawn appeared on the eastern horizon. Roberts turned to Walsh. "Hardy, we'd better find a place to hole up for the day."

"Where do you suggest?"

"I can see a large rock formation to our north and some trees to go with it. Be a good place to take root."

"We should have enough water to get us through today, and when we reach Willow Creek tonight we'll be able to top up," Walsh surmised.

They turned their horses and reached the rocks a few minutes later. "Take care of the horses, Hardy. I'll see if I can blot our trail some and fool our friends if they try to follow us."

Later that morning the two men were sitting talking when Roberts asked, "What's with you and Mary Denham?"

"What do you mean?" Walsh asked.

"You know what I mean, son. You're sparkin' her ain't you?"

The deputy stared at him for a moment then said, "I don't rightly know."

"You know about her pa, don't you?"

Walsh nodded. "Sure, he's going to run for governor."

The old scout pulled a face. "Not that. God knows what'll happen to the damned state if he gets in. No, a couple years back just after the war."

With a shake of his head, the deputy said, "Nope. I know nothing about it."

"Must've been just before you went to work for Deke," Roberts said and spit on the ground. Still can't believe he's gone."

"Come on, Chick. Tell me."

"Well, it was not long after the war, they were still using the Shawnee Trail mostly then. Now the Chisholm has opened, most of the stock goes that way."

"You talking about cattle?"

"Ain't talking about mules," Roberts growled.

"Go on, you old packrat."

"Watch who you're calling old, sonny," Roberts growled glaring at Walsh. "I'll still run rings around the likes of you."

"Just get on with it."

"Fine, fine. It was just after the war and demand was starting to climb. Denham decided to take a herd up to Sedalia. Except his herd wasn't much of anything. He claimed he had at least three-thousand ready to go but from what I heard it was closer to two. Anyway, it was about that time that a band of rustlers moved in. It was blamed on soldiers coming back to Texas and looking for a way to make some money. Eventually, they were broken up and one of them got away. But Deke swore that there was a main man behind it all, but he never could find out who it was."

"Did Denham make his drive?" Walsh asked.

"Sure, he did. Took three-thousand head just like he said he was going to. Two of his and a thousand of everyone else's."

"Surely not."

"I'm telling you, son, old Clive Denham ain't as squeaky clean as he makes out."

Walsh knew what Roberts was saying was true.

"I'd think twice before you go hitching your wagon to that filly of his."

Walsh grunted. "Get some sleep, Chick. I'll take first watch."

"Sorry if I upset your dream some, Hardy, but I'm just telling it the way it is."

The deputy got to his feet. "Forget it, Chick."

The old scout watched as he turned away and climbed higher into the rocks so he could keep a good watch out.

Tejano's Canyon, Texas

Buck and Carmody saddled their horses around mid-morning and made sure that their rifles were fully loaded. This was followed by making sure that their Colts were ready for use as well.

"Where are you going?" Carmella asked them.

Buck turned and looked at her. Her hair was mussed, and she looked like she'd been dragged through a prickly pear patch. However, she was still just as pretty and for a moment Buck found himself staring at her and thinking of Maggie. He cleared his throat. "We're going to check on your place, ma'am."

"Why?"

"Just in case. Never can tell what Conker and the cattlemen might do to it. After we do that, we're going to have a look where they're building this dam. We'll be gone a day or so."

For a moment a look of concern washed over her. Buck said hurriedly, "Don't worry, Carmella. Bert, Lonnie, and Ralph will take care of you."

"We have to do this, ma'am," Carmody told her. "These men need to be stopped. Just because they were here before you, don't make what they're doing right."

"They will kill you. They have no fear of the law. Those badges will not save you."

Buck shrugged. "We've both been shot at more times than we care to think of, ma'am. We're still above ground. Can't say that much about them though."

"What do you mean?"

"Well, there's only one thing that the likes of them understand. That's bullet law." He saw the look on her face. "Don't look so shocked. They're responsible for the death of your man. They tried to kill me, and they're going to try again. We're going to stir the pot a bit in the hope that they'll do just that."

"You be careful," Carmella told them. "Both of you."

"We'll be back by tomorrow supper," Buck told her. "Keep an eye out for us."

They rode from Tejano's Canyon and headed straight to the Ortega Homestead. On their approach, Buck was the first to see the black smudge on the horizon. He'd reined in and said, "That don't look good, Holt."

The deputy sheriff grunted and replied, "You know what they say, Buck."

"Yeah." He leaned down and took his Winchester from the saddle boot. Carmody did the same.

They rode slower now, hoping not to ride into an ambush. When they reached the low rise overlooking the homestead, they saw that the source of the smoke was the barn which was still smoldering, not the house itself. In the corral were four horses.

On the land around the homestead was a small herd of cattle.

"Looks like they've moved in," Carmody said.

"How about we go down there and ask them to leave?"

The deputy sheriff nodded. "Let's."

The two men rode into the yard and called out, "Hey, you in the house. Come on out."

Four men came out of the door and stood on the porch. All of them were armed and had a surly look about them. "What are you men doing here?" Buck asked.

"This land belongs to the cattleman's association," a wiry looking hand said.

"Since when?"

"Since the Mexican woman vacated it," he replied. "She's gone and so are the stinking sheep. So, the association has taken legal possession of it."

Buck shook his head. "The land still belongs to the woman, friend. "You and your pards get your horses saddled and move the cattle back where they belong."

The four men stepped out into the yard, spreading like a woman's paper fan. Thin one said, "Can't do that."

"In case you don't know, or someone forgot to tell you, we're the law," Buck said moving the lapel on his coat so they could see his badge.

"Not around here you ain't," the hand replied. "That honor goes to Troop Quinn and his men."

"Jackass," Carmody muttered.

"You got something to say, friend?" the thin man asked.

Carmody moved his coat so he could access his six-gun with ease. He rested his hand on the butt and said, "If I have something to say to you, friend, you'll know about it."

The man took a step forward.

"Hold it!" Buck snapped. "You fellers don't want

to be starting anything especially over a piece of dirt that ain't yours."

"It's what we were hired to do," the thin man stated unwavering.

Buck gripped the Winchester tighter with his right hand. His thumb eased the hammer back on it as his eyes scanned the group of men. "Is that your last word?"

"That—"

The sentence was never finished before the rifle in Buck's hand erupted. The .44 Henry slug hammered into the thin man's chest with brutal force. He staggered back and sat down hard. While he worked another round into the breech, Carmody drew his six-gun and leveled it in the direction of the three remaining men. They were stunned by the sudden act of violence. "You boys just relax unless you want to join your friend in hell," he said in an even voice.

"You—you killed him," one of the other hands stammered.

"He was given the option of riding away," Buck told them. "Now you'll have to take him away from here face-down over his saddle. And you'll take your cows with you."

"Mister Conker ain't going to like this," another of the men warned.

"If he has a problem, you tell him to come see me. I'll be more than accommodating."

Under the watchful eye of the two men, the hands put their friend over the saddle of his horse and then started to push the cattle off Carmella Ortega's range. Carmody said to Buck, "They ain't going to take this laying down."

"Don't suppose they will," Buck acknowledged. "We'll go to town. I want to check on Antonio."

Carmody shook his head.

"What?" Buck asked.

"You ain't one for poking the bear much, are

you?" the deputy sheriff observed. "Instead you just walk right up to him and slap him on the ass."

"Ma always said I was the more forward of us boys. Our sister was the quiet one."

"Sister? Never knew you had one. Where's she at?"

"She's dead," Buck said and heeled his horse forward.

"Good one, Holt," he muttered to himself. "Maybe you should just mind your own business."

Bell, Texas

"How's he doing, Doc?" Buck asked as he looked down at Antonio.

"I am ready to leave," the Mexican stated, trying to rise.

Carmody placed a restraining hand on his chest. "Just hold it there, Cisco. You don't go nowhere until the doctor says you can."

"You are not going anywhere, Antonio," Walker told the disappointed shepherd. "You're in that bed for at least another week."

"But I feel fine," he protested.

"You stay," Buck told him.

The two lawmen left the room accompanied by Walker. "How's he really doing, Doc?" Buck asked again.

"He'll be fine, but it's got me beat how he lived. Given time he'll be on his feet."

"Good to hear. Now, what's the word around town?"

"The dam has been started," Walker said. "I also heard that Carmella walked off her land. Is that true?"

"Not in so many words," Buck explained. "We took the decision to tuck her and Louisa away somewhere safe."

"Well, you need to know this then, the cattleman's association have moved men and cows onto the land."

"We know that, too," the deputy marshal said.

"You do?"

Carmody said, "We've been out there already."

"What happened?"

"Let's just say they're a man short and they've been moved on."

"Conker isn't going to like that," Walker said.

"I don't much care."

"He's in town, you know. Ever since things started to heat up, he's been spending more and more time in Bell."

"What about his hired law?"

"They spend most of their time at the saloon since the others rode in."

Buck frowned. "What others?"

"He had five more men arrive. There's ten of them now."

Carmody looked at Buck. "I thought he only rode with five men."

"Looks like he called in some more shooters."

"Don't they have enough between the ranchers?" Carmody asked.

Buck smiled. "Let's find out."

The deputy sheriff shook his head. "Life with you could never be called boring, that's for sure."

They bid farewell to Antonio and the doctor and walked along the street to the Stockman's Saloon. Inside they found Troop Quinn and a handful of his men sitting playing cards and entertaining some of the local ladies. The regulator looked up from his hand and said, "I see you're still around, Chaney. Here I was thinking that you might have pulled out along with the woman and her sheep."

Buck and Carmody walked over to the bar. There was a look of uncertainty on the barkeep's face as though he wished the two men would turn around and walk out. Buck said, "Get us a couple of beers."

The man nodded and Buck turned back to face Quinn. "The lady ain't gone nowhere."

"Not what I heard. Story is that she and her sheep are both gone, and the cattlemen have taken over the range."

Buck's eyes scanned the others who were sitting at the table. He'd seen a couple of them with Quinn the first time. The others were new to him. "Got yourself some new friends, Troop?"

"Just some extra deputies just in case things get out of control. Don't look like I'll need them now though, do it?"

Buck paid for the beer and then took a drink of the amber liquid. He winced. "Tastes like mule's piss," he said glaring at the barkeep. "You get the stuff out of your girls' chamber pot?"

"If you don't like it, don't drink it," the barkeep snapped back.

"You ain't answered my question, Marshal," Quinn prodded.

"Which one was that?"

"The one I mentioned before."

Buck shrugged. "Depends I guess."

"On what?" Quinn asked.

Buck pushed his beer away from himself and started to walk towards the door. "Be seeing you, Troop."

The regulator watched them go and one of the newcomers said, "He don't look so tough to me, Troop."

"And an attitude like that will get you killed, Wiley," Quinn snapped at the man. "Our friend the marshal is a very dangerous man. And don't let his friend fool you either. He's just as dangerous."

"What you figure they wanted, Troop?" Crocker asked.

"Just looking us over is my guess," Quinn theorized. "I think he's almost ready to show us his hand."

"What do you suppose he meant when he said the woman ain't gone?"

"No idea. Now, somebody deal me some decent cards this time, I'm sick of losing."

From the saloon, Buck and Carmody ventured across the street to the Cattleman's Association office. They walked in and found Conker inside with Gilbert and Red Samson from the Slash S. The three men glared at them for the intrusion. Conker said, "Why haven't you gone like the woman and her stinking sheep?"

"The woman ain't gone," he answered.

"She sure as hell has," Gilbert grunted. "Her sheep have gone too. We moved men and cattle onto the range yesterday. Damned Mexican whore belongs back below the border. Her and her calf."

Buck felt his blood start to rise. "You did have men trespassing on Ortega land. They ain't there no more."

"What do you mean?" Conker asked through clenched teeth.

"I mean we asked them to leave and they obliged."

The rancher's face changed color as he realized what he'd just been told. "That land belongs to the cattlemen," he grated.

"It belongs to Senora Ortega."

"It don't belong to no Mex bitch and her sheep," Gilbert hissed.

Carmody shook his head in dismay. This feller sure was hell-bent on digging himself a hole with his mouth. But before he could say anything, Buck stepped forward and hit the foreman in the mouth with his right fist.

The blow sounded like an ax biting deep into a log, and the force of it sent Gilbert staggering back until his legs became tangled in a wooden chair and he fell over the top of it. Buck was far from done with the loudmouth foreman. He strode forward and grabbed a handful of his greasy hair and dragged him to his feet. Buck held him there for a moment and hit him again, knocking the Broken C foreman to the floor once more.

"What the hell are you doing?" Samson demanded but the deputy marshal ignored him. Instead, he closed on Gilbert once more.

From where he stood, Carmody noticed Conker open the desk drawer in front of where he was now standing. The Colt on Carmody's hip leaped into his hand, his thumb earing the hammer back. "I'd think again if I were you."

Conker froze and glowered at the deputy.

Meanwhile, Buck was starting to drag Gilbert to his feet once more. "Get up, you son of a bitch."

The foreman came to life with sudden ferocity, dropping his shoulder he drove it forward into Buck's middle and shunted him across the room like a runaway train. Buck's back crashed against the wall causing the whole office to tremble under the impact. Air whooshed from the deputy marshal's lungs with an audible grunt. He raised his arms and made a fist with his hands locked together. Buck brought them crashing down and drove Gilbert to his knees.

The deputy marshal raised his cupped fist to hit him again, but the Broken C foreman rocketed up, straightening his legs until his head smacked into Buck's chin.

Bright lights flashed before Buck's eyes and he rocked back on his heels. Gilbert shook away the pain from his head and swung a punch at Buck. The clenched fist crashed into Buck's lips and he tasted the sudden explosion of blood inside his mouth.

The deputy marshal tried to back away, but was pinned against the wall. Gilbert hit him again and for the first time, Buck was hurt. He gave a wild swing that the Brocken C foreman blocked easily and hit him again.

Damn fool! Buck tried to gather himself as lights flashed from another vicious blow. The deputy marshal shook his head to clear the cobwebs and gave a snarl. He pushed off the wall and wrapped his arms around Gilbert. Using all the strength in his legs he pushed the Broken C foreman backward. The ferocity of it carried them back across the room and through the large front window with a shattering crash.

They hit the boardwalk hard, both men stunned by the fall. Buck climbed to his feet first, shards of glass falling from his clothes, tinkling as they struck the boards, blood appearing from numerous nicks on his person. He staggered away from Gilbert to gather himself, running into an awning post which he grabbed for support and stayed there, blowing hard.

The deputy marshal raised his right hand and wiped at his mouth. The back of it came away bloody. He then spat blood onto the street to his left and waited for Gilbert to struggle to his feet.

As soon as the man was upright once more, Buck lurched forward and swung twice, landing both blows, the impact of each jarring up his arms and into his shoulders. Gilbert rocked back and fell from the boardwalk. His lower back hit the hitch rail and he somersaulted over it, ending up sprawled in the dirt of the hard-packed street.

Buck followed him, unaware of the crowd that was starting to gather. Across the street, men spilled from the saloon. Among them was Troop Quinn. Horses tied to the hitchrail next to the one Gilbert had gone over began tugging nervously at their reins, trying to break loose. As the deputy marshal walked past the closest one, he gave it a shove on the rump to force it out of the way.

The animal snorted angrily and lashed out with a rear hoof, narrowly missing its intended target. Not that Buck noticed. His hard stare was still focused on the fallen Broken C foreman.

Gilbert saw him coming and flung a handful of fine dirt into Buck's face.

Snapping his eyelids closed in a reflex action, Buck was nowhere near fast enough, and temporarily blinded, he blinked furiously trying to clear his vision.

Ever the opportunist, the Broken C foreman launched himself at Buck, his shoulder driving into the deputy marshal's middle. Both men cannoned into the horse at the hitchrail and the animal threw its head back letting out a loud screech. It broke free of its tether and ran along the street at a fast gallop, broken reins trailing beside it.

Buck swung with his right fist and connected with Gilbert's head. The foreman staggered back, and Buck followed him. He lashed out twice more, both blows connecting. The deputy marshal tried for another but Gilbert sensed him coming and ducked low, the swing missing its target.

The Broken C foreman came back up and delivered an uppercut which would have spelled trouble for Buck had it landed flush. As it was, the glancing blow still staggered him.

By now, both men were blowing hard, their exertions becoming more labored. They separated, blood on both their faces, and dirt covering a good portion of their clothing.

"Come on, lawman," Gilbert rumbled. "Is that the best you got?"

Not wanting to waste energy on words, Buck closed the gap between them once more. Gilbert took a wild swing which was designed to finish the fight then and there. But the deputy was expecting it and went in low, having noticed the shift in the foreman's weight. The fist missed high and Buck brought his own up from down near his knees. The stunning blow rocked Gilbert to the core. Buck hit him three more times, the last one superfluous because the Broken C foreman was already out on his feet.

He fell like a tree in the forest, complete with the puff of dust when he hit the ground. Buck stood over him, chest heaving as he sucked in great gulps of air. He looked up and noticed the crowd which had gathered. His eyes settled on Troop Quinn who just stared at him, face impassive.

"Damn it, Troop, do something," Conker shouted from across the street.

The regulator looked over at the rancher and asked, "Like what? All I see is a harmless fistfight in which your man got the tar wailed out of him."

"I pay you to look after my interests, damn it!"

"And that's what I will do," Quinn said and went back inside the saloon.

Buck walked across to where Carmody waited for him. "You OK?" the deputy sheriff asked.

"I'll live."

"We should get our horses and get out of town for a while."

Buck nodded. "Most probably. But we're not going back to the canyon. I have something else in mind."

Carmody studied his battered face for a moment and said, "Why do I get the feeling I'm not going to like this?"

"Come on, things to do."

"What the hell was that?" Conker demanded. "Whose side are you on, exactly?"

Quinn looked up from his cards. "I'm on the side of the law."

"I pay you, so it's my law. Don't forget it."

Quinn's stare grew cold. "How could I? You don't seem to want me to."

"Get a couple of your men out to the dam site. I want extra guards on it."

"I'll see what I can do."

"Get it done, Quinn," Conker growled and walked out of the saloon. He stopped on the boardwalk, shaking his head in anger, then took a deep breath and began thinking. An idea soon came to him and he glanced around to see Gilbert sitting on the steps across the street recovering from the beating he'd just received. Conker hurried over to him and asked, "You all right?"

The battered foreman looked up at his boss. "I been kicked worse by one of your horses."

"Good. I want you to get one of the men you trust the most and do something for me."

"What would that be?"

"Quinn is sending two of his men out to the dam as extra security. I don't want them to make it."

Gilbert stared at him in silence.

"You have a problem, Max?"

"You want me to kill them? I thought they were on our side?"

"Quinn needs some encouragement to move our situation along. This just might help it out."

The Broken C foreman nodded. "All right, I'll do it. But if this goes wrong, you'd best start digging your own grave because that son of a bitch won't stop until you're in it."

CHAPTER 17

Comanche Territory, Texas

Roberts shook Walsh awake. "Come on son, wake up, you ain't going to believe this."

"What is it?" Walsh asked, still half asleep.

The sun was still up which meant the old scout wasn't waking him so they could hit the trail. "Get up and see for yourself."

Walsh climbed to his feet and followed Roberts further up in the rocks. "There, see them."

Two riders were approaching from the west. At first, Walsh had to squint to try and clear his vision. Then his eyes widened. "Is that—

"It sure is, son. Our quarry has ridden right to us."

"Damn it, let's get down there. They're going to ride right past us."

Walsh hurried back down through the gray-faced rocks and picked up his rifle. He checked to make sure there was a round in the breech and then waited for the unsuspecting riders to arrive.

Their wait wasn't a long one, and once the two wanted men were almost upon them, Walsh and Roberts stepped into clear view taking the two riders by surprise. "What the—" Razor started.

"You boys just keep your hands away from your weapons," Walsh snapped.

The pair froze. "All right," Monk said. "You got us."

Razor, however, had other ideas. "Not so fast, lawman. You won't go firing that thing out here. Not with so many Comanches getting about."

"Are you willing to gamble your life on that?"

"Maybe."

There was a long silence as the two men sized each other up before Monk said, "Take it easy, Razor. I think the man just might do it."

The outlaw's eyes sparkled wickedly. "I think he's bluffing. I don't think he's got the stomach."

"Razor," Monk said cautiously.

Walsh adjusted the grip on his rifle. "You men shuck your weapons."

Monk started to move but Razor remained still. Walsh waved the rifle at him. "Don't press me, killer. I'd just as soon take you in face down over your saddle after what you did to the woman."

A cold smile split the outlaw's face as though he was remembering the incident. He licked his lips and his right hand began to move. At first, Walsh thought it was moving to unbuckle the gun belt. But his hand kept moving, speeding up as it went. Finally, as clawed fingers wrapped around the butt of the six-gun Walsh adjusted his aim with the rifle and squeezed the trigger. The slug punched into the killer's chest before his six-gun could come free of its holster. He threw up his arms and tumbled from the saddle.

The deputy swung the Henry around and centered it on Monk. "Wait! No!" he cried out.

But Walsh had already worked the weapon's lever and rammed a fresh round home. He fired once more, and the remaining outlaw died beside his fallen friend.

The gunfire rolled across the plain and eventually, the echoes petered out. Roberts stepped forward. "That's torn it. We need to get out of here now. If there were any Comanches within two miles, they would have heard those shots."

Walsh nodded. "Help me get them on their horses. We'll take them with us."

"Leave them for the buzzards."

"No. They come with us."

Roberts sighed. "All right. Let's get them up."

Ten minutes later, with no sign of Indians anywhere, the two men rode away from the rocks with the two horses and their gruesome loads in tow.

Open Range, Bell, Texas

The two men lay belly down on the low ridge, watching as men worked on the dam. Wagons were loaded with lumber while others were loaded with rocks to help with the construction. Buck figured there were perhaps twenty men working on it and judging by what they'd already achieved, construction was going well. The deputy marshal looked at the ground beyond the worksite. It was quite low at the creek level, the banks on either side rising to higher ground, a natural funnel for water, the high sides perfect for impounding large quantities once the wall was built.

"Them boys have been busy," Carmody observed.

Buck nodded gingerly, wishing immediately that he hadn't as pain shot through his tortured muscles. "With that creek dammed off, the cattlemen will have plenty of water. They'll fill up a lake so large it'll keep every rancher in water even in the toughest of droughts."

"It looks like it'll be solid enough."

Suddenly the sound of gunshots reached their ears. Buck glanced at Carmody who nodded. "I heard it."

"Come on, let's go take a look."

The two men walked back to their horses crouched low as to not skyline themselves. Once out of sight they straightened up and were able to move faster. They mounted their horses and then pointed them in the direction they figured the gunfire came from.

The galloping horses ate up the terrain quickly until they came to a depression in the trail. When they crested the lip they reined in. Before them were two horses standing beside the bodies of two men who'd once been riding them. They rode in closer and dismounted.

Buck leaned over them and checked both. "Dead. Been shot."

"Wonder who they are?" Carmody said.

Buck started to check them and made a discovery that made his blood run cold. Both men were wearing badges. Not deputy badges, or even marshal's badges. They were different and had the word REGULATOR stamped on them.

"Damn it," he cursed softly. "They're Quinn's men."

"Who'd want to shoot them?"

"I don't know," Buck said. "But I do know who they think will have done it."

"Us," Carmody replied. "Quinn's going to want blood."

"Yes. Let's get out of here before someone sees us and puts no doubt in their mind."

"I think it's too late for that," Carmody said and pointed to the east. "Look."

Buck glanced up. "Who is that?"

"Looks like the feller you taught some manners too earlier and—"

Gunshots rang out and the fizz of bullets passing close filled the air. "Sons of bitches are shooting at us."

Buck slid the Winchester from the saddle boot and turned around to shoot back. Carmody stopped him as he was raising his weapon to his shoulder. "Wait. There's more coming from the dam site. They heard the shooting too."

Buck looked along the trail and saw more riders. "Bastard," he cursed and climbed into the saddle as more lead filled the air. "Come on, let's get the hell out of here."

They turned their animals away from the corpses and kicked them into a run. In his mind, Buck knew this was going to change things and he knew exactly where Troop Quinn and his men would start.

Buck and Carmody eased their horses down to a stop to give them a rest. They'd lost their pursuers about three miles back and could afford to give the horses the rest they needed.

"I been thinking, Buck," Carmody said. "Them fellers who come upon us had to be close."

"It figures."

"What if they was the ones who done it?"

"Why would they?" Buck asked with a frown.

"To get Quinn riled enough to come after us. Because he ain't doing it at the moment."

"So, you think the cattlemen had two of Quinn's men killed so he would come after us?" Buck theorized.

"Why not? You said it yourself he's going to think it was us. The last feller who tried to kill you ended up taking a dirt nap. If Quinn thinks it was us who killed his men he's going to come after us with all of the ones he has with him."

"We need to get to him before he learns about this from someone else," Buck said thoughtfully.

"He won't listen, Buck. All that's been done is have this war kicked up another notch."

"We need to prove it then."

"How do propose we do that?"

"We find Gilbert and put him in front of Quinn."

Carmody snorted. "Good luck with that."
"We'll try to get him tonight."
"You mean go to the Broken C?"
"Yes."
Carmody shook his head. "How on earth did you get to be as old as you are?"
Buck smiled. "Just lucky I guess."

Bell, Texas

"Where were they?" Quinn asked, ice in his voice and death in his eyes.

"Not far from the dam site," Gilbert told him. "We heard the shooting."

The regulator looked at the two bodies draped over the saddles. Paulson and Reilly. Two of his better guns, dead. Shot down from ambush. Quinn's harsh stare focused on the Broken C foreman. "Are you sure it was them?"

"We seen them. Got off a few shots at them, too. Right before they lit a shuck out of there."

"Did you follow them?"

Gilbert nodded. "For a time. We lost them before we could catch up."

"Damned useless lot you are," Quinn growled. He turned to Bodie. "Gather the others and saddle the horses. This marshal has just run out of rope."

Bodie hurried off and Quinn turned his attention back to the dead men on the horses. "They look like they were shot in the back."

Gilbert nodded. "Seems that way."

The regulator eyed him suspiciously. "Why would he shoot them in the back?"

"I don't know. Maybe you can ask him when you find him."

"Maybe I'll do that," the regulator stated.

He turned away and walked off not seeing Conker emerge from the gathered crowd. He pulled his foreman aside and said in a harsh whisper, "Did you have to shoot them in the back?"

"Seemed like the safest way of doing it."

"It might well have been, but you seen what Chaney did to Coleman. Does he act like a back shooter to you?"

"First time for everything."

"Damn it, Max. You're a fool. You want to hope that Quinn doesn't talk to Chaney first. You need to take some men and get out there and find them before Quinn does or it's all finished. Understand?"

Gilbert nodded. "Fine. But I only did what you told me to do."

"Go."

After Gilbert was gone Conker walked into the saloon. He bought a bottle and was about to leave for the ranch when he was found by Red Samson and John Peters. "We need to talk," Peters said.

Conker studied him for a moment and knew by the look on the JP Connected owner's face he wasn't about to be deterred. "Let's find a table."

They followed the rancher to a vacant table and sat down. "What is it?"

"Things are getting out of hand," Peters said.

"You think?" Conker asked in a harsh tone. He lowered his voice. "Things have been out of hand for a good damned while now. I seem to be the only one trying to fix it."

"There's too much killing going on, Hank," Samson told him. "Before long we're going to have more marshals snooping around. Let the sheep stay and forget about the dam. It's the only way we can get rid of the law."

"Let the—" Conker started incredulously. "Are you crazy?"

"Listen, Hank. Once the marshal is gone then we can have another go at getting the woman to leave with her sheep. But we've been thinking, and killing a marshal ain't the smartest move."

"We? We've been thinking?" His gaze switched

between the two men. "What does Harv think of this?"

"He feels the same way,"

"Why isn't he here telling me then?"

The two men glanced at each other. Samson opened his mouth to speak but Conker had heard enough. "Get away from me. It's too late to go back now anyway."

The ranchers were confused. "What did you do?"

"Fixed it so our problems will be gone very soon."

Broken C Ranch, Texas

Buck and Carmody kept watch on the ranch until the daylight had burned off and the darkness of night had settled in. They'd watched men come and go and hadn't seen hide nor hair of Gilbert. The only one they recognized was Conker himself.

"You suppose he's there?" Carmody asked out loud.

"No, I don't expect he is."

"What now then?"

Buck stared out into the darkness at the pin-pricks of light made by the lanterns and lamps in the windows. "We go and find out where he is."

"I was afraid you'd say that."

"Come on."

They crept forward keeping as best they could to the shadows. They circled around the corral to the rear of the bunkhouse. They then settled down beside a small clump of brush near the outhouse. The pungent scent of shit floated on the night air and seemed to slap the two men in the face. Carmody wrinkled his nose. "You all could have picked a better place to wait."

"Man's gotta piss and shit sometime," Buck replied ignoring the smell. "Best place to wait."

Somewhere in the darkness, they could hear cows bawling followed by the distant yip of a coyote.

The moon crept slowly higher in the night sky and a cool breeze sprang up pricking at their exposed skin. "I wish they'd hurry up," said Carmody. Or I might have to use their hole in the ground myself."

"Go on then," Buck told him. "I'll keep an eye out."

There was a growling sound from Carmody's guts, and he moaned. "I'm gonna have to."

He crept forward towards the outhouse. Once he reached it the smell became even stronger and he contemplated maybe going back and shitting in the brush. Instead, he swung the door open and it squeaked loudly, causing him to halt momentarily.

Moonlight flooded the interior enough for Carmody to see the plank with the hole cut in it, place precariously above the open pit in the ground. He dropped his pants and sat down half expecting the board to break under his weight.

His brow knitted and relief flooded him as he did his business adding the stink of human excrement. Once finished, the deputy sheriff reached around to find the old sheets of paper which had been left for when the person was finished their business. His hand had just settled upon it when the door swung open and a cowboy stood there staring at his face in the moonlight.

"Who are you?" he asked confused.

Carmody thought fast and words came from his mouth before he realized that they were there. "Go away, I'm shitting."

Stunned, it took the hand a good amount of time to realize that the man in the outhouse didn't belong. Then as he opened his mouth to shout a warning, Buck came up behind him and struck him with the barrel of his Colt. The deputy marshal looked at Carmody and asked, "You done yet?"

The pair dragged the unconscious man out into the brush and then slapped him awake. By the time he was aware of his surroundings, he had the barrel of a six-gun in his middle with the hammer eared back.

"Wh—what's going on?" he stammered.

"I'll ask the questions," said Buck. "Where's Gilbert?"

"Not here."

"Where?"

"He's out looking for the marshal with some of the men."

"Why?"

"I don't know?"

Buck pressed the barrel harder into the hand's middle. "Try again."

"I don't know. All I heard was he had to get to him before Quinn did."

"Why?"

"Damn it, I don't know."

"Who shot the two regulators?" Carmody asked.

The hand said nothing.

"Was it Gilbert?"

"I don't know."

"You don't know much, do you? Where were they going to look?"

The man hesitated again, and Buck pressed the barrel even harder into the man's middle, which made him grimace. "Where?"

"I think over at the homestead. Gilbert figured that you would head for there. Seeing as you run off the others from it."

Having all the information they figured the hand knew, Buck rapped him over the head with the barrel of his Colt. The man collapsed in an untidy heap at their feet.

"It looks like Gilbert is desperate to find us before Quinn because of what he did," Carmody said. "Maybe he's afraid of him talking to us before he tries to kill us."

"Maybe. But let's go find him and see if we can squeeze the truth out of him before Quinn finds us."

CHAPTER 18

Ortega Homestead, Texas

The homestead was still burning when they reached it. Orange tongues of flame licked greedily at charred pieces of wood, desperate for more fuel to keep them sated. Black smoke stained the clear blue sky like a giant beacon.

Obviously angered by not finding their quarry at the homestead, Gilbert had decided to finish what had already been started, and burn it all to the ground. Buck felt the heat of his anger rise into his cheeks. "Rotten son of a bitch."

"I count six of them," Carmody said.

Buck's eyes shifted to the men in the yard. "There's about to be a few less when we ride in."

The deputy marshal was about to climb to his feet when Carmody stopped him. "Wait. More riders coming in."

Buck looked along the main trail to the homestead and saw the cloud of dust with the riders at its base. Before long he could make them out. Eight horsemen. Had to be Quinn.

It was.

They rode into the yard and hauled rein. They all stayed on their horses while Quinn and Gilbert talked. Arms were waved and then there was some more discussion. Then the eight horsemen turned their horses away and rode back out of the yard.

"What do you suppose that was about?" Carmody asked.

"Who knows. Let's go find out."

Using the scattered brush as cover, the two lawmen closed in on the yard. Eventually, they came up behind the six men who seemed more intent on watching the flames instead of their surroundings. Not a very intelligent move on their part.

"Each one of you turn around slowly," Buck ordered.

The men stiffened half expecting a bullet in the back. Then they gradually turned to face Buck and Carmody who covered them with their rifles. When Gilbert saw who it was his lip curled up in a sneer. "Well, well. It's the back shooters themselves."

"Unbuckle the gun belts and step back from them," Buck said ignoring the barb.

After they'd done so, Gilbert asked, "What now? You going to shoot us cold like you did to Quinn's men?"

Buck fixed his cold stare on the Broken C foreman. "I was going to ask you about that. You seemed to get there awful quick to start shooting at us."

"I heard the shooting. I was on the way to the dam site."

Buck nodded. "I was at the dam site when I heard the shooting too. So, there was no way we could shoot Quinn's men."

"We saw you. Me and Bernie."

"Who is Bernie?" the deputy marshal asked.

A thickset man stepped forward. "I'm Bernie."

"You say you saw us shoot the two men?"

"I do."

Buck looked at Carmody. "You're both liars," the Brenham deputy shot back.

"We're what?" Gilbert grated.

"I said you're both liars. You see, while the marshal was checking out the two dead men and I was on my horse, I was still able to see clear tracks. Four men rode that trail. The two regulators and two more. They were the ones who killed them. Not us."

Buck knew that Carmody was lying but he was trying to shake something loose. He studied the two men waiting for a sign.

"Now who's lying?" Gilbert asked.

"Am I? You and your friend shot both of Quinn's regulators in the back. Why else would you be out here trying to find us before anyone else?"

"Prove it," Gilbert sneered.

"Who told you to do it? Was it Conker?"

There was an almost imperceptible flicker in the man's eyes. "No."

"But you did do it."

"No."

"Liar," Carmody snapped and eared back the hammer on the rifle he held.

"What are you doing?" the foreman asked tentatively.

"I'm going to get some answers."

"How?"

"Going to shoot bits of you until I find one which tells me the truth."

"We saw you do it."

"Wrong," the deputy sheriff said and squeezed the trigger.

The rifle whiplashed and dirt erupted between Gilbert's feet. He jumped back, an alarmed expression on his face.

"Consider that your first and last warning, Gilbert."

"No," he gasped.

"Yes," Carmody said working the lever on his Henry.

"No. You can't—"

"Yes, I can."

The foreman's eyes grew wide and his hand streaked for his six-gun. "No!"

The rifle whiplashed and a .44 caliber slug punched into Gilbert's chest. The force of which flung him back mercilessly. He lay flat in the dust of the yard breathing his last when the rifle moved to cover Bernie. "Guess I'm not as good a shot as I thought I was," Carmody said. "Or maybe I am. He shouldn't have gone for his gun."

The hand licked his lips nervously. He opened his mouth to speak and then it snapped shut like a bear trap. Buck sensed he needed some prodding and said, "Come on, Bernie. Spell it out. I might even let you get a head start out of the county."

"All right. It was us. We killed them."

"Why?"

"I don't know. I was just told to do it and I'd be paid extra."

Buck shook his head. "Where was Quinn going when he left here?"

"Tejano's Canyon," Bernie said.

Buck snapped a glance at Carmody before staring hard at the hand. "Why was he going there?"

"He came here looking for you and him. When he found us already here, he asked if there was somewhere that you might be holed up. Max used it as an opportunity to get him out of the way. Send him over there on a wild goose chase."

Except it wasn't a wild goose chase. Quinn would arrive there and stumble across the others. Buck said, "Get gone, Bernie. Don't bother looking back. Expect the law to be on your trail every step of the way."

The hand rushed to his horse and leaped into the saddle. He kicked the animal savagely and put it into a run.

"The rest of you head back to town and wait there. You all heard what he said. You'll be needed to testify at any hearing that is required."

"We ain't going to do that," one man said.

"Then get on your horse and get out of the county too. The same goes for the rest of you."

Only the man who had spoken up moved. The rest stayed put.

"We never wanted any part of this, Marshal," a tall man said. "All we want is to work regular like. Hell, we ain't even got anything against those damned sheep. We just sprout what we're told to."

Buck nodded. "Go to town and wait."

"We'll do that."

The deputy marshal turned to Carmody. "We got to get to that canyon."

"Our horses are spent as it is, Buck," Carmody explained. "If we push them too hard now, we'll kill them."

"I know damn it. I know."

Brenham, Texas

It was late in the afternoon when Walsh and Roberts rode into Brenham. They dropped their loads at the undertaker's and then saw to the horses. After that, the deputy organized to meet up with the old scout at the Railway Saloon for a drink as soon as he got cleaned up and stopped smelling like a horse.

As soon as Walsh entered the saloon Lily saw him. She was wearing a red dress with puffed sleeves and black lace around the neck and bottoms of the sleeves. She hurried over to him and said, "I heard you got them."

The deputy gave her a tired smile. "Word sure does get around fast. Yes, we got them. How's Milt?"

"He's coming along. I'm pleased you got them. Find yourself a table and I'll bring you a bottle."

Walsh did so and sat down. While he waited, Craig Fellows entered and looked around. When the mayor spotted the deputy, he waded between the tables until he reached him. "About time you returned. What were you thinking going off leaving the town to fend for itself?"

"I went after a murderer, Craig," Walsh said his weariness evident.

"Here's your drink, Hardy," Lily said and placed a glass beside the bottle on the tabletop. "Good evening, Mayor."

"What would have happened if outlaws had ridden into town?" Fellows asked, ignoring Lily. "There would be no one here to stop them."

"Did anything happen, Craig?" the deputy asked wearily, too tired to play stupid games.

"No, it—"

"Then good. I, on the other hand, got the murderer."

"That's not the point. What if it did happen?"

"I'm not having this argument, Craig. Go away and leave me alone."

The mayor's face turned red. "I'll not be spoken to like that by some deputy. I'll take this up with the sheriff when he returns."

"You do that."

Fellows huffed and stormed off.

The deputy popped the cork and started to pour himself a drink. "Sometimes I wonder why someone ain't put a slug in him yet."

"Are you OK, Hardy?" Lily asked.

He looked up at the concern on her pretty face and smiled. "I'm fine. Just tired, I guess. You heard from Lance?"

"Not since the other day. Seems he had some trouble on the way up there."

"Did he say when he was going to be back?"

She shook her head. "Mary Denham was in here while you were gone. Came looking for you."

Walsh nodded but remained silent.

Lily pulled out a chair and sat down. "Do I sense trouble in paradise, Hardy?"

"I guess with everything that's going on it's kind

of hard to see past the problems."

"What prob—oh, sorry. You're right."

He tossed back the rest of his drink and poured another. "You want one?"

She shook her head. "Thank you for what you did, Hardy."

"Part of the job. It—" he noticed she was looking towards the doorway. Walsh turned his head and saw Clive Denham. "What's he doing in town at this time of day?"

As they watched, Liam O'Connor entered behind him. The new arrivals looked around the bar and the Irishman pointed in Walsh's direction. "Looks like I'm the popular one, don't it?"

The two men approached the deputy and stopped before the table. Denham nodded. "Hardy. Miss Lily."

"Clive. You want to take a seat?"

The rancher shook his head. "You mind if we go somewhere to talk?"

Walsh gave out a tired sigh. "Can it wait until tomorrow, Clive. I've only not long got back from hunting down a murderer."

"I wish it could, Hardy but it is important."

"All right let's go along to the jail."

"Thank you, Hardy. It won't take long."

Walsh climbed to his feet and said to Lily, "Sorry, Lily."

She reached out, touched his arm and gave him a warm grin. "It's fine, Hardy. I'm used to being stood up."

"Could you tell Chick Roberts when he comes in that I won't be long?"

"Sure."

"Thank you."

Walsh slumped down in the chair behind Lance's desk and looked up at Denham. "All right, Clive, what is it that was so urgent it couldn't wait until morning?"

"Have you heard from the sheriff at all?" he asked.

"Nope, not a word. Mind you, I haven't been here either."

"Do you know what he went up to Grand Valley for?"

Suddenly Walsh's weariness slid away and he sat up in the seat. He let his hand fall to his six-gun as blood began coursing faster through his veins. Perhaps if he'd not been so tired he would have been more alert to start with. But he wasn't and the mistake was made. The pressure of a six-gun barrel pressing into the side of his head just behind his ear told him as much.

"Not so fast, Boyo," the Irishman said in a low, menacing voice. "Put your hands back on the desk for me. I'd hate to be making a mess on the floor with your brains."

"What the hell is going on?" Walsh asked angrily, more at himself than anything.

"We just want to ask you some questions," Denham said. "That's all."

"This is a bad idea, Clive," the deputy told the rancher.

"I guess that's all I've got," Denham said. "But I'm willing to offer you a deal, Hardy."

"What deal?"

"You tell me what Chaney knows and I'm willing to offer you a thousand dollars."

"And if I don't take the deal?"

"I'll let Liam get it from you and then he'll kill you. Think about it. And Mary. My daughter for some reason thinks a lot of you but she sure will be upset if something should befall you."

The deputy ground his teeth together in anger.

"You're a son of a bitch, Denham."

"I guess you could say that."

"I bet it was you who killed your son in jail."

"I did what needed to be done. A Texas State governor can't have things like that appearing from his past."

"You used him to kill the others. I bet your plan was to kill him too, all along."

"Rabid dogs like him deserve what comes to them."

"What happened? Huh? What did he do?"

Denham gave him a cold smile. "You don't need to know."

"Horseshit," Walsh cursed. "You want my help, then you tell me."

The rancher stared at him for a moment before he nodded and said, "All right. I'll tell you. We rode into Grand Valley and set up camp five miles outside of town. We were low on supplies and instead of sending a forage party into town I told them to check the farms. I thought I'd made a good choice by sending Christopher to lead it. I was wrong. The first farm he and the others came across was owned by a man and woman. Chris took a shine to her and things happened. My so-called son raped that poor woman and then left her there holding up her husband trying to save his life while he had a noose around his neck."

Denham paused and let his words sink in before he continued, "When they returned, two of them came to me and told me what happened. I rode to the farm and found the woman naked and her husband dead. I gave her money to ease the pain. To try and make up for what had been done. Then I left."

Walsh felt only disgust for this man standing before him.

"When I arrived back at our camp, I sent the rest of them back out. I told Chris I never wanted to see him again and that he would be declared dead. I should have hung him, but I couldn't."

"What happened this time? Why'd he come back?"

"Money. He appeared at the ranch while I was on my own. It was about the time I decided to run for governor. It was then that I realized that if I wanted to be elected to office, I had to get rid of anything from my past that might threaten it."

"So you got Chris to do it for you in return for money," Walsh theorized. "The only way you were going to pay him was in lead."

"No. I wanted him gone, not dead. But then he was taken in and I knew the only way to fix it was to kill him."

"Uh, huh."

"Now, tell me what Chaney knows."

Walsh shrugged. "I don't know."

The color of Denham's face changed. "You lie."

"I don't know anything."

The rancher nodded at his foreman who swung the barrel of his six-gun. It cracked against the side of Walsh's head and he almost fell from the chair.

"Tell me damn it!" Denham snarled. "We had a deal."

"No, we didn't," Walsh said rubbing at his head. When his hand came away it had traces of blood on it. "I ain't telling you nothing."

"Yes, you will," the rancher replied.

"Go to hell," Walsh sneered.

Denham gave another nod to his foreman. Walsh had been counting on it and came out of his seat and turned to face the Irishman. He grabbed at the arm and missed it but kept moving. The two men struggled, and the sound of a gunshot rocked the room. Walsh stiffened and slumped to the floor, unmoving.

"Damn it!" Denham snarled. "What did you shoot him for?"

"I didn't mean to."

"He's done for, let's get out of here."

The two men hurried out into the darkness before someone could arrive.

"Someone shot the deputy!" the cry echoed through the Railway Saloon and brought uproar to the place. "He's over at the doc's place. It don't look good."

Lily felt her blood run cold and she looked around for Milt before remembering that he too was at the doctor's after being shot. She hurried up to the bar. Tyson Bald was behind the counter and she waved at him to get his attention. He hurried along the bar. "Yes, ma'am?"

"I'm going along to Doc Harding's. Keep an eye on the place."

"Yes, ma'am."

Lily hurried out the door and into the cool night air. She hurried up Second Street until she reached the next street and turned right. She passed the saddler shop which was now dark as Helmut Fritz had long gone home. Then came Doc Harding's home and surgery. Lily rushed through the open gate and up the gravel path to the steps and the porch.

She knocked on the door and waited. Footsteps sounded on the other side of the door and then it swung open to reveal Maggie. "What are you doing here?"

Maggie said, "I thought I could help."

"Me too," Lily replied.

"Come in."

They walked along the hallway and into the room where Walker was working on the unconscious Hardy Walsh, blood on hands, and a frown on his face. He glanced up and saw Lily. "Good, another pair of hands. Get them washed and come back here."

Lily washed her hands in a dish and then came back to stand beside the doctor. "Put your hand in here and feel around until you touch my finger."

Wincing, Lily followed his instructions. The insides of Walsh were wet and warm, almost to the point of being hot. She felt the end of Harding's finger. "I have it."

"Right. Just at the end of the finger, you'll feel a vein which has been nicked by the bullet. You'll be able to feel the blood pulse from it. I'll let it go now."

He withdrew his finger and immediately Lily felt the small spurt of blood. "I feel it."

"Right, put your finger over it. Maggie get me that needle and thread there if you will. I need to get the thing to stop if he's going to have any chance of seeing it through the night."

"What happened?" Lily asked.

"I don't know. Someone heard a shot and then Hardy was found at the jail."

"Didn't anybody see anything?"

"Not as far as I know."

"What about Clive Denham?"

The doctor almost stopped what he was doing. "What do you mean?"

"Hardy went to the jail with Clive Denham and his foreman."

"I wouldn't know about that, Lily."

Harding worked tirelessly to save the deputy's life and almost two hours later he was done. Harding let out a sigh and wiped at his brow. "All we can do now is wait and see. Although, if I'm honest, I don't like his chances."

Lily glanced at Maggie who looked as though she was about to cry. Much the same as Lily herself felt. Trying to sound positive she said, "He's tough. He'll make it."

The doctor looked at her and gave a slight nod. "Sure, he will." But his tone told a different story; it said that he wasn't feeling very confident.

Tejano's Canyon, Texas

It was just on dawn when Buck and Carmody rode into Tejano's Canyon. The first thing they noticed was the lack of a lookout atop the rocks at the entrance. The trail in was all churned up where Quinn had ridden in with his men. Once inside, the two lawmen saw that the sheep were still there. They rode on until they reached the cabin where they were met by Ackerman.

"What happened, Bert?"

"Troop Quinn and his men. They shot Ralph and took the woman and kid."

"Is Ralph—"

"He'll live," Tucker said as he joined his friend out the front.

"That's something, I guess."

"How'd they get in here with a lookout on guard, Bert?" Buck asked.

"It was my fault," Tucker said. "I went to sleep, Captain. I'm sorry."

The deputy marshal gave an angry sigh. "It is what it is. Would have been another time, I'd have shot you for that, Lonnie."

"Yes, sir."

"What did Quinn say?" Carmody asked.

"He was taking the woman and kid to town. Said to tell you that you'd find them at the Stockman's Saloon."

"It'll be a trap, you know?" Carmody said.

Buck nodded. "Yes, I'd say so. That's why we're going to have ourselves a guerilla raid. We'll take them out before they know what's happening. They'll be expecting us to ride along the street. Too bad that ain't going to be what we do."

"They'll be expecting us to come straight away, Buck. How about we make them wait?"

"What's your idea?"

"We go in tomorrow night. The men Quinn has staked out will be starting to get careless by then. We'll take them one at a time."

"I have another idea. We get Conker and take him to town, and he can tell Quinn the truth."

"Or we can do that."

"I'm coming with you," Ralph said from the door of the shack.

Buck stared at him. The man was a pasty gray color and looked like he was about to fall over. No, you stay here. If we don't come back by the day after tomorrow, then it all went wrong."

Ralph grumbled something and Ackerman said, "You leave this to us soldier boys. We'll get it done."

Buck looked at him. "You and Lonnie dealing yourselves in?"

"Yes, sir. I guess we are."

"Too right, Captain. If I hadn't gone to sleep, then we wouldn't be in this fix."

"Alright," Buck agreed. "We'll leave just as soon as the horses have rested. We'll ride over to the Broken C and get our man."

CHAPTER 19

Broken C Ranch

It wasn't going to be easy, especially after having been there the previous night. It would have put the cowhands on edge and no doubt they'd have pickets out.

Pinpricks of light lit the ranch house and there were more from the bunkhouse. Ackerman moved in close to Buck and asked, "What do you want us to do?"

"We're going to walk right in and take him. Tucker, you've got half an hour to go down there and find all the pickets. Then come back here. Before we make our move, I want to know where they all are."

"I can do that, Captain."

Tucker disappeared into the darkness. Carmody asked, "Do you think it was wise to send him?"

"When he served in my cavalry troop, he was a top scout. The man I trusted to find whatever I needed found."

"That's right," Ackerman agreed. "Lonnie was real good He could crawl up behind a Yankee doing his business behind a tree, wipe his buttocks, and then slip away without the Yank knowing he was there."

"I hope he's still that good," Carmody said.

"I guess we'll find out."

It took Tucker twenty of the thirty minutes to return. "You were right, Captain. They got pickets out. There's one by the corral, another by the barn, a third around behind the ranch house, and a sneaky varmint near the bunkhouse that I almost missed. If it hadn't been for the smoke, he was puffing on I'd have missed him for sure."

Buck nodded. "He's yours. I'll take the one near the Barn, Holt, you've got the man near the corral. Ackerman, the man behind the house."

"And when we've done that?" Carmody asked.

"Me and you are going inside. Lonnie and Ackerman will keep watch on the bunkhouse while we do."

"I don't suppose you know if Conker is married at all?"

Buck shrugged. "Never thought to ask."

"I guess we'll find out then."

"I guess we will."

Holt Carmody slipped through the rail of the corral and moved silently through the small herd of horses within. His main worry wasn't getting seen, but rather an errant hoof from a spooked animal that might collect him in the head while he was crouched low. He'd seen what that could do to a man. Either death or rattle his brain so much that he'd just sit there unaware of his surroundings and have to be fed from a spoon.

He pushed a bay gently out of the way and proceeded forward. The animals snorted and started to mill about. Carmody stopped and crouched on one knee. The guard turned and looked into the corral, trying to see why the horses were on edge. Carmody heard him say something not quite audible before turning his back on the corral to face the other way.

The deputy sheriff let out a slow breath and then moved again. The milling horses edged aside as he walked forward toward the rails. He drew his six-gun and raised it into the air.

The guard sensed rather than heard the presence and turned around. His jaw dropped but not a sound escaped his lips before the gun fell like an ax and hit him almost perfectly between the eyes.

The man fell back without a sound and Carmody winced in sympathy. He said in a low voice, "My friend, you are going to have one hell of a headache when you wake up."

Buck crept through the shadows of the barn towards where the guard stood at the corner of the frame building. From within the structure, the scent of fresh hay permeated the air. The deputy marshal gently placed one foot on the ground after the other. Paused, moved it slightly to the right to avoid a small twig, then placed it down. As he reached the corner, he drew his Colt, not bothering to thumb back the hammer. The last thing he needed was the sound of a shot crashing out and warning everyone.

The guard had his back to him as he came around the corner of the barn, Making it easier for Buck to do his work. The Colt fell and so did the cowhand. Buck leaned down and grabbed the man by his shirt collar and dragged him behind the barn.

The others accomplished their jobs with quiet efficiency. Once all the guards were out of action, Buck and Carmody began creeping toward the ranch house.

The front door was open, and as they stepped inside, they stopped in the spacious entrance hall. The first thing they noticed was the pungent smell of a cigar that hung heavily in the air. "Follow the scent like an old coon hound," Carmody said in a hushed tone.

Buck nodded and walked slowly forward.

The further he went the stronger the smell became until he stood outside a closed door showing with a thin strip of light beneath it. The deputy marshal reached out with his left hand, drawing his Colt with his right. The doorknob turned and Buck swung the door open silently on well-oiled hinges.

Inside the den, Conker sat in a leather-backed chair facing away from the door. A small plume of cigar smoke drifted upwards from where he sat. Buck could see the man's right hand resting on the arm of the chair. In it was a cut-glass tumbler of amber liquid. Carmody closed the door silently and the pair moved further into the room.

"I suppose you've come here to kill me," Conker's voice came in a flat tone.

With no further need for stealth, Buck and Carmody moved quickly around in front of the man, both with their six-guns pointed at the rancher. Buck said, "No. We're taking you to town where you can explain how your orders being carried out were what got Quinn's men killed."

The rancher snorted as though he was acknowledging a joke. "I'm going nowhere with you."

"You'll either walk out or be carried out," Carmody explained. "Personally, I don't care which."

"You might as well shoot me now because that's what Quinn will do."

"No, you'll stand trial. That's what the law is about."

"Do I get to at least finish my drink?"

"Sure, why not? Might be the last one you ever get."

Conker tossed back the remnants of what was in his glass and stood up. "Shall we go, gentlemen?"

Bell, Texas

It was amazing how smoothly their plan had gone. They'd disabled the guards, kidnapped Conker, and slipped away from the ranch without any trouble, whatsoever. But as things go in life, something unexpected always pops up.

After crossing the bridge into town, the five

riders turned their mounts right onto Yard Street and continued until reaching The Yards Saloon where they tethered their horses at the hitch rail and walked inside.

The barroom went quiet immediately. All heads turned to stare at the five men standing just inside the doors. The room itself wasn't overly large and the tables were spread out making open space even rarer.

Buck pointed at a table near the rear wall. "Over there, near the stairs."

Carmody led the solemn-looking rancher over to the table while Buck walked to the center of the room and said at the top of his voice, "The saloon is closed. Everyone out."

The uproar was immediate.

"You can't do this," a customer shouted at him.

Buck tapped his badge. "This says I can. Now, like I said, everyone out. Those who refuse to go will be dragged out by their feet."

A well-dressed man in a suit and sporting a pencil-thin mustache approached the deputy Marshal, his countenance a sour expression. "Excuse me, Marshal. I'm Wes Holcroft, I own The Yards. Might I ask why you're overstepping your authority and shutting my saloon?"

The deputy marshal turned his hard gaze on the saloon owner. "Aside from the fact I'm not overstepping my authority, I need somewhere to hole up with my prisoner for a spell. This is it."

The saloon owner stared at Conker and then shifted his gaze back to Buck. "Isn't there somewhere else? The jail, maybe."

"Normally, yes, but not this time. He turned to Tucker. "Get upstairs and pick a window."

"Yes, sir, Captain."

"This is not right," Holcroft protested some more but it fell on deaf ears.

"Holt. Keep an eye out at the front door. Ackerman, you've got the back."

With all his men at their posts, the deputy marshal turned to the saloon owner. "You want to make yourself useful, find Troop Quinn and tell him I want to see him. On his own."

The saloon owner nodded. "Fine. I'll find him."

"Make sure you tell him to come alone."

Holcroft nodded once more and left his saloon.

News has already reached Troop Quinn when the saloon owner found him. The regulator was busy organizing his men to storm the saloon, determined to get even with the man who'd killed his own. Outside the jail, he stood like a beacon in the orange glow from the lamplight shining through the window.

"Bodie and Crocker go in through the back while we sit out the front and keep them busy. Once—"

His words were cut off as he stared at Holcroft who hurried toward him before stopping in front of him. "What do you want?"

"I have a message from the marshal."

"Who are you?"

"Holcroft, I own the saloon."

Quinn stepped closer to the saloon owner. "What did he have to say?"

Holcroft swallowed nervously under the regulator's heated gaze. "Ahh—he said he wanted to see you. Alone."

"Did he now? Why?"

"I don't know but he has Hank Conker with him."

"Willingly?"

The saloon keeper shook his head. "No. He's his prisoner."

Quinn thought for a moment and then said, "Go back and tell the marshal I'll be along directly."

"Yes, sir," Holcroft replied and hurried away.

Bodie called out to Quinn. "Are you really going

down there to see the marshal?"

"I sure am," the regulator replied. "I want to hear what he has to say."

"You want us to come with you?"

"No, I don't think the marshal has anything sneaky in mind. Not while we have the woman and the girl."

"He said he'd be right along," Holcroft told Buck as he walked across the saw dusted floor toward him.

Buck bobbed his head. "Good. Now go upstairs and stay there. Keep your girls up there too."

"You ain't going to do anything that's going to wreck my saloon, are you, Marshal?"

"Not if I don't have to," he replied.

The saloon owner smiled uncertainly before he crossed to the stairs and started to climb them.

"You figure he'll come alone, Buck?" Carmody asked.

"I hope so. But let's assume not. Tell the others to keep an eye out."

Buck moved over to the door and looked out at the street. A cool breeze drifted along the thoroughfare and wafted through the saloon. He could hear cattle lowing from the stockyards behind the butcher. Most likely the next day's kill. Across the street, the blacksmith's was in darkness as was the stage and freight. Along the street to the left, the undertaker's light was still lit. Maybe he was expecting further business that night. Maybe.

Five minutes after the arrival of Holcroft, a shadow could be seen moving along the street towards the saloon. Buck shifted his stance and dropped his hand to the Colt in its holster. The figure walked through a patch of light radiating from the cathouse window, and he could see that it was Quinn. Buck looked across the street and scanned all the shadows and rooftops he could see just in case Quinn's men were moving into position to try something. It made him feel a little better, although not much, that he could see nothing. However, the fact that they weren't visible didn't mean there weren't there.

Satisfied for the time being, Buck turned his gaze back to the Quinn. Carmody appeared beside the deputy sheriff. "Is that him?"

"Yes," Buck informed him. "That's Quinn."

"I'll just go sit at the table with Conker."

Quinn changed direction and walked toward the saloon. After climbing the boardwalk steps he moved toward the door and then stopped. "I heard you wanted to see me."

"I did," replied Buck. "Come inside and let's talk."

"I can do that. I'm interested as to what the killer of my men has to say about it."

When they were both inside, they walked over to the table where Carmody and Conker sat. The regulator studied the rancher before asking, "Are you OK, Hank?"

The man looked up and nodded, but that was all.

"So, Chaney, let's hear what you have to say before I send my men in here to kill you."

"We didn't kill your men," Buck told him flatly.

Quinn snorted derisively. "You were seen. That foreman saw you. Gilbert."

"Gilbert is dead," the deputy marshal stated. "But before he died, he admitted everything. He killed your men."

The regulator still wasn't convinced. "Great plan, Chaney. Blame a dead man so he can't tell any different."

"He can't, but Conker can. It was him that ordered it done."

Quinn shifted his gaze to the rancher. "Is that true?"

"No."

The regulator stared at him thinking, trying to decide if he was lying. Then he said, "My men were both shot in the back. Only a coward does something like that. And quite frankly, I don't see the marshal being one. I saw him face down Coleman. No man with a yellow streak down his spine would even contemplate going against him."

"I want the woman and the child, Troop," Buck said.

"I didn't say I believed you, Chaney."

"You know it's true. As you said, I'm not a back shooter."

"OK, you ain't. But if I'm going to give you the woman and the child, I want something in return."

"Like what?"

Quinn nodded towards Conker. "Him."

Buck gave a slow shake of his head. "Can't do that. He's under arrest."

"Put it this way, Chaney. You either give me Conker or I keep the woman and child until you do. If you take too long, I'll hang them instead."

"Not going to happen, Quinn."

The regulator climbed to his feet. "I'll give you until noon tomorrow. Bring him to the Stockman's Saloon. After that, I'll hang the woman."

Troop Quinn turned and walked from the saloon, leaving Buck to contemplate the ultimatum he'd just been given.

"I think he means it," Carmody stated.

Buck nodded. "Can't afford to think otherwise."

"I guess we're going to need a plan."

"I guess we are."

There was a faint red stain on the eastern horizon when the four men decided it was time. A rooster crowed which in turn set a dog to barking. There were four fully-loaded rifles on the table as well as a sawn-off shotgun that Buck had found behind the bar. Carmody slipped his six-gun into his holster and picked up the messenger gun. "This'll come in handy."

Buck looked at Ackerman and Tucker. "You boys ready?"

"Yes, sir, Captain. Lonnie and me will be in position by the time you all get there."

Ackerman and Tucker were to circle the town and take up position on the bank and the pool hall, while Buck and Carmody walked Conker along the street to where the Stockman's Saloon sat at the intersection of Main and Holt.

They scooped up the rifles and Buck motioned to the rancher. "Get up."

The rancher reluctantly got to his feet and came out from behind the table. "Time to go," the deputy marshal explained.

There was still a chill in the pre-dawn air as they made their way along the street. Buck walked on the rancher's right side while Carmody was on his left. They traversed the street slowly giving the others time to get into position.

When they reached the hotel, Carmody broke off and disappeared along the alley between it and the saddler. "Where's he going?" Conker asked.

"Shut up and keep walking."

When they drew level with the saloon, Buck called out, "Quinn? You in there?"

The dawn silence hung heavy in the air for a drawn-out period before the doors to the saloon swung open and Troop Quinn emerged. His boots sounded loud on the plank boardwalk. Behind him were more men who emerged until there were six of them in total. The regulator gave a mirthless smile. "You've made a decision I see."

"I have. Where's the woman and the girl?"

"They're safe. Send him on over and I'll get them."

Buck looked at him skeptically. "The way I see it, Quinn is that I hand him over to you, you hang him. The thing is you ain't stupid. You know I'll come after you for it. Just because it's murder. So, you can't afford to let me ride away from here either.

Am I right?"

Quinn gave him a mirthless smile. "See, that's why you're a marshal. You're smart."

"But you ain't," Buck shot back at him. "You really think I'll just roll over and go down without a fight?"

"I'd be disappointed if you did." He was about to say more when the throaty roar of a shotgun split the early morning quiet.

Carmody had circled behind the hotel and moved swiftly along to the rear of the saloon, finding the rear stairs that led up to the second floor. He climbed them trying to keep as silent as possible.

The door atop the landing was open and Carmody crept through the opening. The hallway was lit by lamps and led directly toward the stairs from the barroom. A number of doors on each side were closed, signifying the numbered bedrooms on that floor. As he walked along quietly, Carmody paused to listen outside of each door before moving on to repeat his actions.

He made it halfway before finding the one he wanted. He stopped, listened, heard the soothing voice of a woman singing softly in Spanish.

Carmody tried the door and it popped ajar. He was about to push it further when a shout from the top of the stairs drew his attention. "Hey!"

The regulator began to draw his gun but Carmody was a shade faster and pulled the trigger on the sawn-off shotgun in his right hand, the first barrel exploding with a roar.

The charge of buckshot punched into the man and flung him back, arms windmilling in the air. He hit the wall behind him with enough force that it seemed to shake the whole building.

Carmody retreated into the room where Carmella and her daughter were. At first, it took her several moments to work out that Carmody was friendly, but when she saw his identity, the tension on her face eased a little but didn't disappear. "We've come to get you out, ma'am."

"Is it safe?"

"Not really. But if we don't go now then we'll never get out of here."

As he finished speaking, the world outside seemed to explode in violence. He looked at the woman and said, "Sorry, ma'am. You and the girl get down behind the bed."

"Why?"

"Just do it." And with that, he walked over to the window and broke the glass.

Buck swung the Winchester up and around. He snapped off a shot at Quinn, but the regulator was already diving for cover behind a trough at the edge of the street. The shot missed and slapped into the wall of the saloon.

The other regulators began pulling their weapons as the shooting started. From up on the bank, Tucker opened fire with his rifle. He methodically levered and fired the weapon and one of Quinn's men threw up his arms in a yelp of pain, crashing against the saloon wall before sliding down it.

Ackerman joined the battle and shot another man from the pool hall rooftop. The battle had only just started and already Troop Quinn was down three men.

Make that four.

Buck levered and fired at a shooter who was firing up at Ackerman on the pool hall. Having exposed himself too much, that was all it took for the .44 Henry slug to punch his ticket when it hammered into his chest.

The deputy marshal felt the heat of a passing slug close to his face and realized that he was still wide open. He retreated across the street and took shelter, scant as it was, behind a post in front of the cattleman's association building. A bullet chewed splinters from the post, one of the razor-sharp slivers cutting the flesh of Buck's cheek, drawing blood immediately.

Up above the saloon awning on the second floor, Buck caught sight of Carmody but from where he stood there was no clear shot at the rest of the regulators.

A cry of pain drew the deputy marshal's attention and he looked up at the top of the bank. He ground his teeth together as he watched Tucker stagger and fall forward off the rooftop, plunging to the boardwalk below shattering the planks under his weight.

"Damn it," Buck cursed and fired at the man responsible. The shooter's head jerked as the bullet drilled into the side of it and he slumped down out of sight.

That left just three of them.

A shout from Ackerman and a flurry of shots and Buck saw one of the regulators run back inside the saloon. Up at the window on the second floor, Carmody still waited for a target. Buck waved at him to get his attention. The deputy sheriff looked at him and Buck indicated that a shooter had gone inside. Carmody waved in acknowledgment and disappeared from the window.

More splinters were gouged from the post where Buck sheltered and then he felt the burn of a slug that tore through his shirt high up on his side. The deputy marshal ground his teeth against the pain and muttered a curse. The sound of the shotgun crashed out from within the saloon and Buck knew it was Carmody.

The deputy sheriff appeared at the entrance to the saloon, rifle in hand having discarded the empty shotgun. Buck saw him open fire at Bodie, the only one of Quinn's men who remained upright.

Carmody fired three times at the killer and each time the hammer fell and the rifle fired, Bodie jerked violently before he fell to the boardwalk dead.

From behind the trough, Troop Quinn rose with a roar of defiance. He fired twice at Carmody whose left leg buckled and he dropped to his knees. Buck saw the regulator take deliberate aim at him and knew things were about to get even worse if he didn't react quickly.

The Winchester in Buck's hands whiplashed as he fired hurriedly to save Carmody's life. The bullet passed close to the killer and threw off his aim. The shot fired at the vulnerable Carmody flew wide and hammered like a lead nail into the boardwalk beside him.

Buck worked the lever of the Winchester as Quinn turned, an ugly snarl on his face. The regulator brought his gun into line with the deputy marshal and for a moment he thought he might actually get out of it alive.

But that was such a fleeting fancy before a bullet from the Winchester smashed into his chest killing him instantly and the lights for the boss regulator went out forever.

The last of the gun thunder rolled along the street and disappeared out of town. Buck's gaze searched for any more of Quinn's men but realized that there were none. A sense of numbness hung in the air from the brutal display that was now done. Then his gaze found Conker laying in the street where he'd been when the gunfight had erupted.

He was still alive, though the deputy marshal wasn't sure how after the quantity of lead that had been thrown back and forth. Across the street, Carmody climbed to his feet, a large red patch on his pants leg.

"You OK?" Buck asked.

"Ain't nothing to cry about," the deputy sheriff

replied. "I'll go check on Carmella and Louisa."

Buck walked across the intersection towards the bank. Tucker lay on the dusty street, eyes open in death. "He was a good friend, Captain," Ackerman said as he joined Buck.

"Yes, he was."

"Are we done here?"

Buck nodded. "It's just a matter of getting Conker to jail and talking to the other ranchers."

"I'll see to Lonnie."

CHAPTER 20

Brenham, Texas

Lance Chaney climbed down from the train and looked about the station platform. As he walked along the boards the station master moved to intercept him, saying, "Thank heavens you're back, Sheriff."

Lance frowned at the thinly built man with a brush mustache. "What's up, Oliver?"

"Deputy Walsh was shot the night before last. Whoever done it shot him in the jail."

Concern showed on the sheriff's face. "Is he OK?"

The station master shook his head. "I ain't sure. He's over at Doc Harding's."

"Can you see that my valise gets along to my office?"

"Yes, sir."

Lance hurried along several streets, crossing over the dusty thoroughfare when he reached the doctor's home on the corner.

He went inside and found the doctor in his kitchen. "Sorry for not knocking, Doc, but—"

The doctor shook his head. "Don't let it bother you, Lance. I guess you've heard about Hardy?"

The sheriff nodded. "Yeah, how's he doing?"

"He's tough. Any mortal man would have died already. But not Hardy. Hardy by name, and by nature."

"Is he going to make it?"

Harding gave a helpless shrug of his shoulders. "Who knows? I certainly don't."

"What happened?"

"He was shot over at the jail. Don't know by who but rumor has that it was Denham and his foreman."

"Why do people think that?"

"Because they were the last ones to be seen with Hardy," the doctor explained. "They were at the saloon, asked to see Hardy, and the next we know, Hardy is shot."

"Damn it."

"How did your trip go?" Harding asked.

"As I expected. Chris Denham raped a woman in Grand Valley and left the husband hanging. The others were there with him. Old Denham tried to pay her off. The only problem is, if I arrest him, she won't testify to anything."

"Then maybe Hardy getting shot might offer you an alternative."

Lance sighed. "It's a hard way to do it, Doc."

"You're right."

"I'll head off, Doc. Let me know if anything changes."

"I'll come find you."

"Thanks, Doc."

"When you see Lily tell her that Milt Reynolds should be right to go in a couple of days."

Lance frowned. "Sorry?"

"That's right, you weren't here. He was shot the other day when the working girl was murdered."

"I heard about the girl. Did Hardy get the ones who did it?"

"Yes, he did. Followed them out into Comanche territory. Him and Chick Roberts."

"Who's he?"

"Old scout. Good man."
"Fine, I'll let her know. Be seeing you."
Lance left Harding's and walked along the main street to the jail. When he entered, the first thing he noticed was the big dark bloodstain on the boards of the floor. He stood staring at it for a long moment before he stepped outside and glanced about. He saw a young man walking along the street and called him over.
"Hey, Sheriff."
"What's your name?"
"Vern Hicks."
"I want you to go and find—" Lance stopped. Who the hell did he get to do what he wanted? "I want you to find me someone who's a carpenter. You have one in town, don't you?"
"Yes, sir. That would be Chester Pickles."
"Chester Pickles?"
"Yes, sir. Best darn carpenter around. Build anything from a barn to a house, even a hotel, he's that good."
"Well, I don't need a damned hotel. Just go find him for me, will you?"
"Yes, sir, Sheriff."
The young man hurried away, and Lance went back inside. His gaze was drawn once more to the mess on the floor. He tried to ignore it but no matter where he looked, his eyes were always drawn to it.
"I heard you were back," a voice said from the doorway.
Lance looked over his shoulder. Filling the void from outside was Judge Granville Dyson. "Howdy, Judge," Lance said morosely.
"Don't sound so excited to see me," Dyson growled. "Maybe if I was a certain lady, I might get a better reception."
"Sorry, Judge, it's just—" he waved at the floor.
"Yes, bad business. What are you going to do about it?"

"Two things, Judge. I'm going to find out who shot Hardy, and go talk to Clive Denham about another matter."

"His son and the murders?"

Lance nodded. "Uh, huh."

"What did you find out?"

Lance told him.

"You want to deputize someone to go with you?"

The sheriff shook his head. "I'll be fine. It's just a friendly chat."

The expression on Dyson's face was one of skepticism. "You mean that you're going out there alone in the hope he'll do something stupid you can nail his hide for. Especially seeing as that woman from Grand Valley won't testify. Am I right?"

"Wouldn't have any idea what you mean, Judge."

"You know that people have been talking about him being the one who shot Hardy, don't you?"

"I might have heard something like that."

Dyson's face hardened. "Don't go making this all about revenge, Lance. If you get the chance, you bring him in for trial. Understand?"

"Yes, Judge."

"It's about time you got back, blast your eyes," Mayor Craig Fellows blustered from the open doorway.

"Can I shoot him?" Lance asked from the corner of his mouth.

"By all means," Dyson replied.

Fellows continued his tirade. "You ride off at the drop of a hat leaving the town wide open to the lawless—"

"Hardy was here," Lance pointed out.

"And he left too. Chasing after a man who killed some saloon hussy. When more important people of the town were left defenseless."

"Mayor," Lance said in a low, menacing tone. "I advise you to plug that wind hole in the middle of your face before I find something to fill it for you."

"Are you threatening me? Judge, is he threatening me?"

Dyson nodded. "I do believe he is, Craig."

"Then I want him dismissed immediately."

The judge nodded towards the doorway. "There's the door, Mayor. Don't let it hit you in your fat ass on the way out."

After listening to him bluster a little longer, they escorted him out. When he was gone, Dyson said, "I can't see him lasting much longer as mayor. Not after the next election anyway. Every time I see him, I want to poke burning sticks into my eyes. Be a much more pleasant experience."

"You wanted me, Sheriff?" a man asked as he entered the office.

"You Pickles?"

"Yes, sir."

Lance pointed at the floor. "I want that gone."

Pickles looked at the stain. "I'll need to take most of it up."

"Don't care. Just get it done and bill the town."

"Mayor ain't going to like it."

Lance said, "Just give it to me when you're done and I'll enjoy passing it on to him myself."

"When do you want it done?" Pickles asked.

"Today."

"I'll get some tools and come back."

Lance said, "I won't be here, but I'll leave it open. If you have any problems, look for Judge Dyson."

Dyson nodded. "I'll be around."

The sheriff started toward the door. "I'm going down to the Railway."

It took a while for them to separate, but when they did, both were breathing deeply. Lily looked up into Lance's eyes and said, "You should go away more often."

"Maybe I should."

Suddenly the euphoria of his homecoming wore off and her shoulder's slumped. "I'm so glad you're back, Lance. With everything that's happened—"

He placed a finger to her lips. "It's OK. Doc said to tell you that Milt will be up and about in a couple of days."

"Thank God. I was so worried about him. And then Hardy. How's he doing?"

"Still the same, from what the doc said."

Lily escorted him across to her table and they both sat down. "Did you find what you wanted in Grand Valley?"

"Yes."

"And?"

"I'm going out to see Denham after I leave here."

Lily's eyes widened. "Not alone, I hope?"

"I'll be fine. You worry too much."

"Oh, please Lance, take someone with you."

He reached out and patted the back of her hand. "Relax."

Anger flared in Lily's eyes. "Don't you tell me to relax, Lance Chaney. Everyone that I like of late has been getting shot. What makes you so damned different?"

"It's my job. You know that," he growled, losing patience.

Lily came to her feet. "Then go and get yourself damned well shot, you stubborn son of a bitch."

She whirled away and stomped off toward the bar, leaving him sitting there confused about whether he should go after her or not. Eventually, he decided not to. Instead, Lance climbed to his feet and walked from the saloon.

Lily looking on from the bar mirror, watched him go, then slapped a palm down on the polished countertop. Posey walked over to her. "Is everything OK, Miss Lily?"

"No, no it isn't," she said. Her eyes darted back and forth as her mind raced. She asked the barkeep,

"Is Chick Roberts still in town?"
"I think so."
"Find him for me."
"Yes, ma'am."

Circle D Ranch

Lance rode into the yard and was greeted by a smiling Martha Denham. "Sheriff Chaney, how nice to see you. What brings you out to our home?"

Lance hesitated and Martha's face dropped. "Oh, no. It's not that lovely young Hardy Walsh is it?"

The sheriff shook his head. "He's still hanging in there."

"Good. I don't know what we'd do if anything happened to him. Mary has been beside herself."

No sooner had she spoken her daughter's name when Mary appeared. Without so much as a hello, she blurted out, "Is Hardy OK?"

"Still the same."

Mary accepted that, just happy the news wasn't bad. Lance looked at Martha. "Is Clive around?"

"I'm here, Sheriff," the rancher called out.

The sheriff turned in his saddle and saw Denham near the barn. His foreman was with him and both men were armed. "Come to have a talk with you, Clive."

"What about?"

"Hardy being shot. Your son and how he wound up dead in my jail."

"Don't know what you mean."

"Wait," Martha Denham snapped. "What do you mean?"

"Yes, Sheriff," Mary joined.

"For starters, your son didn't die in the warlike you thought," Lance explained.

A look of confusion settled on both women's faces.

"I'm almost certain – am certain he was behind

the deaths that occurred in the county recently. I told your husband, but he denied it. Then the man I had in my jail was killed. But as he was dying, he said something to me that I had to check. Grand Valley."

"That's where my boy was killed," Martha said. "Clive told me."

"That's right," Denham stated.

"Someone died there all right, ma'am. But it wasn't your son."

Martha looked horrified.

"That's enough, Chaney," Denham snapped.

"Do you want to continue?" Lance asked.

Denham pointed his rifle at Lance. "I said, that's enough?"

"Clive, what's going on?" Martha Denham asked her husband. "Why do I get the feeling that you're hiding something?"

"Because he is," the sheriff stated.

"Damn it, Chaney. Keep it up and I'll shoot you."

Lance said no more but the seeds had been sowed and the damage done. He just waited for the fuse to burn down.

"What happened in Grand Valley, Pa?" Mary asked.

"All right!" Denham exploded. "But understand this. It was the war, OK? It was the war that made him do it."

"Do what?"

Denham told his wife and daughter, and Lance could see the emotion on their faces as their expressions changed with the telling of each part. When he'd finished, both women were sheet white.

"How could you let this happen?" Martha demanded. "He was a good boy."

"I told you, it was the war."

"Wasn't the war who killed your son though, was it?" Lance reminded the rancher.

"Shut your mouth," O'Connor snapped.

"Easy, Irish," Lance cautioned him. "Just keep that rifle pointed in another direction or I'm apt to get a might offended."

"Why do you think my brother was in your jail?" Mary asked.

"Because the doc identified him."

"That blind old fool," Denham snapped. "He's half blind."

"What about William Bent. You hire him to bushwhack me up in Grand Valley?" Lance asked.

There was recognition in Martha Denham's eyes at the mention of the name. Her throat constricted and she managed to ask, "Is it true, Clive? Did you hire that man? The one who stole cattle for you?"

"Martha!"

"Oh, don't Martha me. Everyone knows what happened when you came back from the war. How you got that first herd together."

"Shut up, woman."

"Who killed Christopher, Denham?" the sheriff asked. "Was it you or your man here?"

The rifle in Denham's hand shifted and pointed at the mounted sheriff. "He was bad. I couldn't let him go to trial for killing those men because it would have all come out."

Martha and Mary gasped audibly. Lance nodded and said, "I can understand that. Especially when you're going to run for governor."

"Exactly."

"If he went to trial everyone would find out that he killed the others because you told him to. It was the only way you were going to give him money for him to leave."

Denham frowned. "How—"

"It wasn't hard. Why else would the boy come? Unless he wanted money. After all, he was dead."

Silence descended over the ranch yard.

Lance continued. "Why did you shoot Hardy?"

"I thought I could convince him to tell us what you knew because of Mary."

"I guess you were wrong."

"I guess we were."

"You shot him?" Mary cried out.

The rancher nodded. "He knew too much."

"Just like the sheriff does now," O'Connor said and shifted his aim to shoot.

A rifle whiplashed and the Irishman crumpled to the ground as a bullet punched into his chest from the side. The sound rolled over the ranch yard and by the time it had started to fade, Lance had drawn his Colt and had the hammer thumbed back.

Clive Denham stared at his foreman who lay in the dust of the yard, his lifeblood draining from the wound onto the thirsty ground. A snarl came to his face as he looked up at the sheriff. Lance shook his head and shouted, "Don't!"

But the rancher was beyond reason. Everything he loved, built, or wanted was now gone and it was all because of the man on the horse before him. His finger tightened on the rifle's trigger, but he never got past the tension of tripping it before the Navy Colt in Lance's hand thundered.

Denham's mouth dropped open with shock as the bullet hammering into his chest. He rose up onto his toes and teetered for a moment before dropping the rifle as all the strength left his hands, and he fell to the yard not far from his foreman.

Martha cried out and hurried to her fallen husband and dropped to her knees. Mary stared at the sheriff, shocked at having witnessed the death of her father. Lance said in a low voice. "I'm sorry."

She glared at him through eyes filled with tears

then joined her mother beside her dead father.

The sound of a horse drew Lance's attention and he saw the elderly rider, a Henry in his hands. "Your woman was worried about you. Sent me out here to make sure you were OK," Roberts explained.

The sheriff nodded then noticed the small group of ranch hands who had been drawn by the shooting. They moved forward to see what had happened, but Lance stopped them. "Go and do whatever it was you were doing. There's nothing to see here."

EPILOGUE

Brenham, Texas, 10 days later

Lance looked up from where he sat in the sun outside the jail and smiled. "The wayward brother returns."

Buck looked around himself thoughtfully at the town and said, "Not quite what I was expecting."

"Things have changed some," the older brother replied. "Holt, how you doing?"

"Got a hole in my leg that ain't far away from being healed. Other than that, I'm fine."

"Where'd you find him anyway?" Buck asked indicating to Carmody with his thumb. "He's not a bad deputy to have around."

"Found him in a saloon."

"You don't say."

"If you fellers plan on jawing here all day I might go back to that saloon and have me a drink."

"If you see Lily, tell her to give you my bottle."

As Carmody turned his horse away he said, "I'll do that, Sheriff."

"How was it, Buck?" Lance asked, his voice serious.

The younger Chaney climbed down and stomped up the steps onto the boardwalk. "You remember Shiloh?"

"Uh, huh."

"Worse than that."

"You exaggerating again?"

Buck smiled. "Maybe a little. You?"

"Thinking it might have been better to stay in Barlow."

His brother chuckled. "Don't tell Lily."

"Hell no, she'd chase me down Main Street with a sawn-off."

"Too bad about Deke," Buck said seriously.

"Yeah."

"Hardy?"

"Got shot. Laid up, on the mend."

There was a drawn-out silence between the two brothers before Lance said, "Go on, ask what you're trying to avoid."

"I ain't trying to avoid anything."

"Sure, you are. You're just busting to ask about Maggie," Lance said.

Buck was about to deny it but there was no point. "All right, how is she?"

"Worried about you. Good thing she's got something else to take her mind off you dying."

Buck was curious. "Like what?"

"Wedding."

Buck frowned. "Whose?"

"Mine, you big ox."

A broad grin split Buck's face. "Well, I'll be a mule's ass. That's just the best news I've heard in a long time." He leaned forward to shake his brother's hand. "Mighty, fine, Lance. Mighty fine."

"Thank you, brother. Now, how about we go and join Carmody for a drink?"

Lance came to his feet and stepped down off the boardwalk and into the street followed by Buck. The thunder of gunshots echoed from somewhere along the street and Lance cursed. "There's always something ain't there?"

As they broke into a run, Buck replied, "Yeah, there's always something."

A LOOK AT LONG ROAD TO ABILENE

LONG ROAD TO ABILENE, is a classic hero's journey, a western adventure that exemplifies the struggles, the defeats, and the victories that personify the history of the American West. After surviving the bloody battle of Franklin and the hell of a Yankee prison camp, Cade McCall comes home to the woman he loves only to find that she, believing him dead, has married his brother. With nothing left to keep him in Tennessee, Cade journeys to New Orleans where an encounter with a beautiful woman leads to being shanghaied for an unexpected adventure at sea. Returning to Texas, he signs on to drive a herd of cattle to Abilene, where he is drawn into a classic showdown of good versus evil, and a surprising reunion with an old enemy.

AVAILABLE NOW

ABOUT THE AUTHOR

Robert Vaughan sold his first book when he was 19. That was 57 years and nearly 500 books ago. He wrote the novelization for the miniseries Andersonville. Vaughan wrote, produced, and appeared in the History Channel documentary Vietnam Homecoming. His books have hit the NYT bestseller list seven times. He has won the Spur Award, the PORGIE Award (Best Paperback Original), the Western Fictioneers Lifetime Achievement Award, received the Readwest President's Award for Excellence in Western Fiction, is a member of the American Writers Hall of Fame and is a Pulitzer Prize nominee. Vaughn is also a retired army officer, helicopter pilot with three tours in Vietnam. And received the Distinguished Flying Cross, the Purple Heart, The Bronze Star with three oak leaf clusters, the Air Medal for valor with 35 oak leaf clusters, the Army Commendation Medal, the Meritorious Service Medal, and the Vietnamese Cross of Gallantry.